The Maya Pill

ALSO BY GERMAN SADULAEV IN ENGLISH TRANSLATION:

I Am a Chechen!

The Maya Pill

German Sadulaev

Translated and with an afterword by
Carol Apollonio

DALKEY ARCHIVE PRESS
CHAMPAIGN / LONDON / DUBLIN

Originally published in Russian as *Tabletka* by Ad Marginem Press, Moscow, 2008

Library of Congress Cataloging-in-Publication Data

Sadulaev, German.
[Tabletka. English]
The Maya pill / German Sadulaev ; Translated by Carol Apollonio. -- First Edition.
pages cm
"Originally published in Russian as Tabletka by Ad Marginem Press, Moscow, 2008."
ISBN 978-1-56478-906-8 (alk. paper)
I. Flath, Carol A. (Carol Apollonio), translator. II. Title.
PG3493.42.D85T3313 2013
891.73'5--dc23
2013033396

Partially funded by a grant from the Illinois Arts Council, a state agency

Published with the support of the Institute for Literary Translation, Russia

ИНСТИТУТ ПЕРЕВОДА

www.dalkeyarchive.com

Cover: design and composition by Mikhail Iliatov

Printed on permanent/durable acid-free paper

Atan khalam sarvatum

In early spring of the year two thousand and XX from the birth
of the prophet Jesus Christ—peace be unto him—I, Maximus
Semipyatnitsky, have set pen to paper. My goal: to snatch humanity from the talons of Maya, of illusion.

I shall tell the whole truth, reveal hidden verities, openly proclaim treasured secrets. The fortunate among my readers will
profit from the knowledge I reveal here and will find their pathway to freedom. The ignorant, though, will reject the path, the
blind will pass it by, and the world will crumble and plunge down
to hell—as well it should—but my conscience will be clear. I shall
fulfill my duty before those who suffer, and in doing so bring
benefit unto myself. At the preordained hour I shall soar aloft to
higher worlds in an airplane made of flowers, having shaken off
the things of the terrestrial earth, its flawed economic system and
discriminatory social relations, like dust, from my feet.

O'men!

*The only inscription in the Khazar language that has been deciphered by
scholars. Some linguists believe that it means "All things are possible." The
phrase was found inscribed on a stone stela that, some historians say, stood
outside the home of a distinguished family of Khazar merchants; it may have
served as their motto. Mainstream scholarship, however, does not recognize the
stela, believing it to be a later fabrication; does not recognize the inscription
itself, which is an imitation of the Sanskrit Devanagari alphabet; puts no stock
in the belief that the inscription is in the Khazar language; and doesn't think
much of the translation either.

PART I

Itil

CROSSROADS

Bald Britney Spears writhed hysterically, slashed her veins, twisted her hospital bedding into a rope, and attempted to hang herself with it. Then she burst into tears, repented, summoned her former husband Kevin Federline, and promised to bear him a third child. Then she sobbed again, invoked the name of Beelzebub, called herself a fake, sought out the best tattoo artist in the United States of America, and had the number 666 branded onto the crown of her head.

Thirteen years ago, a scrawny old man materialized out of thin air in the bedroom of a pudgy girl. The old man looked like a goat and was wearing a baseball cap with "I♥NY" on the front. The girl was clutching a curling iron in her hands, pretending it was a microphone, and gyrating in front of her mirror to the sounds of a Madonna tune coming from a cheap cassette player. The old man perched on the edge of a chair and with the muted and watery leer of a jaded pedophile observed the girl's fleshy thighs bulging out from under her tight white shorts.

The girl glanced over and saw him, but before she could scream the old man reached over and handed her a bunch of pages torn from a school notebook. The pages were covered with elegant handwriting, with Gothic curlicues. The girl quickly skimmed the writing, then looked up at the old man, her big eyes brimming with greed and disbelief.

"What do you want me to do?" asked the girl.

She didn't know Russian or Latin, or ancient Aramaic—only English, or, rather, American.

The old lecher would have understood her in any language, but he said:

"First just sign the contract."

He could have answered in any language; he knows Russian,

and Latin, and ancient Aramaic, and Greek, and Sanskrit. They say he even knows Albanian.

With the innate clumsiness of an overweight pre-teen, the girl lurched over to her school backpack, emptied its contents onto her bed, and fished out a ballpoint pen of Chinese manufacture.

The old man shook his head: "Blood. This kind of contract must be signed in blood."

The girl was taken aback, but only for a moment. Staring impudently into the pervert's eyes, she undid the button and zipper on her white shorts and lowered them to her knees. Then, hiking her gaudy stretch panties over to one side, she poked her finger between her legs and dug around inside. Without taking her eyes off the man's face, she lifted her stained finger and smeared a crooked, rust-colored cross on the notebook paper with the ink of her first menstrual blood.

The old man gathered up the pages and vanished. Only then did the girl realize that his image hadn't been reflected in the mirror.

The contract stipulated a thirteen-year term.

You might ask how I came to know these details. I learned them firsthand from one of the parties to the contract. And I'm not personally acquainted with Britney, so you can guess who I mean.

If you've read any books about voodoo or know anything about the history of the blues, you know the legend of the Trickster. Outside every city is a crooked crossroads, with a withered tree standing in its southwest corner. Every blues master has visited one of these corners on the night of a new moon. There he met the devil and sold him his soul in exchange for fame and glory. The devil in this particular legend is known as the Trickster, or Deceiver. No one can outwit him; he will steal your soul, dear child, and all you will get in return will be a pile of yellowed newspapers with your photograph on the front page.

The city of St. Petersburg has one of those crooked crossroads, in Vesyoly, at the place where Bloody Bolsheviks Prospect meets International Prostitute Kollontai Street. A withered old tree used to stand there, on the spot now occupied by a Neste gas station.

I used to be in a band with Ilya, who later made it big under the stage name "Devil." We were coming back late from a rehearsal one dark night. Feeble little stars cowered behind a dirty gauze veil of clouds, and alcoholics, plagued with nightmares, tossed and turned on park benches nearby. The Trickster came coasting along in a burgundy-colored Volga, the deluxe model. He pulled up beside us just as we reached the crossroads, and invited us into his car. I immediately realized what was going on and instructed the old goat to kiss my ass. Mama taught me never to get into cars with suspicious-looking strangers.

But Ilya did. He got into the back seat and struck up a conversation with the old scumbag. Now Ilyukha sings his songs in huge stadiums and has his own TV show. Whereas my three solo albums came out in editions of twenty copies each, total, on cassette.

Not too long ago, the old swindler visited me again. He told me about Britney, and a whole slew of other clients too. He had heard that I'd become a writer, and figuring that this might give him another chance, poked his contract under my nose. It reeked of urine from a railway station toilet.

My response to the Source of All Sin, after censoring out the nonstandard vocabulary, could be distilled down to two English words: *get lost*. Rebuffed, the tempter spat malevolently onto my kitchen floor, and his saliva sizzled and scorched a hole in the linoleum. It's still there on the floor, under the cardboard carton that I use as a table for my electric teapot and toaster. You can come over and take a look: With its ragged edges and dark center, it resembles a black hole, like the ones in outer space, and gives off a sulfury smell.

The Adversary was in a pathetic state. He told me a sob story about how he'd been to see K, and P, had dropped in on N, and had even flown out to the middle of nowhere to see G, but everyone had turned him down in more or less insulting terms. The despondent seducer whined that now he would have to make a deal with a client you couldn't even call a writer, a scribbling hack whose opuses even he couldn't stand to look at, much less read, and that everyone in hell would mock him, the so-called Master of Evil, when he dragged that sorry-ass soul down there. O, how low he had fallen, after Goethe and Sorokin!

At that point the Prince of Darkness, drained of all hope, dissolved into a pale gray haze that looked like bus exhaust, and wafted southward in the direction of Moscow.

Literary critics had unanimously identified my latest novel as the most insignificant and forgettable book of the year. Most bookstores don't carry it. Sales experts, following some tyrannical inner voice that they call "the dictates of the market"—though we know that the market has nothing to do with it—loaded the shelves with row upon row of copies of a single book by a different author, which had become a surprise bestseller. They even colonized the bookstore windows, piling up a million more copies in huge stacks that spill over onto the sills.

Verily, vanity of vanities, the things of this earth.

Thus did I twice shame the Enemy of the human race and save my eternal soul.

FAMILY TREE

My name is Maximus. Not Maxim, not Max, but Maximus; you can check my passport and driver's license. I owe the name to my uncle, or rather, to his work buddies, who had marked some milestone in his employment by giving him an old book on the history of Ancient Rome just before I was born. Some random Roman emperor's or general's name came up, and my uncle, who was also my godfather, bestowed it upon me. Could have been worse. I'm eternally grateful to my godfather for not choosing one of those other names the Romans were so fond of, the ones that have both masculine and feminine equivalents in Russian. Like Valerian, Valentinian, Julius, or Claudius. It's scary to think how many schoolmates I would have had to massacre during their tender childhood years for calling me girly names like Valka or Claudia behind my back.

My ancestors acquired the surname Semipyatnitsky during the years of serfdom. Don't believe people with names like Sokolovsky, Tarasovsky, Dubovitsky, or Lebedinsky when they try to claim noble birth. On the contrary. That elegant "-sky" suffix usually marks the descendents of lowly peasants with no status whatsoever, who didn't even know who their parents were, much less their ancestors, and accordingly were listed in the census under their master's name: "Who do you boys belong to?" "We're Colonel Ordyntsev's chattel."

What's known for a fact is that my ancestor, the potent patriarch and founder of the family line, was a stableman on an estate in Saratov province, a carouser and cardsharp whose unreliable character had earned him the nickname Seven Fridays—for him, every day was the beginning of the weekend. It's also known that my ancestors weren't Russian, and might have been of Tatar blood. My father's name is Raul Emilievich. So my full name is

Maximus Raulevich Semipyatnitsky. No one uses my patronymic, though; as is said in such cases, I have not earned it.

Our distant relatives bear the name Saifiddulin. Raul and Émile are French names, as far as I can tell, but though it might seem strange to you, they're extremely popular among Russian Tatars. This supports my family's hypothesis about the Tatar blood.

But there's another story as well, a beautiful legend. Through the ages, generations of Semipyatnitskys have passed down the tale that our family originated not in a Tatar tribe—though my forefathers must have come into close contact with Tatars as a matter of course, as neighbors in the Turkish world—but rather in ancient Khazaria, which at one time was a great power, and which vanished, like Atlantis, in the currents of history. It's even said that our family was related to the Great Khagan.

I don't know how much of this legend is true and how much of it is just inspiring nonsense that my ancestors made up to boost their morale in their demeaning and dependent social position. But whether there's some kind of genetic memory at work, or whether all these tall tales have just seeped into my subconscious, for whatever reason, I'm sometimes visited by strange dreams. Last night, for example.

KHAZAR DEMOCRACY

Once upon a time, in the glorious city of Itil, which stands on the River Volga, in the capital city of the Khazar Tsar-Khagan, there lived a herdsman of horses, the younger son of a man named Nattukh, Saat by name. This is no epic tale; there was nothing heroic about Saat; he was just an ordinary man living an ordinary life. He pastured his mares on the steppe, carried foals in his arms, shoveled manure, and hauled it from the corrals. Of course a poor herdsman like Saat wouldn't live in Itil itself; a square *sazhen* of land an arrow's flight from the Khagan's palace cost way more than he could afford: five weights of silver. No, he lived far away, at the very edge of the steppe. And that is as it should be: Where can you find space to graze your mares in Itil? Half the time you can't even find an open hitching post. Horsemen wander the streets, searching among the stone houses, but the posts are all being used, there's not a single free one to toss your reins over! The steppe, though, is a land of plenty: feather grass and wind. Saat's tent was tattered, draughty, and full of holes. But he did not lose spirit. On a summer night, the stars would shine their way through the rips in his tent roof; their rays caressed and warmed him.

But Saat had no one, only starlight, to caress and warm him. He was lonely. He did not crave gold or silver; it wasn't a big stone mansion he wanted, not glory and fame; his only desire was to have a black-haired maiden by his side, a girl with hazel eyes, a bosom like a young mare's udder, and gentle sloping withers. Long did he crave a wife!

But then that desire, too, passed.

And after that Saat had the perfect life.

Itil held no appeal for Saat; Saat forgot Itil. Even the tax collector forsook the path to Saat's tent. When a man lacks a wife and worldly wealth, when he doesn't go to the bazaar or to the bath-house to gossip; when he doesn't inhale the dust at the Khagan's gate, it is as though he doesn't exist; he is invisible. And free.

Sometimes Saat would think: Great is the Khagan, glory to him and victory over all his foes, what use to him is a poor herds-man and his mares? How can the Khagan, blessed be his name under the moon and sun, be mindful of all the herdsmen in the boundless steppe? Send troops into battle, gather in the taxes, array concubines on thick woolen carpets, manage the affairs of state! And the herdsman, for his part, what need has he of the Khagan? The bay mare has foaled, the milk in the *burdiuk* has fermented wrong and turned all clotty, and yesterday the wolves howled all night long, what if they attack the horses? The Khagan and the herdsman lead separate lives. And so be it.

But every year there was a marvelous and strange occurrence. On the second moonless night after the day when light and dark fell in equal measure upon the spring grass, Saat would rise with the dawn; he wasn't quite awake, but sort of still sleeping, sleep-walking. He would take up his *kizil*-wood staff and set forth in the fog, in the direction of Itil.

If he had been able to see, he would have realized that he was not alone. From all over the steppe, men walked, swaying blankly from side to side in their tattered *beshmets*. Eyes open, but dream-ing. Falling down, bumping into, or even trampling one another. But pressing inexorably forward, onward, like a swarm of ants crossing a ford.

For once a year all of Khazaria is called upon to vow for the Khagan and to elect the Great Kurultai.

So here comes Saat, making his way across the steppe, and his head feeling like a buzzing beehive, but divided into different chambers, each swarming with its own political party, so not just one beehive, politically speaking, but several . . . *peehives*, if you will. And even if you won't.

So Saat feels that three tenths of his head, from the right ear to the crown, are for United Khazaria: this peehive is the biggest and the Khagan himself is in it or nearby. And Saat feels that two tenths of his head, the crown and half the back, are for A Just Khazaria, which is new, and also for the Khagan, but from the other side, as it were. And one tenth of his head, the part by the left ear, is for the Utmost Primordial Communal Peehive Party of Khazaria. This peehive is ancient; it has come down from his forefathers. And one half tenth of his head, behind the ear, just a scratch, really, is for the Robber Bandit Peehive of Khazaria. And this party has no more sense than a pile of rotten straw, but its leader is a bandit they call the Thrush, Solovey, and he's a riot, so much fun! The rest of his head stayed home; it didn't go to vow anything, didn't elect anyone. And fine, so let half an ear come, that should be enough for the Great Kurultai.

Shamans lead a bear around the streets of Itil. The bear jingles its bell, dances. United Khazaria is the winner. Who else is there anyway? It's all just Murzlas in the Kurultai. They're not like Khazars: dark-skinned, curly-haired, with round eyes. There's a saying in the bathhouses: For the Murzlas the Khagan is no law, and the *shaitan* spirit no brother. Though the *shaitan* may very well be their father. But you hear all kinds of things in the bathhouse.

Saat returns at night, collapses in his ragged tent, sinks into a deep slumber. Gets up the next day and remembers nothing! Feet all bloody, but where he has been and what he has been doing?—might as well ask the wind!

The old women whisper that every year the Itil sorcerers and shamans send out a huge cloud of foul air, filled with violet-colored dust, gathering the entire Khazar people together to vow allegiance. The ragged herdsmen come to Itil, trudging on their last legs like the living dead, and they speak their vows, vote in swarms with their voices. Afterward they have no recollection of whom they voted for, or of even voting at all. But the Khagan is eternal, and the Kurultai is with him: you swore allegiance back then, so now obey; go forth: raid, gather taxes for our coffers and maidens for our beds, bow down to the earth before us. For we are blood of your blood, flesh of your flesh and it's all for your sake. And the Khazars live on. They carry on as they can, in their own way. And the Khagan, too, with the Kurultai. Until next spring. This is one way. And it is even a good way. Just so long as there's no war.

RAVENS OF MORNING

Every morning around eight thirty I venture forth. The door to the apartment building closes lazily behind me on its pneumatic hinge. The first thing I hear is the croaking of ravens. They're everywhere; they live here year 'round. They weave their black-branched nests on the treetops in the courtyard, and subsist on a diet of human leavings gleaned from the trash bins.

Sometimes I ask myself: Why is it only the most disgusting, ugly, and nasty creatures that have adapted to live with human beings? Ravens, rats, and cockroaches are man's constant companions in his wanderings through time. They establish their abodes either inside those of humans, or in close proximity to them. For whatever reason, human cities are devoid of proud eagles, noble deer, gorgeous butterflies, and even soft-furred beavers. Could it be that in the Creator's plan these fauna are placed near us so as to enhance the aesthetic effect of man's perfection, by contrast?

Or do they sense that we're kindred spirits, grimy, low birds of a feather?

The ravens croak in the morning. Harken to where the noise is coming from. If it's from the right, no problem. But if a raven croaks three times on your left, no good will come of it. An ancient Khazar omen.

Observe also the position of the waxing moon. If it's on the right, all is well; on the left, you're in trouble.

If you see a bad omen, though, all is not lost; there's a sure way to protect yourself. Immediately spit three times over your left shoulder. Everyone knows that the devil lurks behind a man's left shoulder; there's an angel on the other side. So spit three times into the devil's snout; that'll throw him off. Then make four complete turns clockwise, that is, left to right. That'll make the devil dizzy, and then the angel can give him one in the rear. Last, take off your coat, turn it inside out, and put it back on. It will utterly baffle the demon. And he won't give you any more trouble.

I learned this from my Khazar grandma. She also taught me how to cast spells using a dried branch, how to undo an evil spell using nothing but water, how to draw signs to protect yourself from shape-shifters, and how to distinguish the living dead from the living living, and the living dead from the dead dead.

But I've forgotten just about everything from that distant time, those years when I was a schoolboy, and used to spend my summer vacations on a farm far away, on the shores of a broad, muddy river, with my wise, fairy-tale grandmother. It was so long ago, it feels like another lifetime. Or someone else's.

The past, all that used to be, was burned long ago.
It wasn't our life, it was all just a show.

A line from one of those three cassette albums.

The life I live now is completely different.

HEGEMON

I greet the ravens, and if necessary, I spit the shoulder demon away, and head for the shopping-center parking lot. I go up to my boxy gray car, get the remote key out of my pocket, and press the button. The door locks click, and I open the driver's side door and crawl in.

My car is a 2006 Renault Logan, ultra-economy class, designed for the Turkish market and assembled in Moldova or someplace. Bought on credit with a three-year loan with an insane interest rate. Of course the color caused no end of torment. When the bank agreed to the loan, there was too much variety on the lot: For example, instead of drab gray, you could also choose plain gray. Or drabber gray. And then, there was also plain drab gray. Well, I put a lot of thought into it and finally decided I might as well get a gray one—I liked the color so much.

We could spend some time on this. These days, a man's social status, his identity and place in the world, everything that he has (or has not) achieved in his lifetime, can be gauged quickly and easily with one look at the car he drives.

In one of my previous lives, sometime around 1995, I was walking along the Palace Embankment past the Admiralty one warm summer night, hand in hand with a tall, ravishing brunette, talking big: "Katya, if today, right this minute, the devil came up and let me see into the future, and if I saw that I was destined to become an ordinary man like millions of others, that I would just go to work every day, come home at night and watch TV, spend my weekends shopping, and all the rest of it, and if the devil were to hand me a gun, I would shoot myself right then and there, without a moment's hesitation!"

Over the next couple of years Katya got tired of me, of my tendency to disappear into a black hole for weeks and months on end and then suddenly turn up with no warning, "Hey, you busy tonight?" Katya married a good man. Katya has a job as a senior legal advisor, an assistant prosecutor. She might even have made prosecutor by now.

And here I am getting into my cheap Franco-Turkish car, thinking what a dirty trick it had been for the devil not to show up then and there with that movie about my future life and a loaded pistol in his clawlike hand. But what can you expect from the spawn of hell? Now he can gloat at the sight of me, the man I've become, a fate worse than death, the very man I swore I'd never be. On the other hand, don't forget, I did turn him down twice when he offered his contract—my soul in exchange for a chance at something more. Gloating is all he has.

Yes, I careened across the globe from the White Sea to the Indian Ocean and back again; tried on a monk's cassock, then ragged blue jeans; walked around clutching a string of wooden prayer beads, then the handle of a Makarov pistol. I scrambled the best, formative years of my life in the geometric Brownian motion of an unfathomable fate. Now what's left of me spends its days in voluntary servitude as an ordinary office drudge, a cheap white-collar worker in an off-the-rack business suit, my double chin spilling over the necktie leash around my fleshy neck.

I've merged into a class totally devoid of class consciousness. I've become what is demeaningly designated as "lower middle class," the baseline standard for poor taste and ineptitude, unenvied even by blue-collar workers, who merely detest us for getting to work in warm, dry offices, while manual workers spend their days up to their ears in shit and engine oil, poking around in the guts of broken machines. No, they don't envy us; sometimes they actually earn more than we do. Successful people, the upper middle class, hold us in contempt, whereas for high society we don't even exist at all except as an anonymous throng of pathetic losers, barely visible behind the wheels of the junk cluttering up the road and getting in the way of their limousines and sports cars.

In songs and jokes we're "mid-level managers," MLM for short. The term is not to be taken literally; it implies that there are other managers on an even lower rung, but there's actually no one below us; the next level down is the flames of hell. So when you think about it, we managers don't really manage anyone—there's no one there. But "manage" has another meaning as well: to control. In the strictest sense of the word, we're not really managing—but in fact we sit at the controls of the entire global economy.

I shall now speak out on behalf of the insulted and injured, the proletariat of our new epoch. Lend me your ears!

In stuffy, crowded, overstaffed offices from San Francisco to Qingdao, decrepit air conditioners rattle noisily in the background, or worse, there's no AC at all. Amid the din and shouting, with Windows on the verge of collapse, the MLM presides. A telephone receiver is permanently attached to his ear, and he himself is plugged into the computer network like a mere appendix to the keyboard. There he sits, building the economy, hastening the march of progress, propelling mankind inexorably onward toward its inevitable collapse.

Not stockholders, who care only about their dividends, not the masters of business standing regally over the fray like Kutuzov and Napoleon at Borodino, themselves subject to the flow of history and lacking free will; not the top managers who claw bonuses for themselves out of each and every deal and preen before fitness-club mirrors; and certainly not the actual workers in the factories, who could give a shit about any of that—no, it's the office worker: the manager of sales, procurement, logistics, export, import, marketing, human resources, and whatever the hell else—it is he who determines the fate of the world, he, the very embodiment of efficiency, who implements the laws of economics.

An exhausted and alienated import manager in France compares pricing and supply proposals and selects some product from China after rejecting an Italian company's bid. Meanwhile his director flies to Rome on company money, stays in a Radisson or Hilton, drinks himself under the table at some banquet in an Italian restaurant, and seduces the host's wife, and now he needs to get a contract with the Italian company, if only to justify his own existence and his exorbitant salary. The exhausted and alienated import manager couldn't care less; it makes no impression on him, even when he finds out that it was the director of the Italian company who delivered his own wife to the drunken French director's bed (and she's not his wife anyway, but an "export escort" hired especially to seal the deal). All the import manager did was compare prices and terms and select the Chinese product.

If the director digs in his heels, the import manager won't argue, he'll give in. He has a secret weapon: covert sabotage. Almost immediately things start to go wrong with the Italians. Deliveries are delayed; the paperwork is mixed up, work at the plant grinds to a halt, and the entire transaction comes up a loss. The director gets taken down a peg at the next stockholders' meeting, and deliveries begin coming in from China.

Because that's what made sense from the beginning. And the exhausted and alienated manager, who doesn't stand to gain or earn bonuses from any of these deals, all he wants is for everything to balance out, to make sense, and to benefit the business. It gives him a feeling of functional harmony and insulates him from an awareness of the absurdity of existence.

That's all.

Thousands upon thousands of import managers the world over make the same kinds of decisions, and terrestrial exports soar to celestial heights.

When he's done with the world economy, having finally directed it into the proper channels and calculated all the trends and vectors, the exhausted manager sets off for home.

And immediately starts in on the economy from the other side.

He buys up mass-market clothing, fills the seats in chain restaurants, clears stuff off the supermarket shelves. It's not easy; he can't cram everything in, but he keeps on trying: eating and drinking, drinking and eating. Periodically he stuffs some new, pointless item of clothing into the one miniscule closet that itself takes up nearly all the space in his apartment. And who, if not he, can consume all that stuff coming out of the world's factories? He's tired, he's miserable, but he knows how to laugh, he seeks out entertainment, and after all, who, if not he, will fill the dance clubs and concert halls? Occasionally he'll even buy a book and read it, a bestseller, just to keep up with things, to follow what's going on up there in first class. It was written for him, after all; and he's the one drenched in the toxic spit of their scorn: Yes, I'm a piece of shit, a loser, he agrees, and keeps on reading. Who knows, he might hit the lotto jackpot and wind up in the penthouse of the Tower of Babel, and, if so, he'll be able to take advantage of what his reading has taught him about the difference between a genuine thirty-five thousand-euro watch and the one that's not so genuine, the kind that your basic dimwit can pick up for fifteen hundred American dollars.

He believes in God, believes in the President, believes in the Law, believes in the Market, believes in Science, Santa Claus, and the Tooth Fairy. He takes out loans for his condo and his car, he maxes out his credit card for a serving of yogurt. It's his way of issuing credit to the economy, a bond of trust to the government and to society as a whole.

The most deranged among them even bring children into the world.

He is an optimist.

He is Hegemon, he is mankind in the twenty-first century.

Respect this man, bland and faceless though he may be.

Rejoice in his blandness. For when he becomes aware of his true class interests, he will turn the world upside down, without even reaching for a weapon. Everything is already in his power. And if this million-handed mid-level manager should collectively decide to press the delete key, he will erase the Universe.

THE BOX

Now this is how the story goes:

That day I pulled up to the office as usual in my gray Renault with its funny-looking, stunted little hood, and wedged the car into an improvised parking place on the lawn in front of the building. I got the lanyard with the Smart Card out of my pocket and draped it around my neck. This is my personal collar, the visible mark of my servitude. *Nine-to-five slavery*, they call it in the advanced capitalist countries, where over the course of their many decades at the reins of power the liberal socialist parties have trained employers (i.e., exploiters) to observe the eight-hour working day (including lunch break). In my case that comes to nine-to-six; here in the former land of triumphant socialism those eight hours do not include your lunch break.

The sensor reads my Smart Card and records the times of my arrival in the morning, my departure at the end of the day, my lunch and restroom breaks, and my other personal time, which must not exceed one half hour per day, total. There are fines for tardiness, for leaving work early, and for exceeding the allotted break time.

I passed through the turnstile, swiped the heavy metal door open with my Smart Card, and walked past the secretaries' desks to the Import Department. My desk is next to the door, so people are coming and going behind my back all day long.

Could be worse. This girl I know works in marketing for an office furniture company. Her desk is right in the middle of the showroom. It has a price tag on it. So while she's sitting there do-
ing her work, customers keep coming up to her desk and opening and closing the drawers, peering underneath and feeling the legs (of the table), and knocking on the desk with everything but their teeth to test the quality of the veneer. She says that she's gotten

used to it and doesn't even notice them anymore.

The Import Department is a medium-sized rectangular room with a windowless interior wall; a glass partition separating Import from IT; a partition between the Department and the corridor; and the building's external wall, which has three windows (no AC). There are twenty-four other desks with twenty-four employees (besides me) working at them. The desks are jammed right up next to each other, with narrow aisles leading to the printers, the fax machine, and the copier. Pretty near constantly, all twenty-four employees are yelling into their phones, competing with one another to be heard. A couple of hours into the workday, my head starts to throb from the racket; by lunchtime the oxygen in the room is depleted and we've switched over to a carbon-dioxide diet, like plants. We haven't yet mastered the art of photosynthesis, though, so what we're exhaling is not oxygen, but the same gas we're breathing in, only more concentrated. The windows are open year-round, but that doesn't help: The dense, stifling atmosphere in the room blocks any fresh airflow; if you put a candle on the windowsill, the flame would stand utterly still and vertical, without the slightest movement, like the consciousness of a yogi in a profound meditative state. If fresh air somehow manages to break through, the draughts infect one third of the office population with a whole smorgasbord of upper-respiratory ailments.

My job title is Leading Specialist. That's a great jumping-off place for a career if you're twenty-five. For a man of thirty-five it's the kiss of death, a complete dead end.

I am thirty-five.

That morning I thought about it again, and my soul felt like . . . like a herd of scratching cats. Or, rather, it was more like if the cats had spewed their liquid and solid excrement directly into my soul, and the scratching I felt was them trying to clean up after themselves. Have you ever seen a cat scratching at the linoleum after he's peed on it, imagining that he's covering the evidence?

I tossed my faux-leather briefcase onto my desk, on top of a heap of random papers, sank onto my chair, and, forming the classic Anglo-American fuck-you gesture, jabbed the computer's ON button with my middle finger. It started booting up, and the monitor went white. The face of Jessica Simpson flashed briefly before me (the intermediary desktop graphic I'd installed)—but then the screen showed the standard corporate interface for my workplace, that is, the Cold Plus Corporation.

First thing, I clicked on the bat image to check my e-mail. Everyone else in the department uses Windows Outlook; I'm the only one with The Bat. An involuntary extravagance. The IT People simply forgot to switch my e-mail program over when they installed the office system. I like The Bat.

The computer is full of bats.*

The program reminds me of Grebenshikov's song about the Yellow Moon. It also makes me think of vampires and Pelevin's *Empire V.* But the real advantage is that when you forward letters from contractors to colleagues, they arrive as though they were sent directly from the original sender—no middleman—so you don't have to deal with the fallout.

Several dozen new messages popped up, and as usual I began with the spam. Spam has its own special patterns. A couple of months ago I was being bombarded with ads for Viagra, Vuka-Vuka, and other miraculous substances purporting to enhance male potency. Then I kept getting information about a unique, brand-new method for mastering English. Last week I received an invitation to acquire real estate outside Moscow: a two-story mansion on a two-thousand-square-meter lot on the Rublev side, for a mere one-and-a-half million dollars. Clearly my virtual status is rising. Give it a little time and the circle will close back in on itself; I'll start getting invitations to enroll in professional development courses for sales managers.

*Boris Grebenshikov.

I was just about to delete the next message, but realized just in time that it was from our Dutch supplier of frozen French fries, forwarded to me by our Department Import Manager. The letter was an answer, and as I first thought, just the latest installment in a listless dialogue we'd been having with them about compensation for a loss, to the tune of eight hundred dollars, that Cold Plus had suffered in the Russian port because the forty-foot container had exceeded the maximum stipulated gross weight.

In the previous message, the Dutch export manager had denied responsibility, citing several lengthy provisions from INCOTERMS-2000,* and had repeated three times that, insofar as we were following FCA delivery standards,** "we are not the shipper."

I had put the message aside for several days, biding my time until the mood was right, and after my next regular meeting with the Import Director to go over the different flights, I was blessed with inspiration and composed a response in my best English:

Dear Sir,

I'm quite astonished by your letter. Actually, I get a kind of strange feeling while reading in your message the repeated statement that you are not the shipper of your goods. My poor brains are totally collapsed and I'm wondering: who the hell are you? If you are truly not the shipper then who the hell is the shipper? Aliens, maybe? Or Jesus Christ Himself? Or, as we used to say in Russian, might it be Pushkin? Ah, sorry, in case you don't know, Pushkin was a guy who wrote poetry and stuff in the nineteenth century or something. You may ask: why Pushkin? I'm thinking the same thing.

In every Bill of Lading related to every consignment of your goods I see your company mentioned as the shipper. But you are so convinced that you are not, that I'm starting to doubt my own eyes.

* The compilation of standards and conditions for international trade.

** FCA (free carrier) conditions for delivery specify that the seller fulfill his obligations.

*Or maybe you are just missing the meaning of the words? English
is not your native language, you may not understand everything clearly. In that case please go buy any dictionary, or glossary, whatever, and
find the word "shipper." Learn it and we'll go on with our fantastically
entertaining conversation.*

*Sincerely yours, with best regards, as ever, your well-wisher,
Maximus R. Semipyatnitsky.*

Thinking back to this message, I realized that I'd laid it on
a little thick. So now I'd get some kind of reprimand. I didn't
want to read the message, so I shouted across three desks to the
Import Manager for Potatoes, catching her just as she hung up
her phone.

"Lina! What the hell is he writing now? This time, that he's
not selling, just looking?"

"Who, the Dutch guy?"

"Uh-huh, the Flying Dutchman, and he can stick it up his . . .
You forwarded his message, but damned if I'm going to read it."

"Nah, in fact, they agreed to compensate us fifty-fifty."

"Oh. So I typed two entire volumes of *War and Peace* for a
measly four hundred dollars?"

"That's about right."

"So what's the rest of the message about?"

"Something completely different. Remember the time they
snuck those undeclared samples into a container?"

I did remember. It happens every once in a while: Some item
that isn't declared on the invoice gets slipped into a container, deep
inside, away from the door. Customs can't open and unload all the
containers, so they conduct random inspections. More often than
not that happens if there's a glitch, or if some information comes in
from the higher-ups, or if the customs office has a conflict with the
broker and they want to show him who's boss. So in theory it's possible to bring in entire containers full of contraband, with a couple
of rows of approved goods stacked inside the doors, just in case.

By the way, have you ever wondered why bananas are cheaper here than apples? My guess is it's because the banana companies are a front: If a few bags of pure cocaine were loaded into every container of bananas, profits would far exceed any overhead. Your bananas could even be distributed free of charge.

I try to avoid breaking the rules. So when Lina asked, as she always does, "The Dutch want to load three pallets of samples in the container. Is that okay?" I refused.

"Right. Three pallets, half a ton each. One and a half tons of contraband per container. Maybe we should just give up declaring anything? We'll just declare oxygen. What's the TN VED code for air?* Zero duty?"

"I'm not kidding, Max."

"I'm not Max. My name is Maximus."

"I don't care if it's Caligula, asshole. We need samples. The front office is on our case day in and day out, they're going nuts trying to get the mashed potatoes with mushrooms on the shelves before our competitors. And the broker with the mushrooms doesn't want to declare them—that way the mushrooms will be pure profit. You know that!"

"I do. And I also know that we'll bring in two hundred tons of the mushroom mixture, and it'll just sit in the warehouse taking up space for six months, and then all of a sudden no one will have any use for it."

"So what? At least they'll be off our backs."

"Fine, then, load them up. But why three pallets at once? Let them have ten boxes, that should be enough. If they decide to inspect the whole batch, we can buy the inspectors off for a hundred bucks. But three pallets could get us arrested."

"Okay! Should I tell the broker?"

"No, keep them in the dark as usual."

* Nomenclature for goods in international trade.

"Got it."

"But make sure they get it right—it needs to go on the floor in the very back. And God forbid they include the boxes in the bill of lading and packing list! Tell them exactly how to fill out the forms."

"I know, I know—I'm no virgin."

"Oh, you expect me to believe that?"

"Figure of speech, you dimwit."

"As though anyone would take you!"

"You . . . you yellow-faced Tatar!"

"Khazar. Get it right: My face is Khazar. But really, who'd want you anyway? Haunting the workplace every day till nine P.M. . . ."

"I'm going to throw this hole punch at you!"

"Hole punch, hole punch . . . is that an invitation?"

"Filthy mind. Only you could come up with something like that. I think you're in desperate need of a girlfriend."

"All right, we've had our little laugh. Let's look at the rest of the message."

That's the way it was. More or less. But then something else came up. There's always something coming up with these samples—first they try to cheat us, and then they mount an ambush.

"What is it this time, Lina?"

"They claim something got into a shipment that didn't belong there."

"Meaning?"

"They put in an extra box of something, by mistake, and now they want it back, I guess. They're worried we might accidentally send it out to a retailer or open it ourselves. Rat poison, something like that . . ."

Now that was interesting. I decided to read the message after all. In spite of the insulting tone of my earlier letter, the supplier was proposing to split the expenses down the middle, and was being extremely courteous about it.

The second half of the message had to do with a box labeled PTH-IP-176539/48, twenty kilograms net weight. You could tell that the author of the message was trying too hard to strike a casual tone: We've just made a little mistake, everyone screws up now and then, no? So just set the box to one side, and we'll come and get it, no problem.

But he wasn't doing a very good job of sounding innocent. The wording was too strained, and I could see that there was real panic behind it, barely patched over. This was clearly no ordinary box. And sure enough, the phone on my desk rang and I heard the voice of the Import Director, calling from out on the road.

"Maximus?"

"Yes, Diana Anatolyevna."

Or should I call her "Madam Director"? My boss is three years younger than me. It's demeaning. She addresses me either by my first name or my last, but I use her full name, with the patronymic. It's not required, but some masochistic impulse makes me do it.

"Hello."

"Good afternoon, Diana Anatolyevna."

"These crazy Dutch guys have been calling my cell all morning."

"The swine!"

"They're in a huge rush to sign a supplementary contract to issue bonuses by sales volume."

"Imagine that!"

"Anyway, they're on their way to Russia as we speak. They want to be in the office first thing tomorrow. Can you pick them up at their hotel in the morning?"

"Whatever you say, Diana Anatolyevna."

"Semipyatnitsky, can we do without the excess humility? You know my car's in the shop."

"I said I'd pick them up."

"All right . . . so look: I'll come straight to the office from the airport; they can meet me there. Also, they mentioned a box, something that accidentally got into a container along with the samples. Are you up on this?"

"Yes, I am."

"Have the box brought from the warehouse to the office—the Dutchmen want to take it back with them. Though I'm finding it hard to imagine how they're going to manage that. And why all the fuss?"

That's an awful lot of trouble for a box of rat poison, I thought to myself. This sudden visit by the supplier's representatives had to be about the box. It was the contract about the bonuses that was incidental; that sort of thing can be decided without a face-to-face meeting.

I skimmed the message again. The Dutch were insisting that the box remain sealed, to keep the contents intact. So were they just going to take the box back to Holland with them, seals and all, as checked baggage?

Or would they open it beforehand and pack the contents in their personal luggage?

What was in that box?

I had to take a look. I could justify myself later by claiming that it had fallen off the forklift and broken open, or I could come up with some other story. I couldn't get that box out of my mind. I had to head over and see it for myself.

COLD CORPORATION

Let me say a few words about the organization where I work, its history and the nature of its business.

In its current form, Cold Plus is a conglomerate comprising regional distribution companies, warehouse complexes, and transport and freight enterprises, all administered from one central office. Cold Plus imports frozen food products from all over the world and arranges their processing through customs, transshipping, storage, delivery to processing companies, and distribution onto the retail market. The assortment, or, as they still call it, the product line, is enormous. Everything from potatoes to strawberries, shrimp to octopus, even cakes, candy, and bread, is frozen and freighted in from abroad in refrigerated containers and trucks. Just so you know, the chunks of "fresh fruit" in your morning yogurt are shipped in from China at a controlled temperature of minus eighteen Celsius and defrosted in Russia. The cheesecake that you order in a café was brought in frozen from Australia and thawed in the microwave, just moments before the waiter brought it to your table. The "fresh," "steamed," or "chilled" meat and fish in your supermarket more often than not were frozen a year ago somewhere in Argentina and underwent special processing to give them the appropriate degree of "freshness."

Many years ago, when such products were still a rarity, a group of clever entrepreneurs involved in the food importing business realized the potential for growth in frozen food and poured all their energy and resources into that sector. Demand grew with every passing year, and along with it the business of the Cold Plus Corporation. Now, practically everything we eat is frozen and freezing is the most widespread means of preserving the nutritional quality of food over time. The company's owners are now known as pioneers in the industry and are enjoying the well-deserved fruits of their bold initiative.

Cold Plus is a success story, the kind of thing you read about in glossy magazines aimed at a yuppie readership, but consumed mostly by mid-level managers like me, and students, who take it as an inspirational example of the kind of success they can aspire to in their future careers.

In principle it's a true story—though a few details are missing. And as we know, the devil's in the details.

A more complete reconstruction of the company's "success story" would go as follows:

At the very beginning of the glorious, fabulous, and romantic '90s, a group of Young Communists occupying leadership positions in the City Committee of the Komsomol followed the example of the Communist Party itself, which, according to a slogan posted in the halls of the City Committee Headquarters, was the Committee's helmsman, and steered the conversion of the economy to market principles, plunging fearlessly into the abyss of capitalism.

This period in post-Soviet history is called, to borrow Marxist terminology, the epoch of "primitive capital accumulation." Here the distinctions between good and evil get murky. For some, the phrase summons up visions of the Wild West: gold prospectors, adventurers, prostitutes, hucksters, and reckless cowboys. But in Russia's case, there wasn't much romance to it. Anyone who tells you otherwise is selling you a fantasy.

You see, the epoch of "primitive capital accumulation" in Russia and throughout the Soviet Union actually comprised the years of collectivization and industrialization, and the subsequent construction of "advanced socialism." During this period, capital was accumulated by means of cruel exploitation of the population and the confiscation not only of surplus goods, but necessities too; resources were concentrated in the offices of the bureaucracy and the Party machine, where they underwent processing into the ideal form for use by the country's future leaders. By the time the '90s came along, the only thing left to do was divvy up all that accumulated capital. And this task fell to the self-proclaimed red-carpet cowboys, the movers and shakers on the seats of power.

But let us return to our city Komsomol Committee. One of the country's first commercial banks, Bee Trust, was founded through the patronage of the Komsomol, and with the direct participation of its leaders. There was no need to spend centuries accumulating money, collecting it from thousands of individual depositors, as had been the case in old, backward Europe. Money was decanted directly from the city budget into this private bank in exchange for an utterly mundane transfer of a specified percentage of said funds back into the hands of the budget administrators in the form of hard currency. The same old gang of Party, Komsomol, and administrative functionaries retained their old positions, now "serving" in a new capacity.

After the liberalization of foreign trade, special structures were established under the bank's supervision to manage import operations. Purchases were covered by what still passed as government funds, transferred to the bank from the state budget; the revenue from sales within the country, though, following the age-old rules of the game, became the personal capital of those who had established the business.

Initially, the budding Komsomol capitalists indiscriminately bought up everything they could abroad, paying whatever price they were asked. In those days, even the rank and file involved in these deals on the Russian side could become millionaires after a mere month on the job through the unofficial commissions they received from foreign contractors for deals they signed on behalf of the government at exorbitant prices and with crushing terms.

The leadership cast a blind eye on the growing prosperity of their junior partners; they weren't doing so badly themselves, after all. Economically, the deals had absolutely no significance. All of the expenses were written off the accounts of Bee Trust, and the profits went directly into the owners' pockets.

The Bee Trust group's business realized the eternal dream of farmers everywhere: The two halves of the chicken, the part that consumed resources and the part that provided profit, were kept separate. The front part of the chicken, the part that needed to be fed, remained entirely in the government's chicken coop, whereas the back part, the part that laid the golden eggs, was privatized by Komsomol chicken farmers.

But all good things come to an end. The *dolce vita* of the Bee Trust bank ground to an abrupt halt on the day the Russian state declared bankruptcy. In addition to financing imports and buying up real estate, the Komsomol bankers had also gotten involved (excessively, it turned out) with securities. These securities primarily took the form of notorious short-term government bonds. Essentially, their purpose was to serve as an instrument whereby the state could attract funds to cover the ever-present budget deficit. Given the high and unpredictable levels of inflation at that time, these funds were obtained at unprecedented high interest rates.

Bee Trust, like many other banks, acquired these bonds by taking out subsidized loans from the government-owned Central Bank. They obtained them at an artificially low interest rate, then turned around and basically sold them back to the Russian government, but at a much higher rate. In this way, the Russian state issued credit and then covered that same credit by paying private banks for it.

The delta of this inspired operation allowed Bee Trust to increase its assets and to live high on the hog. The bank's offices occupied a five-story building in the historical city center, a palace that had originally belonged to some prince or count. Immediately after it acquired the building, the bank hired a Finnish company to completely overhaul and remodel it in the European style.

The aged gilding and eighteenth-century plaster moldings were knocked down, the mosaics and frescoes were scraped from the walls, and the decorative columns, crowned with sculptures of ancient heroes and divinities, were dismantled.

Four laid-off museum employees joined forces with a schoolteacher and formed a picket line outside the building to protest the destruction of a monument of historical and cultural value. The demonstrators spread out some pages from the newspaper *Pravda* on the concrete foundation of the palace fence and set out a bottle of vodka, a can of sprats in tomato sauce, and some spiced smelt and black bread. The protest went on for well over two hours. The intrepid defenders of culture invoked the memory of the palace's Italian architect and its original owner, a high-ranking general and patron of the arts, a nobleman, and, as legend would have it, a descendent of Khazar royalty. Periodically they would shout out a slogan, demanding that respect be shown to the cultural treasures within. They then turned to one another and indulged in effusive outbursts of mutual esteem.

The protest came to a halt when the bank's security system summoned the local militia, who proceeded to bundle the exhausted resistance fighters into a Kozel van and truck them off somewhere—most likely to be tortured in some windowless chamber.

The international media ignored the protest; most likely they were preoccupied with covering the meteoric rise of a new pop star—or should we say, pop "idol"?—by the name of Britney Spears.

Whatever the case, in 1998 the Russian government declared bankruptcy; that is, it declined to meet its debt obligations. At that point it was discovered that a critical amount of Bee Trust assets were held in the form of short-term government bonds.

Some time elapsed before everything came crashing down. For over a year the bank continued to occupy its remodeled European palace and maintained its sponsorship of the city hockey team. But the times kept on a-changing. The leading man of the TV drama that is Kremlin politics was replaced; new people moved into city government posts, notably those in charge of disbursing the municipal budget. These people had their own personal banks. Bee Trust was squeezed out.

Actually, the expression "came crashing down" is a little too melodramatic. Yes, Bee Trust, as a legal entity, underwent the bankruptcy and liquidation processes. Yes, bank employees who had become accustomed to an excessively cushy lifestyle lost their jobs. Yes, a few small-account holders—a couple thousand retirees—were ruined. But small stuff, really, in the grand scheme of things.

As for our Young Communist capitalists, they no longer depended exclusively on their bank resources. Each one of them held diversified assets: real estate, large amounts of cash both in hard currency and in accounts in countries with stable banking systems, as well as shares and interests in other branches of business.

One of those branches was import. Previously the Bee Trust group had dealt in the whole spectrum of food products. Now the time had come to break down into narrower areas of specialization. The era when one day you'd buy computers, the next prophylactics, and a week later bananas—all the while transporting non-ferrous metals and timber across the border—was over. Each different business staked out its own territory, with a finite number of players: authorized personnel only. Following the well-established laws of economics, the Russian economy entered the stage of monopoly capitalism.

The Bee Trust group imported all kinds of food products: fresh tropical fruits, vegetables, processed and canned goods, frozen foods, alcoholic beverages. But it didn't have the capacity or means to maintain a full-scale defense along such a broad front. The big corporations got rid of bit players in the banana and mandarin orange business by flooding the market with cheap product. Decisions as to who would be involved in alcohol sales were made at completely different levels of officialdom, with which the Komsomol capitalists fell out of touch. Processed foods were taken over by mass producers, with different brands competing for market share. Bee Trust was left to choose between two alternatives: canned goods or frozen food.

The canned-goods market at the time was large and seemed promising. So the senior partners of Bee Trust went for tin cans and founded the United Preserves International Corporation, which, in spite of the name, entailed a process of division rather than unification.

Four of the young Komsomol capitalists who had made their fortune on kickbacks from foreign suppliers took up the frozen-food business, which had been rejected by their senior colleagues. They founded a small company and called it Cold Plus.

The subsequent fate of United Preserves International is pure decline and fall stuff. The company collapsed within a few years. Some of its owners perished in internecine struggles; others squirreled away some capital and dispatched it abroad; the rest ended their business careers in poverty and squalor after spending the last of their money acquiring Russian companies producing canned meat and condensed milk.

Cold Plus, on the other hand, took advantage of the expanding market and the increase in demand and swelled up like shit on yeast. Its branches and warehouses multiplied, and Cold Plus swallowed up its small competitors and suppliers. By the time I entered the story, it had become a large and successful corporation, the industry leader in frozen food.

Now, this version of the corporation's history would be perfect for expansive documentation in some opposition newspaper, one of the ones that are financed by disgraced oligarchies (such as the rats who ran the notorious United Preserves International) or supported by left-wing enthusiasts. But the story is a lot more interesting than that. As I've already said, the devil's in the details. His goaty snout peers out from backstage during this little drama entitled *The Cold Plus Corporation: An Arduous Path to the Snowy Peaks.*

Because the prime mover behind the introduction of the deep-freeze method was Satan himself. Oh yes. As we know, there are certain regions of hell in which the temperature is maintained at an extremely low level. Satan preserves the fruits of Eden there to this day—just in case.

As part of his campaign to promote the deadly sin of gluttony, Satan arranged for each home to have its own refrigerator, along with a microwave oven. Now each and every sinner can indulge in gluttony twenty-four seven simply by grabbing some food out of the freezer and sticking it in the microwave for a few minutes.

In order to keep each refrigerator full, and to further simplify the life of the glutton, Satan devised a way to freeze every possible comestible on Earth.

And his fantasy expanded beyond mere food. The infernal technology of cryonics began to be promoted as a means of preserving the dead, or just their brains, depending on who you're talking to. Deep-freeze technology also made blood transfusions and organ transplantation possible on a large scale. But that's a different story . . .

Let us return to the Bee Trust bank and the Cold Plus Corporation. The few years of the bank's prosperity were dominated by the contracting führers from the Komsomol. The bank's very name, along with its twisted motto, stolen from the dollar bill—*In God Bee Trust*—hints at the true force behind the throne: B[ee] for Beelzebub. There is no doubt where the Komsomol capitalists placed their full faith and credit.

By the year of the great default, the term of their original satanic contract with the Komsomol was running out, and Beelzebub needed to obtain new signatures in fresh blood on his ancient paper. It was then that his young clients in infernal servitude got the brilliant idea of developing the deep-freeze business.

AT THE WAREHOUSE

The department director wasn't in, so I didn't have to ask permission to leave. I just mentioned to the girls at the front desk that I was going to the warehouse, and signed out at the security desk. Having dispensed with the formalities, I went to the elevator and pressed the down button.

The doors parted, and before my eyes I beheld the Goddess of Sex, Spring, and Fertility, a tanned brunette with a perfectly sculpted bosom and sultry eyes. For a moment I was unable to move, then she asked, "Are you getting in or not?" Her voice sent vibrations down my spine. Well, yes I am. "Hot damn!" I thought, in ecstasy or frustration or some mixture of the two. Most likely the girl was a new hire in one of the other offices in our building. As we rode down, I scrutinized the Rules for Elevator Use on the wall so as to keep from gaping at the goddess's breasts. At the first floor the girl got out and headed down the hall toward the break room; I went in the opposite direction, to the exit. Whew, made it. At ease.

I got in the car and started the engine, then inserted the theft-proof front panel on the radio and surfed the dial until I hit on some acceptable music. Then I backed out, exited the parking area, and set off along the crowded city streets toward the other side of town, where Cold Plus has its warehouses.

Recently I've been choosing stations that play rap, hip-hop, or just *kolbasa* pop without lyrics. The moment I hear the opening chords of a contemporary Russian pop song, I have an irresistible urge to puke all over the dashboard. I devoted many years to rock and roll and was always its biggest fan and connoisseur, but my brand loyalty exhausted itself and has now ricocheted in the opposite direction.

At first I used to be surprised when I heard about a real rock band putting on a joint concert with some commercialized pop act. Or when it would team up with some plastic pop group and go on tour to raise money for the president—yours, theirs, ours, "Nashists"'—and the party in power. Or when it went out to that stinking lakeside campground to perform for rowdy enthusiasts amassed at the big pro-Kremlin youth brigade's annual rally.*

Then I realized that it was unfair to Russian rock musicians to expect them to hew exclusively to their aesthetic principles and commit themselves to being engaged citizens. Why should they? They're not doing anything earthshaking, after all. They're simply paid by the hour to entertain people—as a rule, slackers in synthetic leather jackets drinking beer out of big PVC bottles. The ones whose parents have better salaries listen to R&B—which no longer signifies "Rhythm and Blues," by the way; this new music has nothing to do with real Rhythm and Blues—now it means "Rich and Beautiful."

No ideas in music now—just marketing.

On the whole, pop rock fulfills one social and political function—to take away people's ability to think. In a country where consumer demand increases as production decreases, where elections offer no real choice, and where no yardstick can measure the abyss that awaits, there's no need for people who can use their heads. They're useless, annoying, dangerous.

In an earlier era, they used to ban genetics and cybernetics; now it's garden-variety formal logic that's off limits. Because if a person starts thinking about things using simple syllogisms, it's obvious where it can lead: to revolutionary thoughts. And revolution is a crime. So people need to be protected from logic.

Both the singer Mak$im on the one hand, and the group B-2 on the other, dispense with logical ways of thinking. It's not that

* *Translator's note*: The reference is to the pro-government youth group Nashi—which means "ours" in Russian—and to its annual rally. The author might well be pointing out the happy accident of this name's morphological similarity to "Nazi"—and Nashist to "fascist," for that matter.

their lyrics make no sense; but any meaning they might have just slips away, no matter how much you concentrate. These days it's just impossible to figure out who it was that loved whom, and why they broke up, and then, if the song is so sad, then why are the singers all smiling? Rampant postmodernism. And, actually, Mak$im is better than B-2. Because no one needs these things to make sense. They just have to be a little sad, like how you feel after your second glass of vodka, but positive overall, you know, not too heavy. No need to strain your brain.

Modern art doesn't march at the head of a crowd waving a banner, nor does it thrust its mighty prow through ice-bound seas; it issues no summons, has no regrets, cries no tears. Modern art stands by the side of the road with a bottle of uncarbonated mineral water in its uplifted hand, and when a car pulls over, it leans over and calls into the open window, "Cool drink, anyone?"

Nowadays it's only the occasional rapper who might come up with some interesting lyrics and some semblance of content. There is no real rock and roll any more, and there hasn't been for a long time; what we have instead is rap. And *kolbasa* without lyrics is ideal precisely because there are no words: perfect for driving.

You can of course listen to megahits and oldies. Of course you can. But how many times can you listen to the same ones? I even know all the newer songs by heart. The old ones are just over-kill, brainwashing. "Hotel California" is a great song. No question about it. And the first one thousand six hundred eighty-four or so times I heard it I really liked it. Then I was forced to listen to it three thousand more times. At that point I think my enthusi-asm dimmed just a bit. Another couple thousand more times, and now my system goes into anaphylactic shock at the first chords.

All the good old rock and roll, the Beatles, the Rolling Stones, Led Zeppelin, even Pink Floyd, sets my teeth on edge. It's no one's fault. It's just that rock and roll didn't count on our longevity. Live hard, die young! But we clung to life and overstayed our welcome.

By the time my thoughts reached that point, I had switched over to the CD player, and Kurt Cobain's voice filled the speakers. Now there's someone who did it right.

Nirvana took me as far as the warehouse complex, where I parked in front of the office.

Inside, complete bedlam: Buried in papers, the girl at the front desk was pounding manically on her computer keyboard, correcting invoices. The room was packed full of city delivery drivers, and the noise of their grumbling filled the air. I fought my way through to the girl and asked:

"Where's the warehouse manager? The deputy manager? Where is everyone?"

"They're all out at the loading dock. Gone, every last one, the sons of bitches. Leave me alone! Don't come near me! Don't ask me anything! Fuck off, all of you!"

"Okay, fine. I'm almost done, I'll be out of here in a minute—can I use your phone?"

"Fuck you!"

"All right, okay."

I left the office and lit a cigarette. What was going on out here? Of course there's always something going wrong with deliveries; there are software breakdowns, and human error, and before you know it you're reinventing the space shuttle from scratch, piece by piece, all by yourself. But this chaos was way beyond normal. And not a single manager in the office.

I finished my cigarette and tossed the butt into the urn by the door, crossed the road, and entered the warehouse complex. A forty-foot refrigerated container truck stood at the loading dock, with workers swarming around. Everything looked normal there.

But when I climbed up onto the loading dock and approached the container in question, I realized that it was hardly business as usual. In fact nothing was as usual.

The workmen were moving like sleepwalkers, gliding along with a weird kind of grace, tracing slow-motion dance steps. Their eyes were wide open and they radiated an air of perfect bliss. This obvious state of grace was having a markedly deleterious effect on their efficiency, however. I watched one young guy in blue overalls for several minutes. He would pick up a box in the container, carry it to the forklift, set it down there, and then straighten up. Then he would bend down again and pick up the same box and carry it right back into the container. There he would set it down in the row of boxes, straighten up, again bend over, pick up the same box, and carry it back over to the forklift.

The workers took no notice of my presence. I don't think they'd have noticed Godzilla arriving on the scene, let alone some clerk from the central office.

Trying to avoid colliding with the mesmerized workers, I made my way over to the foreman's booth and peered in through the window, where I beheld an even more curious and striking scene. The foreman—a genuine Frenchman named Jean whose parents the Unclean Spirit had lured into the USSR via the Comintern and abandoned there to gasp their lives away during the era of reforms—was sitting inside the booth. No shirt, "topless," if you can apply that term to a man's hairy chest.

But three females, also topless, were crawling on their hands and knees on the floor around Jean's feet. I recognized one of them, the deputy warehouse director; the others were apparently administrative assistants or accounting clerks. The women were caressing Jean, and one of them was already undoing his pants. All of this was entertaining enough to watch, of course, and it was tempting to stay and see out the orgy, but I turned and headed for the walk-in freezer in search of the warehouse director.

Sure enough, there he was, wandering around between the racks in the walk-in cooler, wearing a quilted coat and an army cap with earflaps.

I went up to him and said, cautiously, "Good afternoon, Victor Stepanovich. How are things going here? Everything okay?"

"Huh? . . . Ah, it's Maxim!"

"Maximus."

"Huh?"

"Nothing, forget it."

"Is something the matter?"

"The matter?"

"Well, I mean . . . in general . . . it's just that . . . you've . . . you've got so much stuff coming in! Where am I supposed to put it all?"

"Have you been unloading potatoes from Holland today?"

"Yes we have! But were can we put them all? Look around you, they're everywhere! Potatoes here, potatoes there, potatoes everywhere! We've got nowhere left!"

Victor Stepanovich gestured wildly at the racks, which were completely empty, and at the empty corners of the walk-in. Then he grabbed me by the sleeve with his right hand and led me to the exit, describing semicircles in the air with his left.

"They're clogging up the aisles! And the loading dock. Potatoes!"

"Victor Stepanovich!"

"Why are there so many potatoes?"

"Victor Stepanovich!"

"Enough for a whole year! Where can we put them all?"

"Victor Stepanovich! There are no potatoes here! None whatsoever!"

"What do you mean, no potatoes?"

"Where is the box, Victor Stepanovich? The box with the rat poison?"

"Oh, the box, yes . . . Lina called and said something."

All right. So Lina had called and told them about the box. Who asked her to get involved? Honestly.

"So? Where is it? Is it still sealed?"

"Yes, it is. It's in the foreman's booth. But it's just that . . . it got a little torn."

"What do you mean, torn??"

"Well, it just . . . kind of slipped off the forklift and got a little torn." Sure it did. Slipped off the forklift. He could have come up with something more original.

Everything was clear now, just about. It wasn't rat poison—no, the box had some kind of narcotic in it. Or maybe hallucinogens, LSD or something along those lines. Some potato-dealers, those Dutch. And everyone out here had popped their fill of whatever it was. That's our guys for you. Call over from the main office and warn them that one of the boxes has rat poison in it, and they immediately want to try some. To hell with them. I'll just check out the box and its contents and be on my way.

"I see how things are. And I just might not say anything back at the office about what's going on out here. But I've been in-structed to bring the box back—the supplier is coming all the way from Holland tomorrow to pick it up."

Victor Stepanovich said that the box was in the foreman's booth, and then he turned and trudged back into the walk-in to resume his count of the pallets with their nonexistent potatoes. I went back to the booth and flung open the wooden door.

During my brief absence, Jean and the ladies had made sig-nificant progress. Jean's blue work pants were down by his knees, and the two administrative assistants (or accounting clerks) were hard at work down there, doing the "double helicopter" maneuver. The deputy director was stationed a little higher up, with Jean's face pressed between the two white mounds of her breasts.

The comradely group didn't react to my presence, which I can't say surprised me in the least. I glanced around the booth. A metal cabinet containing work clothes stood against the opposite wall. The cupboard doors were covered with posters of naked women.

A rickety table stood against the wall by the window, with some dirty mugs and glasses on it. I glanced under the table and there it was: a torn carton with big letters printed on the outside—PTH IP—followed by some numbers.

I crouched down and carefully slid the box out. Some little pink pills spilled from the tear. I scooped up a handful and took a close look. The pills were round, about the size of a No-Spa tablet, but without the diagonal stripe. Each pill had three letters printed on its surface, the same ones as on the box: PTH. Quite a sophisticated rat poison, with its own logo, evidently aimed at attracting a loyal consumer base—oh, right. Obviously, their rat-poison story wasn't worth a second thought.

"Right, if you have no objection, we'll just be on our way."

No one was listening.

There was a roll of packing tape and a pair of scissors on the windowsill. I quickly patched the tear, picked up the box, and pre-pared to make my exit. I took a couple of seconds to inspect the additional gallery of glossy whores on the inside of the door, and it suddenly occurred to me that the security guards wouldn't let me through the front gate without documentation for the box.

Jean was still in his private paradise, in the tender care of what he no doubt imagined to be nubile houris. I couldn't bring my-self to drag him back down to our fallen world, fraught as it is with misery and delusion. Felt sorry for the boy. He would come to before long, and when his vision cleared he would notice the accounting clerks' bowlegs and bulgy noses and the deputy direc-tor's advanced age and life-scarred, hangdog air.

I rummaged around and soon found what I needed in a draw-er of the table next to the metal cupboard: a pen, an invoice form, and an official stamp.

In the same drawer there were some torn condom wrappers— the special kind for anal sex—and then some kind of powder, and a bunch of other junk. I decided to postpone thinking about any of this until later. Elbowing the tea-yellowed mugs on the table to one side, I quickly filled in the invoice—"Samples for the central office, 20 kg."—scrawled a fancy-looking signature, and stamped the page.

I stuffed the invoice into the side pocket of my jacket and carried the box out of the booth.

On the way out I gave the deputy director a little spank on her generous behind, just for laughs. She didn't notice.

I passed through security and crossed the road to the parking lot, unlocked the car with the remote, nestled the box gently onto the back, got into the driver's seat, turned on the music, and started back toward the office.

The office?

ONE MILLION US DOLLARS

No way!

To hell with Cold Plus and its demented Dutchmen. Up Beelzebub's ass with my boring, monotonous, humiliating job. Straight to the flames of hell with my slavery and beggary. *To hell with them*!

I inched along in the flow of skittish cars, reviewing on my internal screen the filmstrip of my life, from my very first memories to the present day. A story of almost unrelenting poverty and need.

The few exceptions cluster at the very beginning of the show. Here I am at three or four years of age. I'm wearing a neat little sailor suit and tooling around the playground in an ivory-colored kiddie Cadillac. The car is made of plastic and cheap metal and was assembled in some factory in Hungary, or possibly Poland. It's pedal-driven; my feet in their light canvas slip-ons propel the car around on the asphalt, a one-kid-power motor under the flimsy hood. My older sister walks along beside me, protecting me and my precious vehicle from thieves and hooligans. The other kids from the apartment building stare at us in mute admiration.

My very first Cadillac, and also my last . . .

Now here I am at five or six. I'm in a little dress coat, with a white dickey and a bow tie on an elastic band around my neck. My handsome father, mustached and decked out in a fine suit, is holding my right hand. My beautiful mother, wearing a fancy dress and with her hair freshly permed, is holding my left hand. We are strolling along the seaside promenade in the resort city of Sochi, a fantastical place where we have access to everything—beaches and swimming pools, amusements and rides, restaurants with their Chicken Tabaka and wondrous Pepsi Cola.

At that time my father had been a man of some authority with a promising career, a government official in the Soviet economic system; my mother was that rarity, a stay-at-home housewife.

Soon afterward, my father's career collapsed due to an excessive and misplaced adherence to principle. After that he became a low-level employee in the statistics department of some pointless agency, and my mother took a job as a schoolteacher. These scenes in my little filmstrip are gray and melancholy.

Now I am seven. Or eight. No, still seven, that's right; it's New Year's Eve. 1980 will be the year of the Moscow Olympics. I've been assigned to play the role of the New Year itself, in the form of a frisky little bear cub. In the store, though, my mother sees the price tag on the bear costume, takes me by the hand, and leads me home without a word. At the pageant I run around inside the circle dance wearing a pair of simple red pedal pushers, with two big cardboard ears attached to my head. Hot tears roll down my cheeks. The first adult tears of my young life.

And my first cardboard ears—I will continue to wear them throughout my life, in one form or another.

After that everything pretty much continues in exactly the same way, just one thing after another.

My next pair of shoes are mud-colored Speedsters. They look utterly ridiculous, like clown shoes on my feet, which are already too big and flat as it is. But I'm only ten, no more, and it's not that big a deal at that point in my life. The problem is that my feet hurt. The shoes chafe and cause bloody calluses. Mom says that I'll get used to it; I have to break them in. But before she can turn away I see the tears in her eyes. Indeed, she was giving me false hope; the strange material that my shoes are made of doesn't stretch or ease with time; it just dries out and forms hard bumps in random places on the inside.

Now comes a longer story. I have a dream: I want to get a bike. An Eaglet or a Stork. With big wheels, a bright shiny frame, and a heavy chain liberally lubricated with motor oil. And of course with orange and red reflectors on the back fender. I already have the reflectors: I swapped a stamp collection for them with a kid at school. My older sister had been collecting stamps for a long time, since she was small, and now she had no use for them. Probably. I mean, she didn't even remember them. So I had the reflectors, just no bike. And my parents didn't have any money to spare. Bikes are expensive—eighty rubles!

I'm no pauper, though. I'm already grown up and I can earn the money all by myself. I'm twelve, almost thirteen. So I manage to get a job over summer vacation at the loading dock at a food processing plant. It's against Soviet labor law; I'm still considered a child. But they write me into the paperwork as sixteen. And indeed even at twelve I'm tall and broad-shouldered and look, if not quite sixteen, fifteen at least. Or no younger than fourteen, that's how I look at twelve. So I spend the whole summer lifting and hauling heavy boxes of canned food.

But it's not so bad, really; since I'm a minor I don't have to work a full eight-hour day. My shift starts around lunchtime; I can sleep in and have breakfast at home. My coworkers and I have lunch at the plant, eating the same canned food that we're hauling from the shop to the warehouse. We're just following the unspoken rule of Socialist production: Eat as much as you want on the job, just don't take any food offsite except in your stomach.

I go home in the evening. The noise of the kids playing outside doesn't tempt me. I'm too tired. I don't have a bike anyway, so I can't join the others in their races or forays into other neighborhoods. Soon, though—soon I will have my own bike and then I can go out at night and ride around with my friends. I take a shower, making big plans, put on my pajamas, and go to bed. I read in bed until I fall asleep with the book still in my hands.

Just before the beginning of the school year, with summer vacation coming to an end, I quit my job and pick up my pay, in cash, at the payroll office. It's a small wad of crumpled, greasy one-ruble bills, sassy green threes, and even a few crisp blue fives. Plus a few nickel and copper coins, every minute accounted for down to the last kopeck.

I went home that day solemn and proud. I'd grown up. I became a man that day as I walked home from work, feeling the money in my pocket, the first money I'd ever earned. An initiation, like in tribes of hunters when a boy becomes a man by making his first kill in the forest and bringing it home to his family's hearth.

I felt nothing like that later, several years later, when for the first time I plunged my jasper root into that moist, quivering crevice, if you will . . . My first time. Nothing poetic, just disgust and a drained, wasted feeling. Thirty seconds, a little friction, and I dispatched my entire arsenal, with its crew of cosmonauts, on a one-way trip into the chasm, that black hole beyond the scarlet petals, never to return. I felt nothing, no communion with a new life, no sense of belonging in a marvelous new world full of potential and bliss. Just disgust and a drained, wasted feeling. Primitive, animal shame.

Because I had become a man long before, that first time I received money for my hard labor and brought it home to my family.

I brought the money home and handed it over to my mother, the bills, that is; the coins remained in my pocket. There had been enough to buy a bike, even with a little left over. I had chosen the bike I wanted long before and had shown it to my mother several times already. It was a blue-frame Stork; they had it in the department store, in the sporting goods section on the first floor.

The next day Mom came into my room and, maintaining a tense silence, without looking at me, started randomly pulling books off my shelf. They were arranged in alphabetical order, side by side. She'd take a few out, wipe nonexistent dust off the clean surface of the shelf, and then put them back, out of order. Without a word. Without looking at me.

"Ma?" I asked.

They weren't going to get me the bike. A pair of second-hand Italian demi boots had turned up, just perfect for my big sister. A rare find, the right size, but there wasn't enough money to cover them. I loved my sister, didn't I?

It was at that moment that I understood what it meant to be a man. No yelling or hysterics; I didn't get upset and wasn't even that surprised. I was already grown up, was a man. Work hard, earn money. The money will go somewhere else, not to you and not for you. Work hard, earn money, and turn it over to women. *Man's burden, white or black, doesn't matter.*

My only reaction was to skip meals and shun my family for three days. I sat in my room and stared at the little pile of coins, the sixty, seventy kopecks I had to show for my whole summer's labor.

Then came adolescence, classmates, weddings, friends in Adidas tracksuits, bleached-out, rolled-up jeans. Me, though—I was big, awkward, blighted with acne, and everything I wore was cheap, gray, and out of fashion. Someone gave my father a bolt of some generic, coarse fabric and took me to the tailor to have a suit made, to make me look more presentable. It was cheaper that way. He did try, my father. But nothing came of it; I don't remember why.

I like music, everyone does, I know a lot about various groups and musical styles, always have. But back then, when people offered to swap cassettes I didn't say anything, just kept my mouth shut. I didn't have a cassette player: Mine was an ancient reel-to-reel, bought long before for my sister.

But then I graduated and enrolled at the Institute. For my first winter as a student I got one of my father's old coats, taken in at the seams. It had been pretty decent at one time, but the tailoring was shoddy and it hung on me like an old sack. My family also gave me a big hat that looked ridiculous with the short "diplomat" style coat; the fur was supposedly raccoon but looked suspiciously like dog pelt, badly dyed.

The student life is easy. A student is poor by definition. Back then all or nearly all of us were broke. Of course I was dressed worse than everyone else, but we all chipped in what we could for vodka and shared equally, that's the main thing, and I felt like I belonged.

Next thing you know I'm married to this wonderful girl Lenochka. No wedding, just a quick trip to the registry office. I'm cooking something in the kitchen of our first-story rented apartment and Lenochka is doing something in the other room. "Bring my watch, babe!" I ask. "Where is it?" My wife's voice rings like a little bell. "On the bedside table!" I answer.

A minute goes by. Lenochka comes into the kitchen, spreads her empty hands, says "I couldn't find it, Poppy!" I shake my head in reproach and go into the bedroom myself, with her tagging along. "Here it is!" The watch is right where I said it was, on the "bedside table."

"Pops, why don't you label these cardboard boxes so I can tell them apart? Which one do you consider to be the bedside table, which the coffee table, and which the dresser or wardrobe?" Lenochka forces a smile, but a tiny involuntary tear glistens in the corner of one eye. Our room is furnished entirely in empty cardboard banana and apple cartons.

My girl will dump me two years later and marry a guy who makes a living buying up government vouchers. The first thing she'll do is order some real furniture and a refrigerator for her apartment.

* *Translator's note:* The word *mak* (as in the nickname "Mack"), in Russian, means "poppy," as in the poppy plant.

Enough already. The rest is just more of the same. Rare spells of relative solvency and then poverty again, need. Like now, with practically all my money going to monthly interest fees, nothing left to cover gas for my gray Renault, itself bought on credit. Just like the refrigerator, the computer, even the smart phone.

The filmstrip is over.

I thought about the box lying at this very moment on my back seat. Twenty kilos of Dutch pills. Illicit drugs, of course. Wholesale, a batch that big would have to be moved at a rock-bottom price. But even so, it would bring in fifty thousand dollars, minimum.

If it was cocaine, real cocaine, then it would be worth a whole lot more. Pure cocaine would cost one hundred forty a gram, retail. You could find cocaine at eighty a gram, but everyone knows that at that price the powder has been laced with speed or simply ground analgene. Pure cocaine, though, on the market, was one hundred forty a gram.

Each intermediary cranks up the price by a hundred percent or more. So a pusher will sell a gram at seventy dollars, or, say, fifty, to use a round figure. The dealer will charge twenty dollars a gram if the batch is big enough. And if I wanted to push coke to a dealer, I'd offer it to him at ten dollars a gram.

Twenty kilograms would come to two hundred thousand dollars.

But that's coke. These were some kind of pills, and most likely they wouldn't sell for that much. And I didn't even know what the stuff was. Some ecstasy clone, maybe?

I'd have to try some and see. Not just push the pills blind. If it turned out to be crap, my client would beat the shit out of me even before any money changed hands.

All of this was whirling around in my head as I headed back to work. By the time I realized I would have to try the pills myself, I was already on the Obvodny Canal embankment, just down from the Cold Plus office.

I smirked. So long, workplace! And instead of exiting the embankment on the right and heading for the office, I merged into the left lane, crossed the bridge over the Obvodny Canal in the other direction, toward the waterfront, and floored it.

The road was clear. Traffic was jammed up on the opposite side, the one leading from the port to the city. I made it to Kanonersky Island in no time and entered the tunnel.

This is one of the darkest, scariest tunnels in the whole wide world, take my word for it. The Kanonersky Island Tunnel is long, poorly illuminated, unventilated, and filled not with air but pure, unadulterated automobile exhaust.

I recalled one time a few years ago when I actually had to go through the tunnel on foot. I needed to get to the St. Petersburg Customs office, to certify some payments or confirm a certificate of origin, I can't remember which. It was before I started working at Cold Plus. I used to earn money on the side processing shipping declarations.

I had to get to the customs office, but I'd missed the bus, or maybe there wasn't a bus—anyway, I had set off walking from Baltic Station in the direction of Kanonersky Island and had entered the tunnel. I think I must be one of very few people who've actually made it through that tunnel as a pedestrian.

I pressed up against the wall like the shade of a dead man in Hades; diesel trucks roared past, deafening me. I could hardly breathe; the exhaust made my head spin and dulled my thoughts. I walked on and on, barely managing to put one foot down in front of the other. It seemed like it would never end. Or that I was already dead. "This is all there is. It will go on like this forever," wrote the poet Nikolai Gumilyov, though at the time I was not thinking of poetry. My mind was completely blank and I just lurched blindly along through the tunnel. And at first I couldn't believe it when the tunnel finally ended and I emerged, squinting into the faded northern sun suspended in the pale northern sky above the faded northern sea. And this drained, pale world blinded me with its brilliance and color!

This time I entered the tunnel by car and surfaced on the other side within a matter of minutes.

"GIVE ME TWO TABLETS"*

I parked in a lot in front of a water treatment plant, descended a set of concrete steps to the shore, and sat on an old tree branch that had fallen near the rippling water.

I knew the place well. I used to go there to wait while the customs officials inspected some document I'd brought, or if I'd shown up during their lunch break. I used to have lunch there myself, whatever I could scrounge up, or takeout from the shop at the bus stop. Those were lean times, even worse than now. But still, I remember those days fondly. I was young, after all. In youth, everything—even poverty—is an adventure. In middle age, poverty is just poverty, pure and simple.

Before clicking on the car alarm I opened the back door and dug around inside the box. I scooped out a few of the pink pills and put them in my jacket pocket. I was in no hurry. And then it occurred to me: What if it was poison, what if it was fatal in the long term? I'm scared of death, but not because I regret leaving life behind; the life I'm leading isn't worth fighting for. But dying itself is scary. And painful too, probably. Even when the person shows no external signs of suffering, even when it looks like he's just going to sleep. That's how it seems to the people around him, sure, but how are they supposed to know what the man himself is experiencing? Maybe every death brings agony and suffering, whether or not anyone else can tell from the outside.

But what will be, will be. I reached into my pocket, took out one of the pills, and held it on my palm. I inspected it for a couple of seconds, then popped it into my mouth and swallowed it. I gave it another moment's thought, then gulped down a second one for good measure. Based on my body weight, I usually need a double dose of anything.

* To quote a song by a Petersburg rock group.

Done. Now all I had to do was wait for the rush. Or some other, less pleasant effect. I leaned back and closed my eyes, tilting my face up into the feeble sunlight.

I'd only tuned out for maybe a minute or so. But I came to with a jolt. I'm not sure whether what I felt had anything to do with the pills; I might just have dozed off for a moment. One way or another, when I opened my eyes . . .
. . . Nothing out of the ordinary.
The gulf water came in little waves that lapped at my feet. Seagulls circled overhead and filled the air with their shrill cries. The northern sun bathed me in warm rays; a cool sea breeze brought fresh air.

I thought, "All is well. Why all the gloom and doom? I'm still young; my whole life is ahead of me. And what I have isn't all that bad! A steady, well-paying job in an office, some potential for professional advancement. A literary debut. That's nothing to sneeze at: I'm alive, healthy, and free—all the prerequisites for true Russian happiness. It's nothing to sneeze at. True success. So chin up. Maintain a positive attitude, and good things will come your way. Right. You know all this already. That demented idea of quitting your job, of selling the pills, it's pointless. No good can come of it. Just get right back in that car and make a beeline for the office. Blame traffic for the delay. Take the box straight to Cold Plus and hand it over, and everything will be fine. Perfect. It's just . . . the potatoes—potatoes everywhere! Viktor Stepanovich is right, we're ordering too many."

Lo, before my very eyes: pallets laden with frozen potatoes, row upon row of them, filling the walk-ins and piling up in the warehouse aisles. And when I got into my car, the interior was packed with boxes of potatoes as well, solid stacks of them rising from the back seat to the roof.

But I blinked, and the vision dissipated.

The Maya Pill

There was just that one box of pills, right where I'd left it on the back seat. It had an unsteady look to it, though; its outlines were blurry and it was sort of hovering a couple of inches above the seat.

It was bound to happen: There I was, standing, waiting for the elevator, all sweaty, the top buttons of my shirt undone, my tie draped over my shoulder, holding that stupid box in my hands, with my face twisted into an idiotic grin (where did that smile come from?). And sure enough, there she was again: the Goddess of Spring, Sex, Fertility, and Related Stuff.

"Making a delivery?" she asked, smiling back at me.

"Yes yes," I said. "I'm the idea delivery man. I travel from ear to ear through the hallways of the mind, spreading profound thoughts."

Hardly my best witty banter. But the goddess seemed to appreciate my little word game. She even gave a little wave—see you!—on her way out of the elevator.

Now I have to talk to you about sex.

It's page 65 already, we're well into the plot, but not a word yet about sex. People might start to wonder about me.

I declare, being of sound mind and body: I Maximus Semipyatnitsky, am neither a pederast nor a metrosexual (is there a difference?), nor indeed am I into cyber-sex or chat-sex or whatever other perversions. Your basic normal guy. At least I used to be, before I went to work at Cold Plus.

I even have a girlfriend. Had, rather. Not all that long ago.

She packed her things and went home to her mom's.

To be more precise, she packed *my* things and threw me out. Because she'd been living in the apartment before I came into the picture; her mother had given us a break on the rent because we were family.

It was really hard for her. I mean the girl, not her mother.

Though maybe it was hard for her mom too, how should I know? But it's more likely she was relieved. Anyway, to hell with her, the mom, serves her right for sticking her nose in. (Forgive me, Lord.)

The girl, I mean. She even cried. "Mack!" she wailed. She was the only one who was allowed to call me that. My name is Maximus, and no one—you hear me?—no one has the right to use nicknames with me: Maxim! Maxi! Max! I'm a human being, not a dog. But she called me Mack, and I let her do it.

So she says, "Mack, Pops, I love you so much, I really do." Hear that? She loves me, said so herself.

"Mack, I love you. But I can't go on this way."

"Why not?"

"I need sex, wild sex every day, ideally four times a day, every single day, not once every two weeks after some three-hour fight! I can't go on this way! We both know it. Would it really be better if I started cheating on you, picking up men in clubs, sleeping with guys my girlfriends introduce me to at birthday parties and shish-kebob weekends at the dacha, or screwing some guy from work? I moved in with you so we could have more sex. I mean with each other, you idiot, because I love you, I still do, but I'll get over it. I thought that if we lived together, nothing would keep us from having sex all the time. I was dreaming of the day! But it turned out just the opposite. First we had sex every day, even when I had my period, then we abstained during my period, and then on Mondays, because Mondays are tough, right? Then the only time left was the weekends, you get so worn out at work. Now even weekends are too much for you. But I'm only twenty-four. I'm still young, I need sex—it's perfectly normal. So good-bye, Mack! So long, don't say anything, not a word, just go, it'll be easier for both of us that way. Just go, Mack!"

Now there's no one to call me Mack anymore.

On the second floor of the Mega Mart I saw a booth where

you could order a T-shirt with any slogan you want written across the front, and I spent a long time trying to make up my mind. There were some great options, all in English: "*I Hate Love and Sex*," hm-m-m . . . too direct, don't you think? "*Sex is boring me to death*"—interesting, but too long. "*Sex sucks*"—just the thing! How come no one ever thought of it before?

Of course, ultimately, I ordered something completely different. Now I have a T-shirt with "Jesus hates me" written across the chest in bold black letters. And if I walk past, and you happen to look at my back, you'll see: "U2."

BEAUTY WILL GRAZE THE WORLD

The world is full of ugliness. Yes, this world is ugly. Disgusting, nasty, foul. And of all the creatures populating this sickening world, the most disgusting and nasty are the human beings.

Take any group of people. Will you see a lot of beautiful, classical, or even just generally nice-looking faces? No way. We are surrounded by freaks. Fat, irregular, clumsy, or gaunt, with gray and sallow faces, their cosmetics—cheap or high end—peeling off like old plaster. Crooked, cross-eyed, wrinkled, pimpled, disgusting, revolting creatures.

Take anyone! Aunt Valya? A creature from a nightmare! Uncle Styopa, the wino next door? I've seen better looking turds. Those prostitutes on the next block? One look and you're impotent for life. Coworkers? Where on earth does our company do its recruiting? The formaldehyde room at the Museum of Natural History?

People don't look at all the way people should. The Winter Garden has statues of creatures that look like people. Some of them are supposedly gods, though we have it on good authority that there are no gods, that sculptors in antiquity used their own friends, neighbors, and acquaintances as models. A centurion served as a model for Mars, the god of war, and a streetwalker posed for a statue of Aphrodite. That's what people were like back then. Look at the classical sculptures and you'll get an idea of what ordinary people looked like a mere couple thousand years ago.

Imagine sculpting statues of the gods using your contemporaries as models. You couldn't even manage a Bacchus or satyr. Not even a parody. Anything you could come up with would be pathetic and disgusting.

A writer is a kind of sculptor. That is why the novel and the epic are dead. Big genres need larger-than-life heroes. All you'll get from our scrawny and mean souls and ratty, ugly bodies will be cheap comedies à la Petrosyan.* Mix in some foul language and a pederast or two and you've got a cheap stand-up routine. Even serious writers—take me, for example—just produce superficial, bloggy stuff.

The Eastern gurus taught: Look not into the faces of the worldly. One glance will earn you a berth in hell.

There's beauty for you.

People are more like animals. The most disgusting and vile ones, in fact. Take a look around: rats, moles, pigs, chickens, frogs—these are our companions.

People are also kind of like Tolkien's mythical creatures. When I'm out on the street I can categorize them by sight: trolls, gnomes, orcs, and of course goblins. Long-eared, evil elves are also out and about.

Beauty is extremely rare in this world. That's why it's so treasured. Beauty commands a high price, in any currency. If you want to find a truly beautiful prostitute, you have to shell out some serious cash. One night will set you back three months' salary. Anything cheaper is counterfeit, a tasteless sham.

If a person, male or female, is born beautiful, then everything will fall into his or her lap. No other virtues or assets are necessary. With minimal effort you can sell beauty anywhere at top price.

Everyone is willing to pay a premium for true beauty, anytime, anywhere. But we can't afford true beauty. Admit it, be honest, your life has abounded in sexual adventures, but how many truly beautiful women or handsome men have you slept with in all that time? Three? Two? I wouldn't be surprised if there hadn't been a single one.

* *Translator's note*: Evgeny Petrosyan (b. 1945) is a famous Soviet/Russian comedian of Armenian and Jewish ancestry.

Long ago, in my distant youth, my classmate Vaska—we called him the Fireman —encapsulated the entire tragedy of our existence, devoid as it is of aesthetic value. We were watching one of the new Russia's first televised beauty contests, and the Fireman pronounced mournfully, with great profundity, "Damn! And there are guys out there who get to fuck those beauties!"

We find no real perfection around us, and so we compromise and accept half-beauty, cheap imitations. If a girl isn't disgusting looking, has some marginally decent features, we're ready to marry her and take care of her for the rest of her life. But even a girl like that is hard to find. So we marry freaks. And we almost love them. Of course we do; we try to be decent human beings.

Still, we always long for beauty, the kind of beauty that we can never really touch.

This fills our lives with suffering—yet another reason for our inner disharmony. We don't realize that true beauty is incredibly rare, that our chances of coming into contact with it are close to zero.

If we just accepted it, things might be easier. We don't suffer, for example, from the knowledge that we will never personally make it to Alpha Centauri. Very few people are disturbed by that realization; those of us with some sense, the majority, know that it's impossible, and so there's no point in worrying about it.

But it's different with beauty. Beauty seems so close, so accessible!

Blame technology.

Art, culture, mass media, advertising—they all disseminate myriad images of the sort of beauty that is in fact extremely rare, creating the illusion—and it is an illusion!—that you can find it anywhere.

Photographers ferret out the one and only beautiful girl out of one hundred thousand ugly ones, and they spend days on end photographing her in an infinite variety of poses and angles, against all kinds of different backgrounds. Then they enlarge the photos into posters and suddenly she's multiplied into a million beautiful girls on billboards, magazine covers, and labels.

But it's a thin, paper image, a product of technology. As a million duplicated images, she can only exist within various forms of media, whereas there's only one original version of the real beauty, the actual girl. And she can only belong to one man at a time. Or two. Three, maximum—there are only so many orifices.

But we forget that. We are deluded, led astray by this reproduction of a beautiful image. We cling to the hope that we will see a beautiful girl in real life; that she's just around the corner or down at the bus stop; we'll run into her in a store and strike up a conversation, and then we'll go home and screw, or, in the rare exception, we'll make her our wife.

In the meantime we sit and wait, we live with our half-beauties, girls we can't love the way we should because of our belief that perfection is within reach. In the depths of our souls we consider them to be temporary measures, stopgap solutions until the day we meet the Aphrodite reserved for us by fate.

It would be better to accept the truth that rejecting our Claudia for the sake of some future magazine-cover Venus makes about as much sense as not changing the oil in our little Hyundai, figuring that in no time we'll have our very own Porsche Boxster. Listen, dude, where are you going to get your hands on a two-hundred-thousand-euro Porsche if you still have five years left on the ten-thousand-euro loan you took out for your Accent?

We understand this, and though we dream of a Porsche, we treat our actual car like a member of the family. We don't have any illusions about trading in the Accent for a Porsche, and yet we cling to the belief that we can plausibly trade Claudia in for Venus.

Venus seems more accessible than the Porsche. There she is, smiling at us from all those advertisements. And unlike a Porsche, absolutely free!

But, listen pals, uh . . . I don't want to startle anyone here with an original thought, but nothing in this world comes for free.

Beauty costs money. Real money. More than people like you and me can scrape together in an entire lifetime. If a shitty Boxster is beyond your means, don't even bother thinking about Aphrodite. Let it go.

To summarize: "Don't believe what you see in art, in advertisements, in beautiful pictures; forget those unrealizable dreams about happiness and perfection. You will never have all that. Value your wives and girlfriends. Love the one you're with."

CHINA TRIP*

All of these thoughts were inspired by my encounter with that Venus-Aphrodite, the goddess of all pleasurable things, in the elevator at the office—but only in retrospect. At the time my mind was far from such abstractions. Aphrodite exited on her floor, and I continued on up to mine, with the box in my hands and that idiotic smile plastered on my face. To avoid trouble I stowed the box in the utility room near the tea stash and the cartons of printer paper. The pills had clearly taken effect, but I couldn't quite put my finger on how, exactly. There had been a shift in my consciousness, but my perceptions hadn't changed. No spatial disorientation or physical effects—just a light euphoria, a sense of gentle optimism. And those persistent images of Dutch potatoes.

I returned to my desk.

The inbox was full of messages that had arrived during my absence. The usual spam, notifications from the systems administrator, inquiries from branch offices, and a message from my favorite correspondent, the Chinese partner who supplied us with fish.

Their manager's name was Ni Guan. Or "Eddie." All Chinese businesspeople who work with foreign partners adopt nicknames. Li, Chan, Su, and Shin become Louis, Victor, Christina, and Tanya—whatever they can come up with. I think that they're assigned those names back in school, in their foreign language classes.

My guess is that they adopt these names so that we won't mangle their real ones and defile them with our poor pronunciation. They don't want to waste time on the pointless and gratuitous labor of explaining their language's phonetic system: "My name is Li Li. No, they're different: Li is my first name, and Li

* That is: Tripping to China, or: A Trip Made of China.

is my family name. No, they're completely different words. My first name Li is pronounced 'Li.' But my family name Li is a little longer and a half tone higher: 'Li.' A completely different meaning . . . Fine, okay, just call me Kolya. It'll be easier for you."

For the one-hundred-eighth time Eddie reminded me about our overdue payment of four hundred thousand dollars and encouraged us not to decrease our orders during the current quarter. He wrote calmly, without hysterics.

I was always struck by the paradoxical and transcendental attitude of Chinese employees toward their business dealings. The first time I came into contact with them was when I was working for a tobacco company. We were supplying unprocessed tobacco to Russian factories, which were failing gradually under the pressure of competition with transnational corporations. One of these semi-moribund factories was in Omsk. When the company entered into bankruptcy proceedings, I attended a meeting of creditors to represent the company and to try to salvage some portion of their delinquent account, which came to somewhere around a hundred thousand dollars.

Everyone assumed that the dominant voice at the meeting would be the representative of the Chinese National Tobacco Corporation, which had supplied over three million dollars' worth of raw tobacco to Omsk.

But no one came from China. And they didn't even submit any claims.

The Chinese had a philosophical attitude toward their client's insolvency. So it didn't work out, they thought; it happens sometimes. The world is not perfect. Or, on the contrary, the world *is* perfect, and the collapse of the Omsk tobacco business is also Tao, the path, part of the universal plan, one chord in the great musical harmony of the world. They wrote off their three million and just kept on doing business.

It's possible that two or three of the company's top managers—

one for each unrecovered million—were dispatched by firing squad in a public square; that's something we'll never know. But they didn't waste time milling about in the throng at the factory turnstile, didn't interfere with the executors and court officials conducting the inventory of the factory's property, and they refrained from hiring local Russian bandits and bureaucrats to solve the problem. Why bother? Too much trouble. It's all Tao.

Cold Plus's Chinese partners are also willing to spend years waiting patiently for their unpaid invoices, stoically enduring our never-ending attempts to obtain extra fees and discounts on any pretext, no matter how flimsy; occasionally they'll even satisfy claims that are utterly without foundation. Just so they can continue supplying their products to Russia.

They have their own logic, their own way of understanding the concept of profit. We plan one or two years ahead, they mark time in centuries. Don't bother paying now; go ahead, haggle for every kopeck, cheat us. But keep on buying our products, consume more and more of what we have to offer. You're only cheating yourselves—and your offspring—enslaving yourselves to whatever we produce, destroying your own country's economy, losing your own capacity to produce things of value. The day will come when we'll take you with our bare hands . . .

I thought that it would be interesting to get inside the mind of a Chinese person, to learn what makes him tick. What goes on in the mind of this Eddie?

I typed out our standard formal response about how we "plan to execute payment this month"; and as for the volume of purchases, it was "currently under discussion in our commercial department"; then I slid the cursor over to "Send." I hesitated for a moment, looking at the monitor, then briskly left-clicked . . .

What happened next, all of it, was very much like a hallucination, but to this day I'm convinced that what I experienced was real.

I looked into the monitor and my consciousness was sucked out of my skull, like a soft-boiled egg, out through my eyes. The egg metaphor comes to mind because my consciousness turned out to be yellow. A clotty, yellow-orange substance. I slipped through the monitor and down the cable to the processor, whirled along the circuit boards, and spiraled down into the telephone cable. Then I whizzed along the copper veins, leaping and bounding across transformers and switchboards until I burst out of a different monitor, flew upward, and squeezed with some effort into the pair of eyes opposite it.

And now I found myself looking at a screen again—but at my own message, this time, in the inbox.

Darkness and a short pause. Feel free to insert your commercial message here.

THE TAO OF THE
MID-LEVEL MANAGER

In a low-ceilinged room with a wall of windows facing the street, an old air-conditioner hummed quietly. The higher frequencies of the acoustic spectrum were taken up with the chirping of female interns chattering on the phone and with one another. Only the middle range was relatively quiet. Ni Guan usually tuned his brain to the middle range and basked in its emptiness. Ni Guan had mastered this technique years ago, akin to distinguishing between the high and low frequencies coming over a telephone line. Without it, the sensory overload would cause his head to explode.

Since Ni Guan had tuned out the higher acoustic range, he didn't hear any ICQ beeps,* but the "new mail" icon flashed in the lower right corner of the screen and caught his eye. The message was from Cindy, Ni Guan's young coworker and assistant, who dealt with contract issues involving the northern barbarians.

Cindy's real name was Tsin Chi. She was twenty-two. She had a nice figure, was smart and fun to be with, and showered rather more attention and care on Ni Guan than was customary in interactions with a senior colleague.

Ni Guan opened the message and read:

I drive my chariot
Out the Upper Eastern gate.
To the north of the settlement
I see a multitude of graves.

Above them aspens
Rustle their leaves.

* An instant messaging program. I-C-Q = "I seek you".

Pines and cypresses
Line the broad roadway.

Below the earth lie bodies
Of men who died in ages past,
They disappeared
Into the infinite night

And slumber there in the mist
Where yellow streams flow,
Where a thousand years pass,
Yet no one awakens.

Like a stream, a stream,
Eternally flowing, yin and yang,
The term allotted us
Is like the morning dew.

A man's lifetime
Flashes by, a short visit:
Flesh in longevity
Is not like stone or metal.

Ten thousand years
Follow end to end.
No sage, nor holy man
Can exceed that term.

As for those who have "partaken,"
Striving to join the immortals,
To them before all others was delivered
The soporific of death.

Is it not, then, better for us
To savor the sweet wine,
and spare no silks
For our own raiment?

And under the "Thirteenth Ancient Verse" of the *Shi Jing*, a small postscript was appended: "Ni, shall we go out for a drink after work?"

Ni Guan turned and looked over at Tsin. She was looking straight at him, smiling immodestly. Ni Guan smiled back and shook his head gently, then briskly tapped out another poem from *Shi Jing*, from memory. The poem, known as "The Cricket," is from the "Odes of the Tang Kingdom" section:

The autumn cricket
Has settled in the hall.
It is clear, the year
Is coming to an end . . .
If today
we are not to make merry,
with the moons the days will pass,
never to return.
But let us not chase
After pleasure;
We must be ever mindful
Of what we owe,
And love merriment
Not to excess:
A man of worth
Must be cautious in his pleasures.

The autumn cricket
Has settled in the hall.

It is clear, the year
Will soon quit us . . .
If today
we are not to make merry,
With the moons the days will pass
In vain.
But let us not chase
After pleasure;
We must be ever mindful
Of what we have left undone,
And love merriment
Not to excess:
A man of worth
Must be zealous in his labors.

The autumn cricket
Has settled in the hall.
The time has come for the carts
To come from the field to their rest . . .
If today
We are not to make merry,
With the moons the days
Will pass, leaving no trace.
But let us not chase
After pleasure;
We must be ever mindful
Of many sorrows,
And love merriment
Not to excess:
A man of worth
Must be imperturbable.

Ni Guan added a note of his own: "Comrade Tsin, tonight

I have to stay late at work. Comrade Luan assigned me to do a report on the contract with the northern barbarians. Speaking of which, send me the memorandum on the interruptions in the timeframes of deliveries to Russia."

When she got his message, the girl tapped furiously on her keyboard, and within a couple of minutes the "new mail" icon again flashed on Ni Guan's screen. Ni Guan opened the message and read:

Swift flies the "Morning Wind" falcon.
Thick grows the northern forest . . .
Long have I not seen my lord,
And my mournful heart
Is inconsolable.
What can I do?
What can I do?
He has forsaken me;
Will he ever think of me again?

On the mountaintop
The oak spreads its branches,
In the lowland, supple elms . . .
Long have I not seen
My lord,
And my mournful heart
Is inconsolable.
What can I do?
What can I do?
He has forsaken me;
Will he ever think of me again?

On the mountaintop
The plum branches spread wide,

In the lowland, wild pears . . .
Long have I not seen
My lord,
And my mournful heart
Is as though intoxicated.
What can I do?
What can I do?
He has forsaken me;
Will he ever think of me again?

No postscripts appeared after this poem from *Odes of the Tang Kingdom*. Ni Guan again looked over at Tsin. Comrade Tsin was concentrating on a pile of papers on her desk; her cheeks were slightly flushed, her lips protruding sulkily. Everything about her said "You are a heartless, dry old shell of a man, Comrade Ni!" Or, more precisely, "You are like a withered stalk of wild rice standing alone outside the farmhouse gate, his fruit untouched, when the time of harvest has already passed and his brothers' white grains have been gathered into sturdy barns; he alone will be buried under cold snow, when the twilight of the year gives way to night and a heavy cloud covers the Mountain of Flowers, Huashan."

Ni Guan heaved a sigh and resumed his work. From the purchasing manager of the Russian company Cold Plus, who went by the name of Maximus Semipyatnitsky (which was some abracadabra!), came one of his typically dull messages, utterly devoid of meaning. They always read as though they'd been written by some computer program. Blatantly false promises to settle their debt; nothing concrete in response to Ni Guan's request to confirm the amount of product to be delivered according to their contract with the barbarians, which had given them a discount and advance credit.

Comrade Luan, the senior export manager, would be upset. But it had nothing to do with Ni Guan. Comrade Luan knew that it was the barbarians' fault; it's always like this with them. But the gurgling stream would flow down from the mountains, would crumble the rocky cliffs, would carve crevasses in the solid stone, and would make its way inexorably out onto the broad plain, where it would spread into a mighty river, bearing abundance to the lands under the vault of heaven.

So too Ni Guan, with every day he spent in the office, with every e-mail he sent, with every telephone call he made to the barbarian cities, with his patient persistence and imperturbability, would eventually bring prosperity to the Chinese people. Even now, thanks to the work of the Tsin-dao Seafood Export Co, Ltd., Ni Guan's place of employment, and of thousands of other export companies, millions of Chinese peasants had jobs and could feed their families.

They cultivate everything that can be eaten. They even cultivate fish and seafood, like rice. Ni Guan had visited fish plantations and had seen how they worked. Fish hatchlings were kept in cages made of netting and submerged in flooded meadowlands. Standing waist-deep in the water, peasant workers scooped the fish out, sorted them by size, and moved them into larger cages. They sprinkled fish fodder into the water and cleaned out the cages. Then they harvested the fish, cleaned them, and chopped them up into edible portions.

Peasants working on the fish plantation earn twenty yuan a day! Not all that much, of course, compared to what people make in Europe, but people are no longer dying of starvation. And someday the Chinese peasant will earn more than a farmer in America. This will absolutely come to pass; all they have to do is persist in their patient labors, day in and day out.

Ni Guan recalled one of Mao's sayings, dating from 1956: "Things develop ceaselessly. It is only forty-five years since the Revolution of 1911, but the face of China has completely changed. In another forty-five years, that is, in the year 2001, or the beginning of the twenty-first century, China will have undergone an even greater change. She will have become a powerful socialist industrial country."

Who can now say that Mao's prediction has not come to pass? China has entered the third millennium with unprecedented economic growth. True, some naysayers complain that China betrayed socialism in the process. But Ni Guan understood that permitting capitalist economic activity is merely the wisdom of the water, which always finds its path to the sea, even if the river does take an occasional loop and appears to be flowing in the opposite direction. As long as the Communist Party remains in power, the ideals of socialism will never be consigned to oblivion, and world imperialism is deluded if it wants to gloat that it has forced China off the Red Path.

But there was one other important thing besides the implementation of the Chinese Communist Party's program, besides the great triumph of Chinese civilization: Ni's own personal struggle. His own private, sacred duty, a secret that no one knew, not his bosses at the company, not even the Executive Committee of his apartment building, which knows everything about everyone.

Ni Guan was scrimping and saving, denying his own needs, putting money away for the sake of his younger brother, to clear a bright future for him.

Yes, Ni had a brother. That very fact was a crime.

A few years after Ni was born in the town of Suifenhe near the Russian border, China proclaimed the "One Family—One Child" policy. From that time on, any second child would be considered illegitimate. Only in rural villages were people permitted to have two children, and only if the first one was a girl. But the first child in the Guan family was a boy, Ni, and so they could not justify a second, even if they were to move out into the country.

When Ni's mother became pregnant again, a dark shadow fell over the family. For breaking the law his parents could be punished and demoted at work, and his father could be kicked out of the Party. But his mother refused to have an abortion. She went away to stay with her relatives in a distant province for several months. Ni's brother was born there and there he remained. They named him Kung, in honor of the great Kung-Fu Tzu.* His mother returned home alone, as though nothing had happened. The apartment building's Executive Committee may have guessed the truth, but they didn't know for sure, and so there were no consequences.

Little Kung grew up in the countryside without a birth certificate, leaving no paper trail, like three million other Chinese bastards. His mother and father, and Ni himself, were occasionally able to visit him secretly, taking money to their relatives so that they could feed and clothe the boy.

And now Kung was grown up. On his deathbed, Ni's father entrusted Kung to his older brother's care, and Ni Guan could never violate this sacred charge. And indeed, Ni was in his brother's debt; it was because they had concealed Kung's existence that his parents were able to retain their position in society and Ni was able to graduate from high school and get a higher education. Now Ni Guan's salary in the export company was much higher than that of peasants and blue-collar workers. He had already managed to save thousands and thousands of yuan.

Soon he would be able to afford a bribe to pay for Kung's documents. Kung would gain all the rights of citizenship, would have access to health care, and would be able to marry.

All Ni had to do was keep on working. And observe the utmost thrift in everything he did.

If Ni was to marry and start a family, he would no longer be able to put away money, and his brother would remain only a

---

* "Teacher of Perfection." Europeans pronounce his name "Confucius."

half-person. Which was why Ni Guan was still a bachelor, even though he was already over thirty—not by much, but still . . .

Ni Guan thought about Tsin Chi. Tsin was a good girl, nice-looking, full of life. Maybe a little too full of life. Ni knew that she liked him. And he liked her too, but what was the hurry? She had only just turned twenty-two, the age at which Chinese girls were permitted to marry. On the streets you could see posters depicting an older couple holding a newborn baby with the slogan "Better later, and later better!" No need for haste when it came to marrying and procreating.

Ni would do the right thing; Ni would right his parents' wrong; Ni would give Kung a new, legitimate identity. To realize this goal he would work, and then he would sin before the state, would bribe the official in the registry office.

But that would be the end to it: no more criminal acts. Ni Guan would eventually be able to marry and have a child, but not yet. If Tsin wanted, she could be patient and wait with him. If she wasn't up to it, then all right; to each his own Tao. Everyone treads their own pathway to hell. She could find another guy to marry.

Still, Ni Guan thought that it would be a good idea to have a talk with Tsin, to explain his situation to her, without revealing, of course, his secret. The poor girl didn't understand why he was avoiding her, and it hurt her feelings.

Ni Guan decided to go out for a smoke; he felt for the packet of cigarettes in his pocket and got up from his desk.

My egg yolk jiggled and slithered out of Ni's skull—back into the monitor, and from there into the wires, the way it had come. In the next instant I was conscious again, as though waking from a dream, and found myself back where I'd started, in the Import Department of the Cold Plus Corporation.

THE ROAD HOME

The rest of the day passed without incident. I have to admit that until evening I felt as though someone had dumped a bag of dust on my head. That's how my Khazar grandmother would have put it. Of course, she'd been known to use stronger language too. My brain was foggy, and I saw the world through something like warped bottle glass. If I turned my head, the picture didn't change right away; the objects in my field of vision left smeared trails of color in their wake as I moved.

The pills were wearing off, presumably.

Without enthusiasm I checked a few invoices from shipping companies, then went out to the Harbin, a Chinese eatery, to utilize fully the lunch hour allotted me by my employment contract.

Why the Harbin? Did it have anything to do with my "business trip" into the head of my distant Chinese colleague?

Maybe yes, maybe no. I often ate Chinese. Not too expensive, and filling, if you get the special, immodestly labeled "Business Lunch," and ask for a double serving of Hong Kong Fried Rice. I'm good with chopsticks and I use a lot of soy sauce.

In the restaurant, while I sat and waited for my order, my eyes rested on the manager behind the counter, a Chinese man. He worked with sober dignity, writing out the checks with furrowed brow and giving meticulous instructions to the waitresses, Russian girls draped in some colorful garment that was supposed to represent a Chinese national costume. It might have actually been authentic, but on our girls the effect was lost.

The waitresses went from table to table with an expression of excruciating boredom on their faces, taking orders with an air of poorly suppressed annoyance and spite. Russians in general are terrible at service. Griboyedov put it best: "I'm happy to oblige, but serving others makes me sick!" Waiting tables, and service of any kind, makes Russians sick, and they can't conceal this instinctual nausea even at the prospect of lavish tips.

A trip east gave me the opportunity to experience the difference myself—viscerally, you might say. In an Indian restaurant—I mean, in a real Indian restaurant, in India—a waiter, a young boy, will lick you all over, from head to toe, for a couple of extra rupees. He'll serve you with enthusiasm; he considers this to be his professional duty. Blame the caste system. The boy is at your beck and call; it wouldn't cross his mind to dream of becoming a doctor or government official; his father, grandfather, great-grandfather, every last one of them, were in service. He, too, will serve. It is his natural state. If he advances in his career and makes senior waiter by forty, he will consider himself a complete success. He gives practically no thought to the idea of becoming a government minister, say, a deputy, or financier. He might perhaps dream of becoming a movie star; that's Bollywood at work, poisoning the minds of poor Indians with hopes that can never be fulfilled.

I'm speaking of the hope of becoming someone different here and now, in this life. As far as the next life is concerned, the sky's the limit; the Indian guy can desire whatever comes into his head.

What is most surprising is that nothing prevents this hereditary servant, this *Sudra*, from taking pride in his work and respecting himself. He pours his creative spirit into his labors, working with dignity and precision, but without the slightest hint of servility.

Once in India I took a ride with a poor rickshaw driver, negotiating a price beforehand. When I reached my destination, I foolishly gave him more than the sum we had agreed on, just out of spite. The driver took me rather roughly by the sleeve as I was climbing out, and firmly pressed the change into my palm. His entire being said "I need nothing extra, I ask only the set fee established by my union."

A Russian waiter or waitress, even while serving your food, will always let you know, subconsciously, by way of his or her face or posture, that he or she is doing you an enormous favor. He or she considers his or her current predicament to be a temporary and unnatural state: I may be a student right now, supporting myself by working in this restaurant, but just you wait. I'll graduate and the moment I do I'll become a top manager or rich businessman, or at the very least, will marry an oligarch.

Assuming the whole time, of course, that they will achieve this goal in their current lifetime. They have no faith in a future life. It's not about belief; the possibility of some future life simply doesn't cross their mind. And at the same time they naively take for the truth the theory that if you "want something badly enough" or if you "just try really hard," then "everything will work out fine."

And in fact that is the way it is.

This formula has become the catechism of modern Western man, conveyed through Hollywood films, articles in glossy magazines and books by the ubiquitous and all-knowing Paolo Coelho. But the wise men of the East who originally came up with the formula proceeded from the premise that we have more than one life to live.

True, the art of customer service is not very advanced in Russia. That said, if a Russian starts licking someone's posterior, then he will find himself getting deeper and deeper in filth, wallowing around in there without the slightest need or profit. And not only that, he'll fight an army of other guys tooth and nail for the right to lick even deeper. A nationwide case of mass sadomasochism.

I watched the Chinese guy ordering the white girls around and marveled at his skill. He was clearly in his element. Before long the ancient Eastern man will come into his own, and when that time comes, we, white tailless monkeys, lazy self-satisfied creatures that we are, will do his bidding in the utmost tedium and servility.

After work I started to make my way home. The traffic was horrendous as usual; the line of cars barely moved. Some drivers, like me, kept to their own lane, creeping submissively along in short lurches and long pauses, surfing the radio dial and glancing dumbly out the side windows, first right, then left, or fixing a blank stare, devoid of emotion or thought, through their front windshields. Others fidgeted, jockeyed for position, or drove up on the sidewalk, attempting to pass on the right, but at the next stoplight found themselves inevitably in the same position as before, relative to the rest of us.

Without particular rancor I muttered my habitual curses at the impatient ones. You'd think they were all rushing to some super-important, earthshaking appointment, or that every wasted minute was costing them a thousand dollars.

I'm quite sure, though, that they're simply going home to collapse on their sofa and watch some TV. The more energetic among them might have something to eat first, or engage in sexual activities with their domestic partners. So what's the big hurry? An hour earlier or later won't change anything.

Soon everything will be perfect: They'll fix the roads, fill in all the potholes, lay down new pavement, set up roundabouts, repaint the white lines, add a parking lane so that parked cars won't clutter up the entire right side of the road, and they'll construct a triple layer of high-speed beltlines around the city for heavy trucks. And everything will be perfect. Maybe not right away. But someday.

In the meantime, the speed of every individual car in a line of traffic is ultimately reduced to the same average speed as the rest of traffic. Showing excessive individuality just gets some more scratches and dents on your car, and more resentment from everybody else.

Traffic is no different from the rest of life.

KNOCKING ON HEAVEN'S DOOR

I made it home and parked the car in the improvised for-profit lot next to the supermarket. A polite, solicitous man with an Armenian air about him guided me in between a Volkswagen and a Toyota. The lot was full as usual. I handed the guard (I can't for the life of me recall his name, let's call him Ashot) forty rubles, the fee for his services overnight.

I used to park by the entrance to the apartment building but in no time the side-view mirrors were stolen. Savvy neighbors explained that it might have nothing to do with the night security guards, but then again, it might. In general, you could do without paying the forty rubles to the guys running the unlicensed parking lot. But then parts of your car might go missing: windshields, mirrors, fenders, and the like. It's simpler just to pay.

Sometimes when I came out to get the car at night, there would be no guard at the lot at all. The services of the bottom feeders on site, evidently under instruction from the guys in charge, were strictly limited to making sure nothing was "disappeared" from the cars under their protection. The cars parked at the entrance, though, were fair game.

Anyway, I began parking my car by the supermarket, paying their paltry tribute and enjoying relatively undisturbed sleep at night.

Ashot took the money in his left hand, with an air of sincere regret on his haggard face.

His cell phone rang and he raised it to his ear with the other hand.

"Hello? Hello? Galya? I come today. Money? I bring it. Wait up, don't sleep, we go to movie. The money? I got some—I bring it."

Let it be said in his defense that Ashot is the most reliable of all the lot's watchmen. He does disappear now and then, naturally, but there are times when he spends the whole night pacing from one end of the lot to the other, humming verses of some Armenian song. I've seen it myself, quite often.

When our locals are on duty, they might as well not be there at all. They just drink themselves into a stupor and sleep the night away in their jalopy right there on the lot.

It occurred to me that Russian women could organize a movement in support of illegal immigration. Those Galyas, Liubas, Klavas, and Nadyas—ladies who have crossed into their forties and who tip the scales at eighty kilos plus—wouldn't have a snowball's chance in hell of catching a partner in life who's occasionally sober, capable of working and bringing home a salary, and of giving her some good times in bed, if it weren't for these Ashots, Tigrans, Dauds, and Sulemans.

Such ladies should lock arms and come out in full force to confront the assembled demonstrators of the Anti-Immigration Movement, forming an impenetrable wall with their massive breasts. They could say, so you want all these non-Russian elements to leave our country? Fine, out they go. But can you satisfy your womenfolk? How about right now? Bring it on, defenders of the Motherland, give it to us till we can't take any more. All these dark-skinned immigrants will be out of the picture, so you can plow us every night like Young Communists conquering virgin lands, all night long. Work all day, and then bring home the bacon and potatoes. How do you like that version of Russia, fellow citizens?

That would put an end to the patriotic Russian Orthodox struggle against the so-called black-assed invaders; our valiant warriors would scatter into the alleyways with their tails between their legs, hiking up their ripped trousers with one hand and crossing themselves plaintively with the other.

This is the sort of serious matter that preoccupies me when

I'm out walking. Sometimes I even move my lips or laugh out loud. Looking like a real moron.

But it only looks that way. Fact is, I'm pretty smart.

Just sensitive.

Sensitive to people, to life, to justice, truth, and art.

Home at last, I turned on my computer and launched the universal player. Opened the special "Knockin' on Heaven's Door" file and moved all the MP3 files in there onto the player.

I said before that I hate oldies. Well, all except for this one. I never get tired of listening to Bob Dylan's "Knock-knock-knockin' on Heaven's Door." I even have a collection of different cover versions. You can't imagine how many artists have recorded "Knockin' on Heaven's Door"! I have thirty-nine on my computer: U2 (live concert), Dana Robbins, Bryan Ferry, Randy Crawford, Daniel Lioneye, Wyclef Jean, Roger Waters (yes, you know the one, from Pink Floyd), Warren Zevon, Avril Lavigne (pop crossover!), the Leningrad Cowboys (worth a listen if only for the group's name), Jerry Garcia, solo, and another one with his band (the Jerry Garcia Band), Calva Y Nada (don't ask), Seliq (from the album of the same name, *Knockin' on Heaven's Door*); and then Ed Robinson recorded it twice, Guns 'n' Roses seven times, Sisters of Mercy five times (just imagine the Sisters of Mercy snarling out the words!), Eric Clapton seven times (IMHO the best is the one on *Crossroads*); and then of course Bob Dylan himself—four times. Especially touching is his creaky old man's voice on the *MTV Unplugged* version.

And of course I have a DVD of the German movie *Knockin' on Heaven's Door*, the story of two guys living with terminal cancer and indulging in a no-holds-barred, hedonistic megabinge before they kick off.

No need to listen to a lot of different songs or read a stack of different books. One is enough, so long as you get to its essence. Take the Hari Krishnas, all they do is sing "Hari Krishna, Hari

Rama" and read the *Bhagavad Gita*, but they each perceive and comprehend more than a full professor.

The main thing is that it be the right song or book. "Knockin' on Heaven's Door" is the right song. That is my opinion. If Old Bob had written nothing else, the pearly gates would still swing open before him.

When I'm done writing my one and only masterpiece, I'll just spend the rest of my days working in an office, and my nights drinking beer, like a regular guy. Hmm . . .

I sipped my beer and meditated to the sound of the song as it cycled through all the different versions. Then I undressed, shut down the computer, and curled up on the sleeper sofa. My insomnia was long gone, a feature of the distant past when I didn't work in an office from nine to six, led a bohemian lifestyle, and had sex whenever, with whomever.

Within ten minutes I was back in that strange dream about long-lost Khazaria.

FALLING STAR

A falling star appears out of the cosmos and, whipping its tail like a cat, traces a trail across the yawning blackness of the southern sky.

Every night closer, hotter.

Saat lies on his back on a hillock with his hands crossed behind his head and stares up at the sky. Misfortune, the old people would say, woe.

What kind of misfortune can befall Khazaria? You name it. A bad harvest. Or the opposite, one that's too good—that too is woe. One year the grain grew as tall as a horse. They harvested with sabers, used maces for threshing. Couldn't eat it all! Piled it on carts until it spilled over the tops, hauled it over the mountains, begged the people on the other side: Take our grain, we have too much! Swap it for your heavy stones! The neighbors traded, helped. Carts clogged the high roads, grain going one way, stones the other. The roads were too narrow, so the carts traveled across the fields. Trampled the rich black earth. No one could get through, on foot or by cart. The milk spoiled in the nomad camps, and mountains of stones filled the cities—nothing to eat or drink! The sick couldn't get through to the *znakhar* healers, they fell to the ground between the carts and died there on the road.

No one was left to do the winter plowing and tend the livestock.

The Khazars spent their days carting grain and piling up stones. Weeds overtook the fields, the livestock ran loose. And they still couldn't get all the grain out! The sheds burst from inside. Attracted by the excess of grain, invisible baby mice multiplied under the floorboards and turned into huge, sleek, nasty adults. They'd attack a man by his shed, gnaw his flesh to the bone, and leave him to groan and rot what was left of his life away. Out of pure malice, but also for a little fun. Every living creature needs more than bread alone. Circuses, the ancient tsar-emperors used to say. Just to entertain themselves; even mice get bored eating the same old thing. So the mice cubs devoured the grain, and famine set in. The Khazars had nothing left—no seed grain, no livestock—for the next spring. They tried to eat the stones, but the stones broke their teeth and ruined their stomachs. Some food is just too heavy.

And death came to Khazaria. Felled multitudes.

Some survived by cleverness; they used the stones to bludgeon the mice, then made fires from the parched weeds, roasted the mice, and ate them.

That's what too good a harvest year does for you. No, for the poor Khazar, less is more. Just a taste, a splash of gruel in his bowl; leave gluttony to the Murzlas.

The next year it was announced that the Murzlas would save the people and lands from any excess, would take it on themselves. Would haul the surplus grain beyond the hills. Would take non-surplus goods too. All with a covert, sovereign aim: to make the mice multiply in the enemy's barns, gnaw their bones, sap their strength. And our people would labor and thrive. A clever plan! And the Murzlas would get their just reward: privileges, blue flashers to attach to their mares' tails, to clear their way on the high road.

If it weren't for the Murzlas, all would be lost.

And for the Great Khagan too, of course.

Anything can happen. Drought or an excess of rain—both bring woe. Heat will destroy, cold will kill. Misfortune, all.

But worst of all, producing graves, widows, floods of tears, mountains of corpses, the stench of decay . . .

Is war.

Saat lies on his little hill, stares up at the falling star, thinks thoughts. Hoofbeats. He sits up, sees: A secret *sotnya* of the

Khagan's horsemen gallops by, in full conspiracy, hunched low over their horses' withers, making not a sound. They swish their whips, gouging the sides of their horses' bellies with their heels, urging them on, faster, faster. In their hands, torches of burning pitch.

In the morning a fire in Itil. Two villages burned to ashes, with their people.

The wind whirls bitter smoke across the steppe.

Children weep, wives wail. Men teem in the ashes, seeking their loved ones' bones. Eyes vacant, dead.

There you have it, fruit of the falling star.

But even that fruit is but the seed of a graver woe.

The shamans disemboweled a duck, extracted its liver for fortunetelling. The liver said that those fires had been set by wicked Chechmeks nesting on high cliffs.

The duck's liver never lies. Just to be sure, they mashed it with greens and ate it.

Sure enough, it was the Chechmeks.

In the morning, in the squares and bazaars the town criers spread the truth to the Khazar people. They recall and retell all the Chechmek wrongdoings of the past, the long enmity with our people. The Khagan's words go around to all the households: We will not allow this insult to Khazar unity! We will subdue the evil Chechmeks, restore the eternal and proper order of things.

But for that, troops must be dispatched to the Tatar land, to the cliff-side nests where the Chechmeks lurk, boiling up evil in their cauldrons, honing their hatred on rough whetstones.

They even remember Saat, sniff out the overgrown path to his ragged tent. The requisitions man comes to confiscate all of Saat's mares for military use. He even takes a little colt, tethers him to the back of his cart. The little creature's legs are fragile, slender as reeds in the stream, they will break.

Saat wails: What do you need him for, what good is he for

military transport? You can't put anything on his tiny back—the thinnest Chinese silk handkerchief, much less a saddle—try it, it'll weigh the little horse down to the ground! But the officer silences him, waves the scroll with the Khagan's requisition order in Saat's face. The man wants a cute little colt for his own children, is all. Such are the ways of war.

Saat sits, weeps. All night long, cursing the falling star. The star is close—any closer and it will singe his beard.

But his grief for the mares passes by morning. For Saat now has to grieve for himself.

A *tysiachnik* with a smooth round belly comes and mobilizes Saat, all of him, body and soul. Sends him into a slingshot regiment, issues him a sack on a string and a handful of stones—ammunition.

Troops amass in an endless throng.

Flutes whistle at dawn, the army sets off.

They march for a day, and Itil vanishes behind them.

By the roadside only small settlements. They march on through the night.

A light flickers, or there is only darkness. They march another day. The road leading through the steppe, vast, empty land on all sides, grass rustling in waves like the ocean.

No sign of plow, no trace of man, empty expanse, virgin earth!

Again night, a short rest, then back on the march.

Then the road comes to an end. The men march on over grassland, sun at their backs. March on and on.

After that Saat loses count of the days.

O how vast the Khazar lands! Walk your legs off to the hips, you'll still not reach the end.

And nothing there. Emptiness. *Pustota.*

Saat stamps, jiggles his ammunition bag, thinks.

His body is strong but his head is sick. Too much thinking.

Thoughts bubble up in his head, like gas in the stomach. Swell up more and more. His eyes bug out and his ears emit clouds of steam. God forbid he blurt something out—things are bad enough already.

Wondrous! In Itil you can't squeeze through edgewise. Houses press right up against one another. Take turns breathing, there's not enough oxygen to go around. Here, though, nothing.

Pustosh. Void.

Days on end, no human habitation. Woods, fields, steppe, ravines.

An animal might lope by, a bird in the distant sky.

Not a single Khazar soul, nothing human in sight.

What do we need all this land for? Take some. So much of it, all empty. *Pustaya.* Empty.

At last the vast horde reaches the cliffside nests of the Chechmeks, at the very edge of the Khazar world.

And the fighting begins.

The time has come. The Chechmeks must pay for their evil deeds. Their dwellings are made of clay and straw like the nests of little birds. The Khazars pulverize the nests with their stones and arrows. The heroic warriors clamber up the cliffs, build fires, and sling Chechmek children into the flames by their hands and feet. You will not forget, O seed of the enemy, the fires of Itil!

They eat meat, drink wine, mark their victory with a raucous celebration, and sink into slumber.

And the Chechmeks creep out of the cliff-side crevasses with their stone knives, slaughter the sentries, and hack off the heads of the sleeping Khazars. By morning the blood runs knee-deep.

Again they take the cliffs, send clouds of smoke into the cliff-side crevasses. The Chechmeks come out shrieking and biting like animals. Arrows soar through the air, spears crackle, corpses pile up in huge heaps. Ten Khazars fall on every square cubit of cliffside, but they take back the Chechmek heights.

But in the night the Chechmeks creep out again with their knives.

Where do they all come from? Do they dwell inside the very stone?

On and on they fight, two springs come and go.

Half the army lies in the earth, but they finally subdue the Chechmeks.

Defend the integrity of the Khazar land.

They choose the meanest Chechmek of all and make him chief, and he kisses the Khagan's ring.

And then they start off for home. Bearing news to the new Khazar widows and orphans. Even the survivors aren't whole, some missing an arm or leg. How can they live and provide for a family, crippled like that? Grief, pain, fear, surely the Khagan will care for these brave warriors.

But Saat survives, and with all his parts. Just an injury due to some friendly fire: a stone from a fellow Khazar sling that hit him on the head. Even before that his head hadn't been all that perfect. It's just a little worse now, that's all. And he had had them before, those harmful thoughts. Living in his head like tapeworms in his ass.

Only now they've started to expand, gotten a little full of themselves.

Indulging themselves, in fact.

Saat drags himself along through Khazaria and there's a scraping, a nagging between his ears.

And what did we expect to gain mucking around in all that Chechmek crap anyway? Like we needed their shitty cliff-sides when we have our own vast, rich, fertile land—as much as we could ever want, as much as God has gingerbread. Head out just a little ways from Itil, a verst's walk, and it will unfold before you, all you could ever possibly need, open lands across all of Khazaria! Plows to lift, horses to ride, womenfolk to screw, and not enough men to do the job! But we went and laid down our bones among the stones of other lands. Poured out our blood, fertilized their earth with our flesh.

Is it devils luring us to our ruin,
or radiant God leading us to the throne of paradise?

Tell me, O Mother—O steppe grasslands, what will become of my Khazaria when a thousand springs have come and gone?

PART II

Samandar

THE DUTCH VISITORS

At six thirty in the morning in a semi-vacant, meagerly furnished cage of a room, an efficiency apartment on the seventh floor of a big prefab building on Dybenko Street, in Vseyoly—such being the name of this bedroom suburb of the Venice of the North, the Northern Palmira, Athens, Babylon, and Itil all rolled together—whose windows look out on an identical prefab building with walls that had once been sky blue in color like the Cabriolet in the movie *Knocking on Heaven's Door*, but are now faded and peeling, at six thirty A.M., when all is silent except for the loud cawing of crows, and people still have that preoccupied and sullen morning look about them, the air suddenly fills with music.

A six-piece audio system, complete with subwoofer and surround sound, screeches and lets out a howl that rends the silence of the morning like a burglar's penknife slicing through an old woman's soiled mattress in quest of family heirlooms and cash set aside from her pension to pay for her funeral; yes, a mighty chorus erupts, emitting a great gush of vocal sound:

> *Arise, ye branded with a curse,*
> *Enslaved and starving rabble,*
> *At last our reason seethes and stirs,*
> *And arms itself for battle!*

In a corner of the room, on the cold north side, on ancient lumpy linoleum that bears the traces not only of the passage of time but the effects of the unique non-Euclidean geometry of the epoch of advanced Socialism, is strewn a disorderly pile of blankets, on which a man lies sprawled like some Parisian bum. He stirs, rolls over, and leaps abruptly to his feet.

* Revolutionary song.

Leaps to his feet and immediately doubles over, clutching his aching side with one hand; with the other hand he rubs his face, blotchy from sleep, its features blurred and indistinct, physiognomy dubious at best. Hunched over, bowlegged, he totters with uneven, splayed steps out of his room into the minuscule foyer, whose entire square footage is taken up with two pairs of shoes, proceeds into the bathroom, stops in front of the dim mirror, and straightens up, relatively speaking.

Behold Maximus Semipyatnitsky, leading import specialist, microchip in the great mainframe processor of economic globalization, irresponsible tenant and debtor, signatory of loan number 17593876/LD-8367, and also of loan number 84989874-XXVI, and also of loan number GHM02057585485433498, though, as concerns the latter, already long since in arrears. Also, too, holder of a bank account containing a measly one thousand rubles, longing in vain for a royalty transfer from Portugal, an honorarium payment from the journal *Eurasian Literature*, and a disbursement from the Denis Davydov Prize Committee; writer, novice in perpetuity, forever young, of whose youth, however, his own bones and joints (not to mention his worn-out internal organs, first and foremost, his liver, et cetera) are unfortunately unaware.

"*Aina me,*" thought Semipyatnitsky. "*Aina me tulm bylat sheikel rastan. Karan du khalim chovichi duon sakhyz patalakon gydy, chevataro mukham khyn dez laol, kemam du kan terekat. Faran kulguz etu, faran bumolchi khotamor. Serkel. Buvakhi posturanzhi paiteli, vongaa du karam serkel.*"

Semipyatnitsky turned the blue-handled faucet, filled his cupped palms with water, and, snorting like a horse, splashed his flat face. The cold water rinsed off the remains of sleep, and Semipyatnitsky instantly forgot the language in which he had just been thinking.

"What the devil?" Semipyatnitsky opined.

The abracadabra still remained, in the form of a jumble of

sounds rattling around in his head, but their sense had evaporated. All Maximus could recall, or maybe he knew it from somewhere already, was that *serkel* meant "white house." What house had he recalled that morning, why it was white, and what any of it had to do with Maximus Semipyatnitsky, leading import specialist, and all the rest of it, see above, remained a mystery.

The moon was waxing. During the time of the waning moon, Maximus's facial hair grew slowly and reluctantly. He could shave every other day. But the moon was waxing, and the bristle had sprouted overnight and was prickling his palms as they washed his face. Any other morning he could yield to sloth and skip shaving; he could just scrape off the one longish strand of hair that sprouted out of a papilloma on his left cheek, but leave the stubble on for a Bruce Willis look. Cold Plus was not all that picky about how the staff in the Import Department looked; they really didn't care. But today Maximus was supposed to meet the Dutch partners, and he needed to make an effort.

Maximus turned the red faucet, filled the sink with hot water, lathered his face with shaving cream, and mowed even rows into his chin and cheeks with a plastic disposable razor. When he was finished, he brushed his teeth meticulously, turned on the water in the shower, slipped off his boxers and tossed them directly into the basket under the sink, then stepped into the shower, sliding the plastic curtain closed behind him to protect the floor from spatters.

The Red Banner Chorus, which served as his standard wake-up call, continued to roar in the other room, their song now punctuated by the thumps of the neighbors banging angrily on the hot water pipes. Shower over, Maximus wrapped the towel around his dripping waist, went back into his room, and turned off the music. The whole building was awake now.

Maximus had gotten up earlier than usual so that he could pick up the Dutch visitors and get them to the office on time.

Yesterday he'd been told that there were three of them and that they had checked into the Corinthia Nevsky Palace Hotel. Maximus immediately objected: He could fit three people in his car, but where was he supposed to put their luggage? The trunk could hold only one suitcase. But he had no choice; no one else could do the job. He'd have to figure something out when he got there.

Maximus dressed and boiled some water in the electric teapot, mixed a cup of instant coffee in his thermos, added some sugar and twisted on the lid, checked the contents of his briefcase, and crammed the coffee in along with everything else. Finally he slipped on his shoes, set the burglar alarm, and went out, locking both doors behind him.

The elevator arrived immediately. Maximus rode down to the first floor and stepped outside. The fresh air energized him, bringing on a light, celebratory mood. Such is the effect of morning sometimes: All that has come before remains in the past, out there beyond the dark Styx of the night, a million light years away, beyond the galaxy of sleep. A new day has arrived; everything will be different now. Yesterday's failures will be successes today; whatever caused the sorrows of the past will no longer stand in your way. Quite the opposite: What you've been waiting for so long will finally come to pass, roaring in on an express train from the Province of Joy, tumbling exuberantly into your life with an armload of red roses and fistfuls of greenbacks.

Such is the effect, sometimes, of a new day.

Or could it be the effect of the pink pill that Maximus had swallowed just after brushing his teeth?

In his inspired state of mind Maximus cranked up the radio, pulled out of the parking lot, and started off in the direction of the hotel, periodically lifting the thermos of coffee from the cupholder between the two front seats to take a sip.

If you've ever stayed in the Nevsky Palace Hotel in Petersburg you know that it's located right on Nevsky Prospect, just before it crosses Liteyny. It was too early for there to be much traffic, and Maximus made it to the hotel in under thirty minutes. But there were no parking spots left on Nevsky. As he passed the hotel on the opposite side of the street, Maximus spotted an open space right in front of the entrance, but by the time he U-turned at the stoplight and wheeled back, it had been already taken by a long, sleek white limousine.

"What the devil?" For the second time that morning Maximus blurted out the name of the unclean spirit, and slipped his automobile in between the limousine and a bus stop. He waited ten minutes, until it was precisely the time he'd agreed to meet the Dutch visitors, then clicked on his hazards, got out, locked the car, and made his way into the hotel lobby.

They weren't down yet. Maximus paced back and forth by the glass doors, checking at the end of each lap to be sure his car was all right. A bus could come along and crush his tiny vehicle at any moment. Or else the demonic hordes of the traffic police could summon their hellish tow truck, every driver's nightmare, and drag his darling off to the impoundment lot . . . from which it would be about as difficult to retrieve as to extract a soul from Hades after it had made its descent.

At last three thin, young-looking men appeared at the front desk and began to check out. Maximus recognized them immediately and tried to catch their eye, smiling, moving closer, holding out his right hand:

"Good morning!" he said in his best English. "My name is Maximus, I'm taking you from here to our office."

"Oh, great! Hello, I'm Peter. You wrote me several e-mails."

"Yeah, nice to meet you, Peter."

"Nice to meet you too, Maximus. Here are my two colleagues, Nick and Joseph."

"Hello, Nick! Nice to meet you, Joseph."

The two silent Dutch colleagues smiled broadly at him, baring their glistening white metal-and-ceramic-capped teeth.

"My car is right here, near the entrance. The only problem is your luggage. I'm afraid my car is too small for three big suitcases, if you have any."

"Ah, no worry. See, these bags are all we have."

"Oh, fantastic! You are traveling light!"

"It's true."

The Dutchmen were indeed traveling light, just three small carry-ons. Maximus tucked the bags in his minuscule trunk, hustled his guests into the car, and set off. The three visitors spent the entire trip to the office chattering loudly in their own language, which Maximus didn't understand. They only reverted to English when they had one of the standard tourist questions for their driver:

"Do you always have traffic like this?"

"What you see now we call the open road. Real traffic will start in couple of hours."

"Oh, horrible! Nick and Joseph have to fly back to Europe this evening."

"They'd better plan to leave extra time before departure. And you?"

"Me? I'm going to Moscow. I have a ticket for the train tonight."

That meant that the two dumber ones would go back to Europe today, and Petya would head for Moscow on the night train. Which one of them would take the pills? How would they do it, and where would they take them? Well, thought Maximus, everything will become clear at the office.

Three people would be meeting with the Dutch visitors: the Import Director, Diana Anatolyevna—whose acquaintance we've already made; the Commerce Director; and someone from Marketing. Maximus was not invited. Management decided what, how much, and how, to import; all the Import Department did was carry out the orders that came down from Management, whatever it took.

They called Maximus only after the meeting in the conference room was over, and for the obvious reason.

Diana Anatolyevna dialed Maximus's number on the internal line and asked:

"Semipyatnitsky, where's that box with the rat poison?"

"I'll bring it right away, Diana Anatolyevna."

"That's not necessary. Just tell me where it is and the secretaries can bring it."

"No, I can do it, it's no problem at all, Diana Anatolyevna."

Maximus had given up on the idea of pilfering the pills and starting his own drug-dealing business. But he still wanted to know what sort of pills they were and what the Dutch guys intended to do with the box. As he carried it into the room, Maximus was hoping to learn which of the three visitors would take charge of it.

The Dutch didn't disappoint. While Maximus was in the room, Peter immediately took out a large opaque bag with string handles and dropped the box inside, smiling happily.

Maximus resolved to demonstrate an even greater sense of company spirit and asked the Import Director, "Diana Anatolyevna, is someone taking our guests to the airport?"

"Yes, Maximus, we've already reserved a taxi. But Peter will be leaving later, he's taking the night train to Moscow."

"Really? So he'll be here by himself? Does he have anything to do until then?"

Maximus made it seem as though he hadn't known that Peter was leaving separately from his colleagues. It looked as though he was trying to come up with a pretext to slip out of the office for a while. And maybe get some extra money to cover entertainment expenses.

The Import Director intercepted his feeble scheming.

"Don't worry, the guys from Commerce will take Peter around to some supermarkets to see how the merchandising is going. I'm sure that you have more important work to do than drive them around town."

"Yes, Diana Anatolyevna, you're right. I'm up to my ears in work. May I go now?"

"Of course, thank you very much."

"All right . . . well, if anything comes up and our esteemed partner could use my help . . ."

Maximus turned to Peter and switched back to English:

"Do you have my mobile number?"

"Yeah."

"After you finish with inspections of retail, please call me. This evening I'll be at your disposal."

"Oh, how nice! Sure, I'll call you."

Diana Anatolyevna exchanged quizzical glances with the Commerce Director. On his own initiative, Semipyatnitsky was volunteering to devote his free time to hosting the company's partner. It wasn't like him. Maximus had never shown any particular zeal for Cold Plus—he just clocked in, did his work, and left the moment the little hand reached six; on the weekends he either turned off his cell phone or simply ignored calls from the office.

DON'T GET SHAT ON

A computer game. Maximus thought it up, put together a description, and some guy from IT made it a reality—virtual, anyway.

It operates on a very simple principle, like all those other rudimentary games for computers and smart phones and the like, where the goal is to gather pieces of fruit or, perhaps, dodge flying balls.

The theme, though, is what's original. The interface, as Maximus designed it, consists of eight outhouses arrayed across the lower part of the screen, on what is supposed to represent the ground, with bombs falling down from the "sky." The player uses the cursor to move his avatar back and forth from right to left. When he presses *Enter*, for example, the avatar goes into one of the outhouses; pushing *Shift* makes him drop his pants and sit on the toilet; *Page Down* elicits a big number two.

The challenge of the game is that the bombs fall in random patterns onto one of the eight outhouses. If a bomb lands on an outhouse while your avatar is inside, that's the end, and you receive the following message: "Game Over. You got shat on, Loser!" If the avatar manages to complete his business successfully, though, and run out of the outhouse before it gets bombed to smithereens (*Page Up*: He gets up and pulls up his trousers; *Escape*: He gets out), he earns a point, which flashes in the lower left of the screen. The inscription appears: "Congratulations, Shitter! One Point!"

The graphics are pretty simple. The avatar has a beard and is wearing camouflage combat fatigues. The outhouses have a rustic look to them. The musical accompaniment is a MIDI file playing some patriotic tripe or other. (Go ahead and search for patriotic tripe on YouTube. We'll wait.) When a bomb hits one of the outhouses there's a hissing sound and an explosion, and every successful shit comes with a sort of ineffable creaking sound.

The game has a few different levels. On the first and most elementary, the bombs fall one at a time, and it's a simple enough matter to get your guy to shit successfully, gain a point, and move him to the next outhouse. As the levels advance, however, the bombs fall faster and faster, and the player has to gauge the intervals correctly and make lightning-fast decisions about where to shit next.

In order to move up to a higher level, the player has to accumulate eight points—one for each outhouse. An hour after closing time, when the aggrieved-looking janitress came to empty Maximus's trash basket, he had advanced to level three. Once he even managed to get to level four. The game had six levels in all, but it took a great deal of focus and diligent practice to get past four.

Maximus's cell phone rang, interrupting his game: The ringtone was a polyphonic version of the melody of the Russian (Soviet) National Anthem. It was Peter calling to report that he was free and back at his hotel. Semipyatnitsky gathered his things, went down to the parking lot, got in his car, and headed along the embankment to Nevsky Prospect.

The evening traffic had dissipated, and the road was relatively clear. Maximus drove in the middle lane, his favorite, without undue haste. Vicious jeeps and arrogant sedans whizzed by on both sides. Go ahead, thought Semipyatnitsky, torture yourselves, pedal to the metal, what you don't know is that the traffic police are lurking around every corner, brandishing their bristly clubs. Semipyatnitsky liked that bit about the bristly clubs, and he smiled to himself.

When Maximus drove up, Peter was waiting on the street outside the hotel. He was holding only a small overnight bag; apparently he had left the box of pills in his room. On his way over, Maximus had thought about trying to sneak into Peter's brain, as he had done with Ni Guan. But he resolved to utilize the traditional, tried and true Russian method to get information: Ply his guest with vodka. Once drunk, Peter would readily reveal whatever secrets he was keeping locked up in his Dutch brain. There wasn't much time before Peter's train, not a minute to lose.

Semipyatnitsky offered to show Peter St. Petersburg's most famous feature, the monument to Peter the Great, who had opened the window to Europe. Maximus himself had always felt that it would have been better for the tsar to install actual doors, so that people wouldn't have to keep climbing to Europe through a window, but he withheld this insight from his guest.

They arrived at the Bronze Horseman. Peter naturally asked Maximus to take a few photos of him with the statue in the background, and then Maximus, as though the idea had just occurred to him, suggested casually that they stop into the bar across the street. And his guest, with an equally spontaneous air, agreed.

If you know Petersburg, then you know that this bar can be none other than the Tribunal. Yes, that's the one, where girls— some plump and unattractive, others gangly and awkward—sit on tall revolving stools at the bar, casting welcoming glances at the foreign tourists who come in. Somewhere nearby sits their so-called *mamka*, a bulky woman of forty-five or thereabouts, who hasn't changed her makeup since the age of twenty, when she herself was sitting on a stool just like those she now oversees, back at the Intourist Hotel bar.

Ultimately, everyone has a right to a career. You may be just a simple low-level manager today, but before you know it twenty-five years will go by, and you'll become a respected supervisor yourself, applying all those sensitive leadership skills you've picked up, mentoring the youngsters in sales. In honor of your lost youth and of the thorny path you followed to the top, you'll wear the very same bright-yellow necktie as when you began; jabbing at it with your gnarled finger, you'll harangue your subordinates: "Listen, guys, I wasn't born a supervisor, I started out just like you, and you too—at least some of you, the very best—will also get promoted someday, if you work with diligence and enthusiasm."

But yes—the Tribunal, where couples who drop in off the street and drunken Finns alike listen to live music in the smaller room on the left, or gyrate to disco music on the dance floor to the right, or else stare in silence at the strippers hired from the White Breeze Agency: shockingly beautiful, exquisite, and inaccessible, as though their heavenly bodies had descended to earth from some heavenly body.

Of course, everything is relative, including the inaccessibility of celestial strippers.

Maximus and Peter claimed a table near a small podium with a pole rising from the center, where with twitching fingers a blonde girl toyed with a thin string around her hips, which was evidently supposed to be standing in for an undergarment, but fell far short.

Maximus watched the show, but his heart wasn't in it. He'd just been to Omsk, Russia's sex capital, where in one joint he'd recruited all seven dancers for a private session, with two more summoned in for an encore, and your basic run-of-the-mill stripper had no more appeal for him. After the sincere and remarkably accessible Omsk girls, none of the beauties from Moscow, Petersburg, Minsk, or any other city could measure up.

The Omsk strippers had finished Maximus off right in his pants; he hadn't made it past the third one, who straddled his lap, grinding and gyrating rhythmically on his priapal bulge; he came and immediately panicked that she would call in the bouncer to throw him out, pervert that he was, but all she did was smile as though she'd just aced an exam. "Why did I hold back?" wondered Maximus at the time. And proceeded to climax five more times in that one night.

The icy beauties of St. Petersburg had no such power over Maximus.

But Peter stared at the stripper's legs and licked his arid chops.

Maximus ordered a carafe of Absolut. They refrained from excess conversation. Semipyatnitsky kept pouring the vodka. Peter downed his shots before the ice could melt, frowning and staring at the podium as girl after girl stepped up with each new song.

"Do you like Russian girls?" Maximus asked politely in English.

But rather than responding with equal politeness, making observations about the exceptional beauty of Russian girls, etc., Peter got right to the point:

"Yeah. Could you arrange for her to visit my hotel? If you know what I mean . . ."

"Nothing is impossible, dear Peter. Nothing is impossible in this fucking world. But some things are costly. Very costly. That's the truth."

"How much?" he asked impatiently.

Maximus had noticed a grim-looking guy near the podium, who was obviously with the girls; he shrugged, got up, and went over to him. Now, the White Breeze girls aren't prostitutes. They get paid two or three hundred dollars a dance, and have no particular need to put out for just anybody. They earn more than enough for their tuition and sports car payments. But if the money is good . . .

In a couple of minutes Maximus came back and reported:

"Six hundred."

"What?"

"Euros. Per hour."

"This is . . . ridiculous!"

"Whatever."

Baffled, Peter looked away from the podium and surveyed his surroundings. Maximus understood his surprise: It's a basic principle of business that goods ought to be cheaper in their country of origin. Russian girls are exported to bordellos all over Europe, where they cost a hundred or a hundred fifty euros at most. Once you take away customs fees and transportation and operational expenses, the price in Russia ought to be half that at most. But no, it turns out that Russian girls are more expensive in Russia than in Europe. At least the ones with a good shelf life.

Maximus hastened to comfort his foreign colleague:

"See, they're not professionals. Just dancers. It's like a side business for them. They don't do it too often, only when they get a really good offer."

"Really ..."

"Sure. But you could get another girl for fifty Euros or something. Look over there."

"You mean ..."

"Yeah, those."

"No, they're ugly."

"You think so?"

"I do! In Thailand I could get a super model for fifty euros! Not an animal like that ... Maybe we can negotiate? I'm ready to pay fifty euros, but I want one of the dancers."

Maximus caught himself looking at Peter as though he were a complete idiot. He said nothing and just shook his head.

Their carafe was already half-empty, and Maximus decided that it was time to redirect the conversation to the matter at hand, which would also serve as a handy distraction from the question of the girls' fee.

"Peter, I hope we're good friends now."

"Sure we are!"

"In Russia we ask each other after each bottle of vodka, Do you respect me?"

"Yes, I do! But why are you asking this strange question?"

"It's a kind of ritual. Say it in Russian: '*Ty menia uvazhaesh?*'"

"*Ty ... menya ...*"

"*Uvazhaesh?* Do you respect me?"

"*Ty mena uvadjaesh?*"

"Great! And yes, I respect you: *Ya tebia uvazhaiu.*"

"*Ya . . . teba . . . uvadjaiu . . .*"

"So that means you're respecting me and I'm respecting you. We're respecting each other. Therefore we're drinking together. Let's drink!"

"Cheers!"

Maximus and Peter drank another glass of vodka each.

"That being the case, I'm sure you wouldn't want to fuck over your friend, whom you respect, Peter."

"Never, I'll never do that, Maximus!"

"So, please, tell me about the pills."

"What pills?"

"Those pills, Peter, pink pills in the box I brought you today, fucking pink pills."

"Fucking pills?"

"Yes, fucking pills!"

"Fucking pills?"

"Come on, talk to your friend about the pills!"

"Fucking pills! Fuck those pills! It's a fucking business!"

"No kidding, drug dealing is . . ."

"What . . . ?"

Peter even sobered up slightly, glanced right, then left, and lifted his index finger to his lips, making the international sign for "let's keep it between us."

"No, Maximus. No drugs. Drugs are not our business. Our business is potatoes."

"Then why are you smuggling pills . . ."

"The pills are potatoes."

"What does that mean?"

"The fucking pills are fucking potato pills. Our business. Haven't you seen the ads? PTH-IP. Positive Thinking—Illusory Potatoes. That is what our pills are. First you have to think positive. To be a happy consumer. Then you can dream of particular goods."

It was Maximus's turn to be flabbergasted. Peter explained, speaking enthusiastically and loudly:

"Can you believe that we really grow these millions of tons of potatoes for feeding the entire world in our little country? Imagine—how could it be possible? Have you ever been to Holland? We have no space for farms. But we're great at chemistry."

"You mean, we're swallowing these pills and hallucinating potatoes?"

"Hallucinating, yes. But you don't have to swallow them . . . it's a complicated process . . . sometimes it's enough to smell . . . or hear a commercial . . . radio waves . . . though pills are best. I'm not much into details. I'm just a salesman. Our engineers know better . . . you think of eating potatoes . . . and you even get fat because of it . . . then you buy another pill to lose weight . . . and again . . . full circle . . . that's our business . . . and everyone does it, in Europe."

"Everyone?"

"Sure, some people are selling the illusion of cars, others are selling the illusion of designer clothes, or drinks . . . You drink but only get thirstier. Everything is like that. We produce ideas, thoughts, illusions. Ever since Marx and Freud. And now we can concentrate ideas into pills. For easier transportation and consumption."

He fell silent and let his forehead drop to the sticky tabletop. Maximus stared in stunned silence into the space above the heads of the drinkers and dancers. He'd always suspected something along those lines. But still, what Peter had said filled him with anguish and spite.

Semipyatnitsky shook Peter awake and told him it was time to go to the train station. The foreigner obediently got out his credit card. Maximus didn't bother to protest and used Peter's card to pay for the vodka, even signed the slip for him. The waiter averted his eyes tactfully, an act that earned him a reward to the tune of one hundred rubles, cash, from Maximus's own wallet.

Rather than get behind the wheel in his state, Semipyatnitsky flagged down a cab and settled Peter in the back seat. The latter quickly came to his senses once he'd lowered the window and taken a few breaths of fresh air. Maximus asked whether he needed to stop by the hotel to pick up his things.

"No," answered Peter. "I've already checked out."

When they got to the station, Maximus, with poorly concealed spite, said to his newfound friend.

"You know what, Peter? Next time, why don't you get a girl for fifty euros and not worry about any six-hundred-euro girls? I'll tell you a secret: There's no difference!"

"Why not?"

"I'll explain. Have you ever heard anyone talk about the 'mysterious Russian soul'?"

"I think I've heard something of the sort . . ."

"Let me tell you about this mystery of ours. The fact is, you can never fuck a Russian girl."

"No, I've fucked them many times . . ."

"You didn't. It was a dream. Every Russian girl learns the knack from her mother. She takes your money and you fuck yourself while *dreaming* about Russian girl. So what's the difference, after all? Why pay a lot of money for it?"

"Ah . . ."

"That's not all. You can just save your money and fuck yourself alone in your hotel room for free, there's no need to invite a Russian girl in and pay even five euros. All you'll be doing is masturbating either way. Don't let Russians cheat you."

"This is . . . shocking to me . . ."

"Yes, my friend. You can never really fuck Russia. Only in your dreams . . ."

THE FALL OF KHAZARIA

The victorious host made its way homeward, flowed across the Khazar steppe in the direction of Itil-City . . .

Dissipating into smaller rivulets along the way. Meet a widow and set up house; build a mud hut and march no more. A man gets tired of war. The generals, all Murzlas, had galloped off ahead on their spirited steeds, changing horses when their mounts got tired, hastening to the city to pick up their medals from the Khagan, along with deeds to conquered lands for pillage. But the common soldiers just dragged themselves along—what's the rush? They'd already spent more time marching than fighting. They spent four springs on the march. They stopped, took breaks: Hunt down steppe gophers, shake the apples off a tree, catch fish in the river using your trousers as a trap. There was nothing else to eat.

And the process dissipated even more.

Only a few made it back to Itil.

And with them Saat. No interest in widows, gophers. Maybe he figured they would give him back one of his mares now that the war was over.

They arrived at the city walls. No welcoming ceremonies, no laurel wreaths and flute bands playing music, no sweet congratulatory speeches. Initially the people inside even refused to open the gates. They shouted, "What are you, a band of gypsies?" The march home had run them ragged: They were filthy, covered in rags, bedraggled.

Of course they were. Four years of war will do that to you. But then good people let them in. Maybe they thought, What's the point of them dying out there in the steppe, they might come in handy for cleaning the slop ditches or hauling stones to pave our courtyards.

The horde entered Itil, and—holy shit!—you wouldn't recognize it; it had become a completely different town. Not a single Khazar left.

A feral people, a mass of black and yellow.

Little shops piled up everywhere, one on top of the other, daytime for trade, nighttime for dancing—the bad kind. And their language, it'd destroy your tongue. Sort of like Khazar, but strange, the sounds all twisted. And who was maintaining order? You could get clubbed in the back of the head just walking down the street. Chechmek *sotnyas* prancing around everywhere. Executive and judicial branches all rolled up in one. Their chief, the one who kissed the Khagan's ring, now stood on every street corner, embracing the Khagan. Statues, that is.

The Khagan himself was nowhere to be seen. Voiced his will through the Chechmek. People were whispering: There's no Khagan, only the word itself remains: Khaganate! But no Khagan.

Maybe there had never been one.

What about the Murzlas? Where were they?

Gone, gone to the lands beyond the sea, gone to the places where they'd taken all that grain, poured it into their own barns and bins. Grain makes the man.

Abandoned the Khazar land.

So they weren't Khazars after all, but a different people, nomadic.

Saat made his way home to his tent, and there were new people living there, children running and crawling like kittens in the yard, howling. Guess he wasn't going to get back his mare. Home full of strangers. Who needed him now? And where could he go?

Saat sat on a hill, mourned.

The falling star?

Passed him by.

WASTELAND

The events of the previous day—the Dutch pills and the trip into Ni Guan's head—had shaken Maximus out of his usual dazed state, his preoccupation with the mundane: his commute to work every morning, his beer drinking and TV every night. The mind-body interface in his brain had shifted, something had changed forever. And there was something alarming in that change.

The day after his excursion with Peter was Saturday, and he didn't have to be at work. Semipyatnitsky slept until noon. Just before awakening he had the next dream in his Khazaria series, a sad little installment.

Maximus took a shower, boiled himself four eggs for breakfast (lunch?), and decided to take a drive. Somewhere, anywhere. One of his magazines had an article in it about an archaeological site, a three- or four-hour drive away. Though of course he had to figure out where he'd left the car.

Maximus dressed, went out, and hailed a taxi heading downtown. He found the car right where he had left it the night before, near the Tribunal. Untouched by thieves, hooligans, or the tow truck. A good omen. And Semipyatnitsky headed north.

The Murmansk Highway begins just after Vesyoly. At the city line the driver encounters a row of Cyclopean bulletin boards advertising the Mega Mart. After that the road broadens out into a divided highway with a tree-lined median, but that lasts only as far as Sinyavino. The road that continues on to Murmansk after Sinyavino bears little resemblance to a national highway. Resembles it even less than that string on the stripper's hips resembled panties. Narrow, just one lane going each way, no stripe down the middle. Nightmarish pavement, nothing but potholes. Maximus clutched the wheel, shuddering as trucks roared past his window a mere arm's distance away, pondering the sobering truth that this transport artery was the only road linking an entire oblast to the rest of Russia. Other than that there was one railroad line and a seaport that iced up every winter. That was all. Considering the high cost of railway tariffs it was clear that most of Murmansk oblast was supplied by truck transport using this one narrow, pitted road. And there are so many other regions like this in Russia, essentially cut off from the capitals! And no one cares. Not until one of them rises up and demands its independence or one of their neighbors starts to show too much interest. There was that incident where the Finns claimed a village, and the president offered them the ears of a dead donkey instead. But we're talking about an entire oblast here. Do we really need to keep it? Well, if so, you'd think they'd at least put down a decent road.

It's only on the map that we're one big united country, all one color. But the land isn't a map, it's forests and rivers, fields and ravines. And for one place to be united with another, you need a road.

Centuries ago people on the flatlands settled along rivers, mostly because the rivers served as highways linking one world to another. You can't get far traveling through the great slumbering forest or across the vast empty steppe, especially if you're hauling goods for trade. The Varangians, those bandits and traders who founded the Russian state, had traveled by river, if you buy that theory about the Norse origins of Rus, that is.

Semipyatnitsky had no intention of going all the way to Murmansk. His destination was the village of Staraya Ladoga, Russia's first capital, the place where the Varangians had begun their expansion onto the Central European highlands. He wanted to see that landscape for himself, to feel what those energetic Norse adventurers had felt so long ago. To unwind the scroll of the country's history back to zero. To understand how and why things had turned out the way they had.

The road was long. Nothing on either side. Semipyatnitsky recalled a phrase from a guidebook for tourists: "Some ten percent of Russian territory is densely populated; twenty percent is relatively civilized, and seventy percent is virgin land." *Tselina*, in Russian. The land is a young girl. A virgin, you say? But what if she's an embittered widow, an old trollop?

What do we need all this space for? For nothing—all that emptiness just gets in the way. We cross it in haste and in shame as we travel from one oasis to another in our busy lives. Indeed, if Moscow were closer to St. Petersburg, and Rostov-on-Don to Moscow, with Novosibirsk nearby, it would be a lot easier to govern and supply. You can see why the tsar unloaded Alaska in exchange for a couple of glass beads: He knew that the cord binding it to Russia would unravel.

Yes, in the big cities people fight to the death for every square meter; the buildings cram in closer and closer together and rise higher and higher, grasping at the last remaining breathable air, reaching up to the heavens. Along Russia's horizontal axis, however, the only things that grow and multiply are cemeteries and wasteland: *pustosh*. You could cover four or five cities with the palm of your hand, and all the rest of Russia is one giant empty wasteland.

And it's all the same: above and below, outside and inside. Above the scorched, burned-out land is an empty sky, devoid of color. And inside your heart too: nothing there, just parched, wretched emptiness: *pustota*.

Wasteland, *pustosh*. The word entered Semipyatnitsky's head and surrounded itself with other thoughts. An ancient word, conveying an exact meaning: *pustosh*, wasteland, not *pustota*, emptiness. Emptiness entails something Buddhist, a vacuum, there is something postmodern and pretensions about it. But *pustosh* is primordial. Like a pagan divinity: *Mokosh . . . Pustosh . . .* God of Emptiness.

Emptiness, though, *pustota* . . . is just emptiness. It is and always has been, from the beginning. And will remain so, permanently. Emptiness is cold, no way out. Wise: Chinese, Hindu. Eternal, indifferent.

Whereas *pustosh* is warm and melancholy. It contains the past, what's gone by. In what is now *pustosh*, grain used to be harvested, great households stood, gardens and lush orchards grew and flourished. Then everything burned to the ground. Weeds grew tall and covered the arid soil. It's abandoned now: no one there, just an old wino digging a hole in the earth. Planting sunflowers, maybe, on a whim, or digging a grave for his dead dog.

Then there's *pustinya*, desert. That's different too. *Pustinya* is sand, wind, a white camel, the Prophet on her back—peace be unto Him—she's taking him from Mecca to Medina, or is it from Medina to Mecca, whatever, bearing Him on her back, and along with Him, salvation to all mankind.

Maybe it's a bad thing that the land is so empty, but emptiness is necessary, because emptiness is a space that can be filled. Though everyone's emptiness is different.

For the Chinese, the entire world is emptiness, *pustota*. Sewing Dolce and Gabbana labels onto trousers in some basement sweatshop, stealing the design for a concept car from Toyota—nothing is sacred. It's all emptiness, and emptiness is Tao. Emptiness is the inner essence of things. And any form is simply a label pasted on emptiness, predetermining the way our untrustworthy senses will perceive it. So what's the point of copyright, of defending someone's asinine trademarks?

For the Arab, the whole world is a desert. *Pustinya*. And he couldn't give a damn that there are other people living on the globe who've built great cities and roads, who have something that they consider to be civilization and culture. No, they're all savages, heathens. The Arab rides alone in all his glory, regal and handsome on that white camel, a sack of petrodollars in one hand

and an Kalashnikov automatic in the other, bearing either the Prophet's teachings—peace be unto him—or salvation through death, take your choice, O infidels who wander in the darkness.

Whereas your European hates emptiness in whatever form. He covers it with construction projects, divides it into plots, parcels them out, maps everything, and presto, no more emptiness! Or so it seems. But no, it's emptiness nonetheless: *pustota*.

For a Russian, though, wherever you make your home is wasteland. *Pustosh* is the Russian natural landscape. And any other terrain a Russian finds beneath his feet inevitably turns into that same wasteland which is so dear to his heart. Even his apartment becomes *pustosh*.

Because when you find yourself in a wasteland, it's only natural that your thoughts turn to the futility of life.

There they are, the remains of empires, the bygone glory of kingdoms, and what now? Futility. From wasteland we emerged, into wasteland we shall return, empty on the inside, on the outside empty too.

At that point it might seem fitting to try and free yourself from the trammels of the material world, but such a quest requires emptiness, *pustota*. Sitting on *pustosh*, though, you think: What are all paths? Many have trod and fallen, many have plummeted into the abyss. That too, futility!

But "even if I do not fall into the abyss, the poison will still find me," sings the bard.* And pours the poison into the glass himself. It is all one path, all Tao, and this glass is Tao, Russian style. He drinks. And imagines himself wandering on roads paved with diamonds, then plummeting into the black abyss . . .

They say that this is Russia's unique path. The Russian path to God. Through wasteland . . .

And so it is. For any road leads to God.

* Ilya Kormiltsev (lyricist for the band Nautilus Pompilius), from the song "Diamond Roads."

Maximus recalled something he'd read in Blavatsky or Roerich, a verse they claimed was translated from the Upanishads or something like that: All mountain roads lead to God, who lives on the mountain tops . . .

The Romans thought that all roads led to Rome . . .

And the Bhaktivedanta Swami used to tell his disciples that if they got on the train to Calcutta, they would never reach Bombay.

Funny, and true. But perhaps there is another truth: Any road leads to God.

Though it has two ends.

Semipyatnitsky drove slowly, trying to protect his car's suspension from the road's abundant potholes and ruts. He came to a fork in the road, with a 24/7 fish market, a café, a hotel, and a highway patrol station, and headed to the right, onto the road to Staraya Ladoga. When he reached the village, it was already dark.

The white nights retained their calendar rights; the sun still set late and its whitish light lingered in the pale sky long after the clock indicated darkness. But in this strange time, when night came on, it came suddenly. A dark hood would descend without warning, covering the entire world, blocking out even the stars. And when dawn glimmered early and drove the night away, it left the night even darker in memory.

The village nestled along the banks of the Volkhov River. Maximus drove down the right bank until he reached a hotel on the small town square. The square was deserted. Maximus parked, entered the hotel through a dark doorway, and climbed a stairway with carved wooden banisters to the second floor. The door into the hotel lobby was closed and Maximus pressed the buzzer to summon the desk clerk.

The clerk told him that a room would cost 1,500 rubles, but that there were no vacancies. The rooms were reserved a month in advance: A lot of visitors, tourists as well as pilgrims, were coming to visit the monastery and churches of Staraya Ladoga.

Semipyatnitsky drove on to the very end of the village, then turned and headed back the way he'd come. He took a secondary road and followed it to the monastery gate. The gate was locked and the monastery was dark. In front of the gate was a convenient paved parking area, enough for a few dozen vehicles. A couple of cars drowsed there; around a third, a group of young people had gathered. The car's windows were open, and its speakers were blaring a song to the entire town—something about a girl, a student, a sweet piece of candy—violating the spiritual grandeur of the place. Maximus spat and drove away in annoyance, retracing his steps.

The second road on the right was narrow and led up a steep hill. On top, in a grassy clearing, stood an old chapel, or maybe it was a church—religious architecture not being one of Maximus's strong points. A cat, evidently the church's caretaker, appeared and meowed a loud greeting. Maximus regretted that he hadn't picked up some smoked fish at the market he'd passed on the way. All he had in the trunk was a milk chocolate bar. The cat demonstrated an admirable lack of fastidiousness and accepted his gift gratefully. She ate the treat, and then, meowing loudly, led Semipyatnitsky on a tour of the grounds, showing him a hill that sloped down to the river and a mowed lawn behind the church. Maximus took a liking to the animal; he had a soft spot for cats anyway, and this one projected an air of reverence and spiritual dignity.

Maximus stroked the vociferous cat one more time, delivered an eloquent and verbose farewell, got in his car, and descended cautiously back to the highway. He was now quite close to the entrance to Staraya Ladoga, with its cupola-shaped hills rising over a bend in the river.

THE KURGANS OF
STARAYA LADOGA

Their proper name is mounds, *sopki*, from the Russian word meaning to pour or pile up . . . The word *kurgan* came later; it's Turkish.

Semipyatnitsky left his car by the side of the road, which was practically deserted except for the occasional vehicle passing by every half hour or so, the great eyes of its headlights blazing as it rounded the curve. He walked out onto the grass and followed a clay path up to the top of one of the bigger mounds. And looked out onto the world.

His breath caught in his chest, his head spun. The grandeur of the landscape that opened out before him blinded and paralyzed him. The Volkhov's dark, motionless, glossy surface reflected the newly risen moon and stars in the infinite expanse of the sky, making the river itself seem billions of light years deep. Gentle, warm spots of light twinkled from the dachas and cottages on the opposite shore. A light breeze stirred the trees and bushes, like puffs of down on a black swan whose wings rustled, barely audibly, in the summer night.

For a few minutes, maybe more, Maximus couldn't move, then he sank down onto the grassy earth. He closed his eyes, unable to bear the beauty. And when he opened them again . . .

Remembering that moment later, Maximus was inclined to explain his vision as a drug flashback of some kind. That can happen. You go for days, weeks, or even months without taking anything, and then suddenly, completely unexpectedly and in the most unlikely time and place, you're back where you had been back then. Maximus hadn't taken any of the pink pills that day, but evidently there was enough of the drug left in his system to bring on a hefty hallucination.

When he opened his eyes, Maximus saw the same landscape. But it was also not the same. The Volkhov was broader, the water came up to the very base of the *kurgan*. The contours of the trees and the lights from the other shore looked different too. But most importantly . . .

People. Throngs of them, even now, in the middle of the night. A sailboat glided down the river; fishing boats rocked gently near the shores. Sounds wafted up from all directions: people laughing and talking, voices singing, the splash of rigging, the occasional knock of hammer against anvil. Maximus looked first to one side, then to the other, then back again. No hint of *pustosh* now: All the land was in use. In the town, stone mansions crowded up to the water's edge, and beyond them wooden buildings, settlements and farmsteads stretching all the way to the horizon. Even the open fields showed signs of human habitation: waves of ripening rye and dark patches in the grass where flocks of livestock grazed. A caravan of ox carts moved along the well-trodden, smooth surface of the road, accompanied by a convoy of horsemen, their swords and armor gleaming in the white light of the moon. Everything was vibrant and alive, and everything was of this place.

Maximus fell onto the grass, roaring with laughter, then leaped to his feet and shouted in what he thought was a booming, resonant voice, though in fact what came from his dry throat was a hoarse croak:

"So this is what you are, O Russian land, your true origin and essence! Not sad wasteland, not *pustosh*, but fertile, rich *Gardarika*!"

KHAGAN

Saat resumed his life on the steppe in the same place he'd lived before. New people were living there, yes. They had him groom the horses and muck out the corrals, and in exchange they gave him food to eat and mare's milk to drink. Now and then they would take a whip and give him a beating, for not working hard enough or just because they felt like it. And afterward they would send him away, into the steppe. But why go to the trouble of finding another place? A man always feels most at home and free in the place where he was born and lived most of his life. At home even the switches are sweet, the whippings tender, and hunger is like one of the family.

Where is there to go, anyway? Man is not a bird who can fly away and seek warmth and food in some distant land. If he were a star, he could just twinkle in the sky, high above it all. But Saat was a man. He would go on sending roots deep into his native earth, deeper and deeper with every passing year, until his time came and he would lie down on the ground at last and take his rest. And the land would cover him. Land of his birth, native land.

But a new sorrow befell Khazaria: The Khagan died. You'd think, what difference would that make to an ordinary herdsman? Saat had never even seen the Khagan in person. Maybe the Khagan died a natural death. People of all walks of life die of natural causes. Or maybe he'd outlived his preordained time. That's what the old women said, whispering, with dull eyes. Or maybe he was done away with, according to custom.

In the old days, when there was a bad harvest, they would take the Khagan out into the fields during the plowing and stab him to death right there, to make grain grow in the next season. And when there was an excess of grain, they would pile up stones and bury the Khagan alive. When the Chechmeks set fires in Itil, they burned the Khagan at the stake. And if their foes triumphed in battle, they would cut the Khagan to pieces with their sabers. Short is the lifespan of the Khagan, from one misfortune to the next. And there is so much misfortune in my homeland; all of our history is woven from it, like a wanderer's ragged garment, all rips and tears, held together by mere threads.

But the people are not given to know that. Eternal is the Khagan, no more need be said. There is one Khagan; and there can be no other. He rules for thousands upon thousands of years. The Khagan is not a private individual; he is an immortal figure, and his role in our land is akin to a heavenly duty.

Saat lay exhausted, covered in horseshit, in the tall steppeland grass. Lay there on his back after the day's work was done, as was his custom, and stared up at the sky. Suddenly above him there appeared a multitude of faces, a throng of officials!

"Are you Saat, son of Nattukh, herdsman of horses?" they asked. Nowhere to run, nowhere to hide. Even if you could find some woodcarvers to whittle changes into the plank of wood that served as your passport, still your face would give you away, anyone could tell who you were.

"The Great Bek has commanded that you be brought to the palace. It is an important matter of State!"

O how Saat wept! A matter of State—everyone knows what that means: shootings and hangings. Or beheadings, or drownings in the river, or boilings in a copper kettle, after the pulling out of veins and tearing off of fingernails.

Saat knew of no sins staining his soul. He had not wealth enough, nor power, for great sins. Nor even enough strength for a small sin, like flirting. But who is ever taken to the gallows for sinning? Sin is awash in silver and gold and has been from the beginnings of time. When they say that "virtue abhors a vacuum," "an empty place must fill with holiness," it's just words; it must, in fact, *not* be filled; it's the emptiness that makes it holy. But if there's a place of execution, then there indeed "nature abhors a vacuum": That emptiness must be filled. Verily, it will not stay empty long! And if not, then what need is there for law and rulers? Judges cast their ivory dice, and if they wind up with the number on your passport board, then you are designated the guilty man, the sinner. Lo, Saat's number tumbled out onto the table. Such is divine providence!

So thought Saat.

The officials took him gently under the arms, bundled him in soft cloth, stuffed a soft piece of bread, no crust, into his mouth, laid him crosswise across a saddle, and bore him away from his home. Saat saw nothing, heard nothing, and made no sound, until the great bolts of the fortress gate thundered sevenfold and clattered open and he found himself standing, unswaddled, in a great hall. Saat had eaten the bread; no point in dying on an empty stomach.

Saat opened his eyes and beheld, ten paces before him, two golden thrones. The officials stepped back, forming two rows along the walls on either side of the great hall, and stood motionless, heads bowed.

On one of the thrones sat the Great Bek, white of face, black of hair, yellow of teeth, beaming a broad smile of welcome. The Great Bek's robe was embroidered with peacocks in gold thread and adorned with rubies. A great belly had the Great Bek, it rested on his thighs. Must eat a lot, thought Saat. And why not? He holds all of Khazaria in his mouth, like a soft piece of bread!

The Great Bek arose from his shiny throne, descended from the podium, went down on his knees, and knelt on the floor in front of Saat. The officials along the walls immediately all dropped to their knees, and their weapons made a great clattering noise on the floor!

And the Great Bek spoke:

"Glory and honor to you, Saat, son of Nattukh! Following the Khazar custom, having duly meditated at the fire, having made offerings to our sorcerers and sacrifices to our gods, we, the Great Bek and Executive of Khazaria, have determined that there is no better Khagan for our realm than yourself. For you are of the generation of Ashin, son of the Khagan, uncle of the Khagan and brother of the Khagan, and you are the one to raise the golden *kamcha* and take your place on the throne of Ashin, at our left side."

A great trembling overcame the son of Nattukh. But he managed to speak nonetheless: "Allow me, O Great Bek, defender of the peoples, sharp saber in the scabbard of Khazaria, heavenly light, Khagan's equal, to speak a word in my defense! Spare my life, poor herdsman that I am, and order that my passport board be reread carefully, for this is all a simple misunderstanding! I am a widow's son, a poor beggar! How could the blood of Ashin be flowing in me?"

The Great Bek laughed. "Do you know your own father, Saat, that you can speak thus?"

Saat was puzzled at this. "I never saw my father with my own eyes, no, but my mother spoke of the herdsman Nattukh. And my mother was an honorable woman, she only ever knew one man. And that man, her husband, died of the belly sickness when I still slumbered curled up in her womb. And my mother died too, when I was seven springs from birth. And I grew up thus, an orphan."

"Know, Saat, that your father was the Khagan, and his brother before him was Khagan as well, and after him the son of his brother became the Khagan, and all of you are scions of the ancient Khan Ashin. But do not judge your father, for so it is ordained: The Khagan is taken from his family and they are told that he has died. The doctors carve a death certificate and return it to the family in place of a body, saying that the corpse has been requisitioned for medical study. They give the widow and orphans a copper coin, and this satisfies them. And the court's legend keepers devise a different biography and a different genealogy, in accordance with legend."

Saat raised his hands aloft and clutched his head. If the Great Bek wasn't just making all of this up for his own amusement, then this was a great secret indeed! But Saat's heart would not be still, and he spoke again:

"Great Bek! Sun in the night of history! How am I to govern a great realm, when I have not been taught? I have not known a noble education, I have not even been to trade school! Governing is a great and intricate science!"

"Who said you had to govern? To govern, issue judgment, gather tribute, make war—that is my, the Bek's, task. You will sit by my side on this as yet empty throne, and you will keep silent. On your right I shall sit and receive ambassadors and warriors and give commands in your name. Such is our way! Yours it is to taste ripe fruits, to listen to marvelous melodies, and to visit the harem, where your wives await, seven tens of them, each one shaming the next with her beauty!"

Joy flooded over Saat, and he began to believe in his good fortune. But fear came as well: "Great Bek! I am not accustomed to such a life—how will I manage? For are not palaces the Khagan's cradle, must he not from his infancy partake of the very best, so that it will be second nature to him? Will I not bring dishonor on myself? I have eaten only hard crusts and water from the streams and steppe grasses! My only loves were the horses! And how can I wear brocades, when my only garments have been of the coarsest cloth?"

The Great Bek grew solemn. And spoke. "It is not true that Khagans multiply in palaces. The Khagan must know how to braid a horse's tail, must spend nights outside beneath the cold sky, must know hunger and need, must march against the enemy bearing only a sling and with no armor covering his chest. Otherwise how can he be a martyr for the Khazar land? For this is our way in Khazaria: There is the Great Bek with his warriors, and they are the zealous benefactors—they govern. And then there is the Khagan, he does not govern, but suffers day and night, prays and weeps for his homeland! And this sustains Khazaria. Rise, then, Khagan, and take your place on the shining throne! And pray that the heavens will not witness our lawlessness, and that misfortune will pass us by. And if misfortune does strike, then do not complain. For you will be the first to die; you will die a martyr's death, washing away our sins with your tears, like salt rinsing a stain away from a white tablecloth! Such is your destiny!"

Saat nodded. To take on suffering, was this anything new for him? And to know that it is for the sake of his native land!

Then Great Bek asked: "Tell me, Saat—only be honest— what did you think of during those dark nights, as you tossed and turned on the cold steppe, with your empty belly grumbling and your exhausted muscles aching from the day's unbearable labor?"

Saat went numb and replied truthfully: "I pondered, Great Bek, the fate of Khazaria. How to ensure that the simple people would labor without thieving, that the doctors would heal without quackery, that teachers would teach with wise words and not with damp birch rods, that those in high positions would not forget their duties and obligations before society, that our warriors would be so strong that the very sight of them and their valor would keep foes far from the borders of Khazaria, that wealth would grow within from our industries and trade relations, doubling every year, that we should have peace and prosperity among ourselves, and should live in loving respect with our neighbors . . . This I pondered day and night, miserable, foolish herdsman that I am!"

The Great Bek did not laugh at Saat's thoughts, but folded his hands piously and expressed his approval: "Spoken like the true

Khagan! Proof indeed that you are seed of Ashin, blood of the Khagans! Even as you starve, to be thinking of the economy of the land, of doubling the country's wealth!

"O, Saat, son of Nattukh! Only the Khagan, the Khagan, blood, mind, and spirit, is concerned with this! Know now that the Murzlas, whose task it is to gather wealth for the realm, care only for their own bins of grain! The warlords share the spoils. Even I myself, the Great Bek, concern myself with intrigues, with maintaining my own power and position. This is what power means to us. And the simple people are no saints either: One poor man dreams of swindling another for a kopeck, the farmer cares only for his field; his neighbor's melons can wither on the vine as far as he is concerned! Each is concerned only with his own personal well-being and pleasure! Only the Khagan can, forgetting about himself, give thought to the country and the people as a whole! By this is the true Khagan to be recognized!"

THE CHINESE QUESTION

"I hate my life."

Maximus heard the words and awoke. Awoke and realized that it was he who had spoken. Not that he'd awakened with the thought; rather, the thought awoke first and woke Semipyatnitsky in turn.

"I hate my life. I hate my job."

The words whirled in his head like a mantra. And occasionally they spoke themselves aloud, without Maximus's help. But that didn't make any of it any easier.

The night before, after he came down from his flashback on the hill, Maximus had set back for home. He drove for a long time along the dark night road, drove slowly, peering out into the darkness ahead, verifying the route by lights near and far, proceeding hesitantly like a blind man tapping the untrustworthy sidewalk before him with his white cane; the path ahead hides so many unwelcome surprises, so many steep curbs and open manholes. Maximus arrived at his apartment just before dawn. And only got up again with the greatest reluctance, a half-hour later than usual.

It takes a long time to get to work by car during rush hour. And Semipyatnitsky had had enough driving yesterday. So he set off on foot and took public transit.

When he descended into the metro, Semipyatnitsky noticed that there were a lot fewer people around than there used to be before he'd gotten a car and stopped using the train. Even in the morning rush hour the crowd was sparse, like hairs in a Khazar's beard.

The crowds had migrated onto the surface, where they now idled in tin boxes clogging up the streets leading from St. Petersburg's residential suburbs to the commercial center. Within just a couple of years, all the luckless commuters had moved from trams and metro cars into automobiles, used and new, bought on credit. Every eighteen-year-old chick has her own car nowadays: If she's poor, her car is a Daewoo Matiz; if the girl has a rich Dad—or Daddy, which is not at all the same thing—she can aspire to a huge SUV, a monster that takes up half the road. And only after she's had enough of playing tank driver, and has overcome her childish fears, does she acquire a tiny, predatory little convertible—thereby holding traffic up more than ever, as it turns out.

And if the girl is still carless, well, that only means that she's still taking driving lessons and working to get her license, without the least doubt that she is on the verge of becoming a full-fledged driver.

The workplace is overflowing with young women from universities out in Barnaul who have come to the big city with the conscious goal of career advancement, and the subconscious goal of finding a good husband (and isn't that the best way to advance your career anyhow?). Subconscious because, ultimately, what else do you need a diploma and work experience for, really, if not to burst into tears and throw it back in your husband's face in response to some incautious statement on his part about the grocery bill: "I'm not just some run-of-the-mill trade-school girl! I have a higher education! And if I hadn't devoted my whole life to you, I would have become the CFO of some big corporation long ago, and would now be earning more than you do! I had real potential! How dare you get on my case about these petty expenses, you ingrate!" (Of course, some girls get the short end of the stick: They actually do have to become executives and make more money than men, which puts a damper on this particular attack. But their time, too, will come . . .) And so now here they are in the northern capital, where they spend half the workday scrolling through car ads on the Internet and discussing the pros and cons of all the different models with their friends.

At one point Maximus had tried to cool the acquisitional zeal of his young female colleagues, asking them where they thought they were going to get enough money to buy and maintain an automobile. Blondes and brunettes alike performed the same arithmetical operation, which was shockingly simple: Loan payments are 12,000 rubles a month, right? And I earn 16,000, right? That'll cover it. And there will even be some left over. Hm . . . maybe I should look into a more expensive model?

In vain did Semipyatnitsky remind them that there is more to owning a car than just the loan payments; what were they going to put in their refrigerators, for one? And a car wouldn't relieve them of the desire to dress in the latest fashions each season. Or did they think they would drive naked? Though that of course would be interesting . . .

An automobile, over and above its purchase price, necessitates endless expenditures for fuel, insurance, parking, and repair. Maximus came up with an apt metaphor, one that every woman was bound to understand. It was like adding another person to your life. Like having a baby. So now everything—food, drink, shoes, medical care, housing—had to cover two. Not to mention all the time and worry. Maximus watched the girls' eyes go all moist, and realized that his example had hit a little too close to home, and that now they would be all the more eager to become car owners.

The real reason a girl suddenly wants a car the moment she hits puberty is that she can't have a baby yet. That's what she really wants, but she has to suppress that desire. She has to work on an equal basis with men. In exchange for her sacrifice, the modern economy offers her the option of buying a car—a cute little Tamagotchi on wheels that she can love like her firstborn.

Thus is the maternal instinct exploited for the expansion of the automobile industry.

Maximus thought that the underpopulation crisis could be solved by banning auto purchases by women and denying them drivers' licenses. There would be nothing left for them to do but have babies.

Maximus often pondered issues of global importance. He was quite sure that if he were the Khagan he could fix everything that was wrong in the country. Not just the country—the whole world!

Clinging onto the overhead strap in the metro car, Semipyatnitsky found himself empathizing with the Chinese. It's even worse over there. Thanks to the wise and flexible leadership of the Chinese Communist Party, everyone's standard of living has improved. It's not so obvious in the provinces, but in the capital, Beijing, and other big cities the changes are striking. The problem is that prosperity has brought along with it Western ideas about the good life, which decree that everyone must have his or her own car. And if there are one and a half billion of those car-hungry people?

A thick cloud of exhaust hovers in the air over Beijing, visible even from outer space, and it will never clear.

And where are you going to come up with enough fuel to supply all of China?

Even if the government of the People's Republic manages to buy up all the oil deposits and refineries in Africa, it still won't be enough.

Semipyatnitsky had watched a show on the Euronews channel about the Chinese automobile crisis.

This problem, like many others, Semipyatnitsky believed, required a solution not patterned after the American notion that "bigger and faster," ever-increasing growth would save the day— this was already leading civilization into a dead end—but rather a Completely Different Principle (CDP). And he had come up with what he considered to be a very good one.

Long before the advent of the pseudo-science of marketing people like Philip Kotler, the writer Mark Twain (or was it O. Henry?) taught that if there was no demand, then demand must be created. And he'd written a great short novel in which a young man, a diplomat representing the United States of America on some tropical island, comes up against what would seem to be an impossible challenge: The inhabitants of the island go barefoot year 'round. His fiancée's father is obsessed with the idea of starting a shoe business, and has had an entire shipload of footwear delivered to the tropical paradise. So as not to disappoint his future father-in-law, the diplomat, American to the marrow, comes up with an elegant solution: He buys up tons of prickly thorn seed pods from farmers on the continent and secretly, overnight, with the help of some friends, strews them all over the island's lawns and pathways. He then follows up with a PR campaign teaching the islanders that these prickly pods, which they have never seen before, are in fact a swarm of poisonous insects that has flown in from across the ocean. And the only way to protect themselves is to wear shoes at all times . . .

The reverse theorem must also be true. Call it anti-marketing, a theory devised by Maximus Semipyatnitsky, mid-level manager, writer on the side.

If demand cannot be satisfied, it must be destroyed.

What do we need cars for? I've already dealt with the female side of the problem; let's talk about men now. If we discard the nonessential, quasi-religious views propagated by aggressive advertisers, automobiles serve one basic purpose: driving people around. Primarily to and from work.

Every morning employees flood out of the residential districts to their offices, and every evening they head back home. Sociologists call this phenomenon "pendulum migration" and consider it to be one of the most serious problems facing modern society.

But why go to the office in the first place? Who even needs an office?

Ninety percent of office work can be done anywhere, any place that has Internet and phone connections—at home for example. And even the remaining ten percent—briefings and business meetings—can be conducted virtually, using modern technology, from any distance.

People also use cars to do their shopping, though. But this problem will disappear on its own when, as Semipyatnitsky predicts in another as yet uncompleted book, everyone leaves their apartments and houses to live in the malls full time.

Semipyatnitsky hurried from the metro station toward the office, his head teeming with these profound thoughts on the ways of the corporate world. They weren't at all abstract; on the contrary, they were utterly practical. You see, the Cold Plus corporation had made a unilateral wager with its employees: "I bet you can't make it to work by nine A.M.!" If an employee loses, he has to pay a fine. His paycheck will be docked, without right of appeal. If the employee wins, his reward is that nothing will happen to him.

"So what demon chases me out of the house every morning, makes me dash out onto the street, rushing all the while, in a lather like a race horse, to reach a stuffy, crowded workplace on time, when I could do everything, make those calls and send those e-mails, from home?"

Maximus blurted this out loud, having lost control of himself yet again, while standing at the crosswalk waiting for the green "walk" light.

At that precise moment Maximus heard a malicious cackling just behind his left shoulder. Semipyatnitsky turned and saw a spry-looking old man of indeterminate age and curious appearance behind him. The old man was garbed in an ill-fitting blue double-breasted jacket, green trousers, and red shoes with pointed toes. A venomous-looking yellow necktie completed the picture.

"Late for work, young man?"

The forced sympathy in the old man's voice surpassed the heaviest sarcasm. Maximus's glance slid across a large round badge pinned to his new acquaintance's chest, identifying him as a sidewalk marketing specialist. Fiery red letters against a white background spelled out a bold invitation: "Get rich quick: Ask me how."

"You don't have to go, you know. That is, you brought this on yourself. Going to the office, sitting at the computer, putting up with a stupid boss . . . But you can still change everything. And right now you have a unique opportunity! We have a special offer, just for you."

"O God!" thought Semipyatnitsky. The old man seemed to twitch momentarily, though Maximus might have just imagined it. All in all, the encounter was a surprise, if a mild one. It had been several years since he'd encountered this particular brand of street salesman; not so long ago they had thronged the sidewalks, accosting naïve passersby, besetting them with get-rich-quick schemes and fleecing them for easy cash.

Maximus smirked and interrupted the peddler of illusions:

"You're right, it *is* a unique opportunity. I didn't expect to run into you. I must confess, I had assumed that your type had gone extinct, had died of starvation and disillusionment, leaving your bodies draped on top of stacks of boxes of miracle powders in communal apartments that in the Soviet days used to belong to distant aunts with heart diseases, and which you acquired, along with the job title of supreme supervisor, in exchange for the powder. Do you know how we used to deal with your brand of so-called businessmen back then? Ask me if I want to lose weight, and I'll tell you where you can go."

Contrary to Semipyatnitsky's expectations, the geezer didn't take offense. He smiled even more broadly, exposing a row of fake yellow fangs, and emitted a stream of words:

"Oh no, it's not at all what you think! This is a completely new system! And yet it's as old as the world itself, and has truly passed the test of time! Success is guaranteed; all you have to do is decide! No gimmicks whatsoever, it's all completely legal and legitimate! All I need from you is your signature on this splendid contract!"

The old man reached into his leather briefcase and produced a few sheets of paper, covered with fine print and held together with a metallic green paper clip. Maximus could have sworn that the man hadn't been holding a leather briefcase a second before. He cast a nervous, hopeful glance at the stoplight. It was still red.

"This is the longest light I've ever . . . " muttered Maximus, baffled, to himself.

"I know, you're about to ask: 'What about the deposit?'" the agent rattled on. "I have great news for you! No initial expenditures are required! Absolutely no material investments on your part. You won't believe me—you'll ask, 'How can that be? Is it really possible?' And I will answer, 'Yes!' But only here and now, and only through our company! What you will provide is absolutely without material substance; in a certain sense, it doesn't even exist! You have it, but you're not using it—you don't even notice it! And what will you get in return? Completely tangible, material things! Those very things that you're striving to acquire by going to work every day and performing hard labor that will bring you nothing in return. All we need from you is sound, air, an empty concept, fluff! Thinner than a hair! And even that, I repeat, absolutely nonmaterial investment is not required up front—no! And not in installments, either! Only later, only at the very end, when you've already fully savored all the riches that our contract will provide you!"

Maximus's head was spinning; he felt numb all over. The huckster clearly was taking advantage of his weakened state.

"Well, what do you say? I see you're ready! Just sign here and here. Use this pen!"

A syringe sprang out of the old man's jacket sleeve, and he poked it into Maximus's free hand, drawing a tiny drop of blood.

"Oh, how clumsy! Please forgive me!" chirped the old man.

The syringe instantly mutated into a massive pen with fake gilding, and wedged itself between Semipyatnitsky's writing fingers.

But the pain brought Maximus to his senses. Stunned, he stared at the tiny red spot on his hand and then raised his head and shrieked to the people standing next to him at the crosswalk, involuntary witnesses to Semipyatnitsky's conversation with the street hawker.

"Help! This maniac stabbed my hand! He's probably spreading AIDS!"

The crowd recoiled. A few girls, who had evidently heard urban myths about men who went around spreading the virus by sticking needles into people in nightclubs, started screaming at the top of their voices.

At that moment a beat-up Gazelle municipal passenger van emerged from the line of vehicles on the street and squealed to a halt right in the middle of the crosswalk's zebra stripes.

"Oh here's my ride!" announced the old man joyfully, as though nothing had happened. "So pleasant to chat with you! Bye! Until we meet again!"

And with that he sprang through the open door into the empty back of the van. The briefcase was gone; instead, he was clutching a shopping bag against his belly, crammed full of red vegetables that looked something like turnips. The turnips were shaped like human hearts and were throbbing, or at least it looked that way to Maximus. But the door slid shut and the van lurched into motion. The driver, a brunet with a long hook-nose, cast a brief venomous glance Semipyatnitsky's way.

One eye was green, the other was made of glass.

The Gazelle merged back into traffic and disappeared. The walk light flashed green, and Maximus joined the crowd walking briskly across the street. The pedestrians jostled one another carelessly, as though they had forgotten that one of them had perhaps just been infected with an incurable, highly contagious disease.

The gilded pen was gone, and there was no sign on Maximus's hand of the red spot. But he wondered: How do one-eyed men get chauffeur's licenses and jobs driving passenger vans? It doesn't exactly fill you with faith in public transportation, does it?

WHAT DO STRAWBERRIES
HAVE TO DO WITH IT?

That morning, the usual spirit of liveliness reigned in the office . . .

The words came naturally, or, rather, they arose spontaneously and appeared on the monitor of Maximus's inner consciousness.

"Now that's a nice turn of phrase!" he thought. "'The spirit of liveliness reigned.'"

The fact that somebody was writing down every detail of his life, day after day, evidently didn't surprise or trouble Semipyatnitsky. His only concern was that the author's style be up to snuff, and that he acted in a professional manner.

Maximus lowered himself onto the chair in front of his computer, turned it on, and gathered up several sheets of paper from the desk, going through them while giving himself over to abstract and mournful thoughts.

First Pelevin, now this Herbalife devil, it's like something out of Bulgakov . . . what next? Gogol? Quite the eclectic mix. Or, as they say these days, *fusion*. Yes, Maximus, your life is profoundly derivative—you can find every detail in Franz Kafka, who, by the way, was the favorite writer of Vladislav (Aslanbek) Surkov (Dudaev), who had such a friendly chat with you that time in an office in the Kremlin.

Semipyatnitsky recalled his dreams of Khazaria, especially the last one, and he asked himself: Who would be our present-day Khagan and who would be our Bek? Surkov the Khagan, and Putin the Bek? Or the reverse: Putin the Khagan and Surkov the Bek? A fat red line of letters appeared and began scrolling across the internal monitor of Maximus's consciousness, interrupting these musings:

"You idiot! Weren't you told in no uncertain terms that *you* are the Khagan? What does Dudaev have to do with it?"

"All right, but who's the Bek, then?" Maximus tried to make his little contribution.

"The Cat in the Hat!"

His Inner Author was obviously not interested in having a constructive dialogue. Maximus would have to get to work. Begin, as always, by sorting the mail and purging spam. Today's spam contained messages that seemed particularly deranged. Maximus read:

> Stuck in a boring, unfulfilling job? Thwarted in your life's dreams? Betrayed by your lover? No friends? Living a life without meaning, purpose, devoid of even the simplest pleasures? . . . Why not try NARCOTICS?
> That's no solution. Better just kill yourself.

But what really caught Maximus's eye was the footnote at the end:

> This is a public service announcement. Sponsored by the Russian Ministry of Health and Social Welfare.

The next message was an insurance ad, aggressively infernal in tone:

> Better dead than poor! Sell a kidney and invest the proceeds in optional medical insurance!

And another one, an offer from a hard-currency broker:

> While you were wasting time on porn sites, the Arabian dirham gained two points against the Japanese yen. Would you rather throw your life away on photographs of virtual-reality whores or make money on the forex market and buy

yourself any whores you want—real ones? The decision is yours!

But the next message was the most interesting of all:

We are NOT trying to sell you imaginary real estate on the moon for real money. We are NOT trying to trade you a bottle of vodka for your share in the socialist economy of a great country. We are NOT trying to persuade you to vote for that band of carpetbaggers masquerading as the government. Simply turn over your mythical "soul," and in exchange you will receive a real Visa Gold card with $30,000 worth of overdraft protection!
—Beelzebub Trust Unltd.

Maximus smirked maliciously and dispatched the entire batch of spam into the trash.

There was a short message from Peter, writing from Holland, in English as usual. It had a businesslike, even dry, tone: "Hi Maximus! It was great to meet you in Saint Petersburg. Hope our conversation and disputes will help us strengthen our companies' business relationships. Best regards, Peter."

The letter's tone gave Semipyatnitsky the impression that Peter was biting his own elbows out of fear that he'd said too much when he was in St. Petersburg, terrified that Maximus would get him in trouble.

The PS, though, adopted a more personal and friendly tone: "PS I took your kind advice, thank you! Now I have (you know what) for free (or almost free)."

Maximus opened the database and examined the purchase figures for Dutch frozen potatoes. Volume was growing fifteen to twenty percent per year. The peak came in summer, when the sidewalk cafés were open and serving French fries, which came over from Europe already cleaned and sliced into strips, crinkle style.

Lina was sitting in a stupor, staring at her phone. Obviously the aftereffects of whatever she'd been doing the night before.

Semipyatnitsky risked an attempt to rouse her.

"Lina!"

The girl shuddered and gave a grunt.

"Everything all right?"

"Yes."

"Strange. You look like the 'before' picture in an anti-drug campaign. You have that overdose look. Or, worse, like after you got laid for the first time after losing your virginity on graduation night sixteen years ago . . . when was that again, a couple of weeks ago, was it?"

"Tatar bastard." But her heart wasn't really in it.

"Khazar," corrected Maximus, as usual.

"So what did you want?"

"Oh, I wanted to ask you something. About the potatoes."

"So?"

"Lina, look at these numbers: We import up to thirty tons from a single supplier. And we're not even the biggest importer of Dutch frozen potatoes. And that's not counting potatoes imported fresh and sold in supermarkets year 'round. And, think about it, Holland exports to other countries too. Off the top of my head, that would have to come to millions of tons of potatoes every year. It says here that in 1997 Holland produced eight million tons of potatoes. That's their official statistic. Here in the Black Earth Region two hundred centners per hectare is considered a good yield. But the Dutch supposedly get seven hundred. How do they do it? All right, maybe it has to do with different weight standards. A Russian centner is equal to one hundred kilograms or 0.1 ton, but a German centner is one hundred pfunds, or fifty kilograms, or 0.05 ton. That means that their yield is still 350 centners per hectare—I mean, according to our standard. To get, say, seven million tons of potatoes, you need to plant two hundred thousand hectares. That is, two thousand square kilometers just for potatoes. The territory of the Netherlands is just short of forty-two thousand square kilometers—all right, accounting for rivers and lakes, canals, roads, and cities, there's enough for that volume of potatoes. But only if all that land is used *just* for potatoes! But the area also exports all kinds of other agricultural products, from beef to tulips! So where do they grow all that? Where do all those Dutch potatoes come from?"

"Was all that meant for me?"

"Don't act dumb. You know it was."

"All right. Okay."

"My dad was an agronomist."

"I see."

"What do you mean, 'I see'? Answer the question. How can they manage to grow all that in one tiny country?"

"What makes you so sure they grow them all within their own borders?"

Maximus froze. Did Lina know about the pills? And here she was acting like it was no big deal.

But Lina was on a different track:

"Were you born yesterday? The Dutch and other European vegetables, fruits, and berries are imported from China—everyone knows that!"

"Everyone-everyone?"

"Of course! Even our clients! And our clients' clients, everyone knows. Apparently you're the only one who doesn't."

"But why do they import the Chinese vegetables into Europe?"

"What do you mean, 'why'? Europe is where they put on the labels."

"You mean they can't do that in China?"

"They can, and some already do. They sell Italian strawberries straight from China. But we don't want to encourage that."

"Why not?"

"Maximus, are you pulling my leg?"

Lina was completely awake now. Why was Semipyatnitsky interested in these details all of a sudden? He never used to care. But she was basically a decent, patient, person, so she explained it to him decently, patiently:

"It's risky, because then you'd have the market flooded with counterfeit labels on counterfeit strawberries."

"So Italian strawberries grow in China too?"

"Yes."

"What about Chinese strawberries?"

"Where else would they grow?"

"So what's the difference?"

"Maximus, what is this, Stupid Questions Day? What's the difference in what? It's one thing for an Italian name-brand product to go for five dollars a kilo—it doesn't matter if it's produced in China. But it's something else entirely when someone tries to sell you ordinary Chinese strawberries for four dollars, when the actual price is two dollars, simply because they come in a nice cellophane pack with a fake Italian label!"

"But it's the same strawberries!"

"What do strawberries have to do with it?"

Semipyatnitsky lapsed into eloquent silence. Lina started tapping on her keyboard, filling out a new order for potatoes.

Maximus had the overwhelming urge to confide in someone. But who? Then he recalled the letters on his inner monitor.

He slid open his desk drawer and felt around for his pack of cigarettes and lighter. He draped his smart-card lanyard around his neck and headed outside for a smoke. And a conversation with himself.

"Mr. Author, are you there?"

"No."

"Good. Let's work this out."

"All right. Work what out?"

"You know what."

"I do. But formulating the question is half the answer."

"I don't need half an answer. Half an answer is worse than no answer at all."

"Well put!"

"I can put it even better! Is there anything at all in the world that's actually real? Or is it all just pills and hallucinations? And what exactly is a hallucination, anyway? Is it when we see something that doesn't actually exist, or when what we see *does* exist, but we don't see it as it really is? So we think that we're eating potatoes, but there aren't really any potatoes at all . . . we're just taking some pill? Or we think that we're eating Dutch potatoes, and we are indeed eating potatoes, but they're actually Chinese, and the only thing Dutch about them are the labels and the drug. And what are we actually buying and eating, anyway, potatoes or labels?"

"I see . . . All of your questions boil down to the subject of a famous dispute that took place in medieval India, involving three different philosophical schools, whose names . . . well, will mean nothing to you. There were two basic questions. The first was whether the world was real. The second was whether our conception of the world was real.

"According to the first school, the world wasn't real, since it lacked any substantial foundation. The world is based on indivisible particles that cannot be weighed or measured. Under the Karmic law of cause and effect—that is, relative and in reaction to living beings' sinful actions—atoms join together into compounds, which give the appearance of substantiality. So our conception of the world as material is equally unreal. We have been taught that consciousness is a feature of highly organized matter, but the philosophers of the first school believed that matter was a feature of *primitively* organized consciousness. When a living creature breaks the chain of illusion, the world itself—and its conceptions about the world—cease to exist for it. In other words, there are no potatoes, and no pills either.

"Adherents to the second school, however, held that the world was indeed real, based in real substance, that is to say Brahma. In essence, they said, Brahma was the only reality. As for our conception of the world as something existing within time and space and occurring in a variety of forms, for them it did not correspond to reality. They cited the example of the rope and the snake: When a man in the dark assumes that a rope is a poisonous snake, his conceptions are illusory, though the rope itself exists. An enlightened individual is not distracted when it comes to reality, and sees everything as it is, as all Brahma. That is, all potatoes *and* no pills.

"Theoretically speaking, there is another answer to these basic questions: that the world is unreal, and that only our conceptions about it are real. According to that scheme, there are no potatoes, only hallucinogenic pills. But the adherents to this way of thinking were physically annihilated long before this particular dispute began. They were given the opportunity to drink a lethal dose of an elixir made from poisonous mushrooms, after having been told that it was divine nectar. They agreed, and everyone present witnessed a quintessentially physical spectacle: philosophers turning blue and dying in horrible torment."

"What about the third school?"

"What 'third school'?"

"You said that there were three philosophical schools participating in the dispute. You set forth the positions of two schools, then mentioned another one that did not take part in the dispute. What did the philosophers of this third school have to say?"

"Oh, them . . . Well, they said that all of that was of course very interesting. And that under different circumstances they would have participated in those debates with the greatest of pleasure. But when a house is burning is not the time to go through all of its architectural specifications—it's the time to take foot in hand, so to speak, reason in heart, make a break for it, and start living."

"What do you mean?"

"Dance and sing. And pray to God to release us from our entrapment in physical matter."

"So then what? How did it end?"

"It didn't, really. Like all disputes. Both the main schools, and the other group, the ones who were poisoned before they had a chance to participate, are taught in university courses on the history of Indian philosophy. While the third group, to this day . . ."

"What?"

"They sing and dance."

"Why did you tell me all of this?"

"That's funny. I knew why until you asked. Lina is right, today really is Stupid Questions Day."

Maximus lit up another cigarette—his fourth. It made the inside of his mouth taste bitter, and he tossed it away after a couple of puffs.

The inner author continued:

"I would put it this way: The material world is real. And our conceptions of the world are also real. But the world is made in China, and our conceptions of the world are made in Holland."

"But why?"

"What do you mean, why? To crank up the profit margin!"

"But why does the world made in China have any need for conceptions about it being made in Holland?"

"Because this conception of the world is made in Holland."

NACH DRACHTEN

The northern sun peered out from behind the shroud of clouds on the horizon and shone into a little house on the outskirts of the town of Drachten, in the Netherlands. Its gentle rays slid across the cheap Swedish furniture and, observing maximum courtesy, brushed the rumpled face lying there on a green pillow. Peter Nils awoke.

"Ah, shit," Mr. Nils cursed, not without pleasure, in English, and stretched out on the orthopedic mattress of the sleeper sofa.

By the way, it's incorrect to call the Netherlands "Holland," as some people do, and we've been doing. The provinces of Holland are just a part of the Netherlands, which also includes Friesland. Frieslanders consider themselves to be a different national group and have their own language, which is a close relative to English. Nils was a Frieslander. And he swore only in English.

Peter Nils was an export manager, responsible for deliveries to Russia by the Frozen French Fries (or FFF) company. People who know their way around frozen food call the company "Triple F." Triple F is the industry leader for the production and sale of frozen French fries in the Netherlands. According to its own official history, the company traces its roots to the distant, glorious past, to a time even before the Norman Conquest, when pirates invaded and occupied the British Isles. *A furore Normannorum libera nos Domine!**

As the venerable Bede writes in his *Ecclesiastical History of the English People*: "IN the year of our Lord 449, Martian being made emperor with Valentinian, and the forty-sixth from Augustus, ruled the empire seven years. Then the nation of the Angles, or Saxons, being invited by the aforesaid king, arrived in Britain with three long ships, and had a place assigned them to

---

* God save us from the fierce Normans! (Latin).

reside in by the same king, in the eastern part of the island, that they might thus appear to be fighting for their country, whilst their real intentions were to enslave it. Accordingly they engaged with the enemy, who were come from the north to give battle, and obtained the victory; which, being known at home in their own country, as also the fertility of the country, and the cowardice of the Britons, a more considerable fleet was quickly sent over, bringing a still greater number of men, which, being added to the former, made up an invincible army. The newcomers received of the Britons a place to inhabit, upon condition that they should wage war against their enemies for the peace and security of the country, whilst the Britons agreed to furnish them with pay. Those who came over were of the three most powerful nations of Germany: Saxons, Angles, and Jutes. The two first commanders are said to have been Hengist and Horsa. Of whom Horsa, being afterwards slain in battle by the Britons, was buried in the eastern parts of Kent, where a monument, bearing his name, is still in existence. They were the sons of Victgilsus, whose father was Vecta, son of Woden; from whose stock the royal race of many provinces deduce their original."

The founders of the Triple F Company traced their genealogy either from Hengist or from Horsa, one of them, anyway, thus their start-up capital originated in British war booty.

The Bede continues his account of the feats of the continental invaders on the isles:

". . . In a short time, swarms of the aforesaid nations came over into the island, and they began to increase so much, that they became terrible to the natives themselves who had invited them. Then, having on a sudden entered into league with the Picts, whom they had by this time repelled by the force of their arms, they began to turn their weapons against their confederates. At first, they obliged them to furnish a greater quantity of provisions; and, seeking an occasion to quarrel, protested, that unless more plentiful supplies were brought them, they would break the confederacy, and ravage all the island; nor were they backward in putting their threats in execution. In short, the fire kindled by the hands of these pagans proved God's just revenge for the crimes of the people; not unlike that which, being once lighted by the Chaldeans, consumed the walls and city of Jerusalem. For the barbarous conquerors acting here in the same manner, or rather the just Judge ordaining that they should so act, they plundered all the neighbouring cities and country, spread the conflagration from the eastern to the western sea, without any opposition, and covered almost every part of the devoted island. Public as well as private structures were overturned; the priests were everywhere slain before the altars; the prelates and the people, without any respect of persons, were destroyed with fire and sword; nor was there any to bury those who had been thus cruelly slaughtered.

WHEN the victorious army, having destroyed and dispersed the natives, had returned home to their own settlements . . ."

According to Triple F's official version, it was from these victorious warriors, who returned to the continent with their rich booty, that the Frieslander family who founded the frozen potato company in the twentieth century traced their genealogy.

Historians working on contract for the company left unmentioned the fact that the Vergistus branch of the family on the continent had fallen into decline as early as the twelfth century. The last daughter, heiress to the blood of the noble plunderers, was taken to wife by a fugitive merchant from Khazaria entirely without dowry, like the lowest peasant. For a sack of silver, which made its way into the pocket of the suzerain, the merchant acquired his wife's family name and established himself in Europe as a nobleman. Soon thereafter his wife died from a sudden infectious illness, and the newly ennobled merchant married a woman of his own tribe, and in the veins of their offspring there flowed not a single drop of English blood.

In Russian translation, Triple F could very well come across as analogous to "Triple H," conveying both a Russian expletive and the names the company's founding fathers: Hengist, Horsa, and Hazars.

The management of Triple F, as in many other corporations, had long understood that it was not at all necessary to maintain a headquarters in the capital city with its crowding and high real-estate prices. No, you didn't need to be in a capital in order to stay connected to businesses the world over. Doesn't the Internet work just as well out in the country, not to mention the telephone? Triple F chose the sleepy little town of Drachten as the site for their central office, 140 kilometers northeast of Amsterdam.

In Drachten, medieval brick buildings stand side by side with modern glass and concrete structures, and the population (not counting immigrant workers) is under 50,000. In the early 2000s Drachten became world famous when the town government took down all its traffic signals and street signs. From then on, the town's 20,000 automobiles, along with bicycles and pedestrian traffic, were regulated exclusively by mutual courtesy and deference. And from that time on there hasn't been a single traffic jam or serious accident with human casualties.

Peter Nils, himself a pureblood Frieslander with an MBA, easily got a job in the central office of Triple F and had been with the same employer for several years.

That morning, which was utterly ordinary in all respects, he went into the kitchen, kissed his wife—a somewhat angular and dry lady, who was getting ready to leave for her own job at a telecommunications company—tousled his pudgy son's hair as the boy headed out the door on his way to school, and, after a breakfast of vitamin-enriched corn flakes with skim milk, backed his blue Toyota out of the garage and headed for the office.

The trip along the anarchical streets took no more than fifteen minutes, even factoring in the long interval that Peter spent waiting as a little old lady with a white cane crossed the roadway. Nils left his car in the convenient parking lot and proceeded up to the company's floor, where he entered his tiny but private cubicle, which was partitioned off by a translucent, soundproof glass wall from the rest of the office, where the lower-level employees worked.

Nils quickly sorted through his e-mail and sent a few notes to each of the company's business partners, including a short message to Maximus, his Russian colleague at Cold Plus. Nils indulged in a moment's silence, recalling his adventures in St. Petersburg. He'd probably told Maximus a little too much about the pills. But no matter, that was better than letting him know the real truth about what Triple F was selling.

Nils went through his e-mail, signed some shipping documents and held a five-minute briefing for his staff. Having dispensed with his regular morning routine, Peter closed his office door, sank down on the chair in front of his monitor and entered a web address into his browser: www.i-xxx.com.

SEX WITHOUT BORDERS

The site's welcome page was plastered with photographs of half-naked models and invitations to enter virtual sex video chat rooms. Uninhibited Latin American, Nigerian, Thai, even Aleut girls were available to talk to you in real time. Nils was a member; he typed in his password and clicked on the banner for the "Russian Girls" room.

An auburn-haired girl with a clipped-on hair extension, wearing a skimpy slip, sat on a sofa in front of her computer, fanning herself with an out-of-date issue of *Liza* magazine. She looked bored.

Noticing that a member had logged on, she perked up, bared a mouthful of even, white teeth, and waved seductively into her webcam. There was picture, but no sound. Smiling, she began typing her own brand of broken English into the chat box:

Hi cowboy! What's your name?

Peter typed in his answer: *My name is Peter. I'm from the Netherlands. Let's talk!*

Sure Peter! With all my pleasure . . . What do you want me . . . to tell about?

The girl cast an anxious glance at the clock displayed in the lower right corner of her screen. Every hour of commercial chat cost the "member" fifty euros. The girls got forty percent of the final tally. But her contract specified that unless she can keep the client online for at least ten minutes, she gets nothing.

My name is Tanya. I'm 19 years old. And I like to talk with guys about desires . . . Also I like to show my body . . .

To keep Peter's attention, the girl somewhat abruptly lowered the left strap of her slip, exposing half of her breast.

That's nice. U R beautiful.

Nils scooted his chair back slightly, loosened his belt and

slipped his hand through his fly.

I don't have much experience in love and sex. Indeed, I'm just a little girl, you see. Do you like foolish little girls like me?

The girl lowered the other strap and exposed the upper part of her breasts down to the edge of her bra, which, modest girl that she was, she evidently never removed, even in the tanning booth.

Yeah, baby, go on!

I think that you are very handsome. Oh, let me imagine, you are a big man with great gadget. And you know how to do all these nasty things with girls.

Yessss, I do, baby.

Can you teach me? Please, say to me, how can I give pleasure to you?

The model hitched up her slip, and the edge of her white panties peeked out from underneath.

Tell me about your country.

Sorry?

Tell me about Russia, baby.

Oh . . . Russia, yes . . .

The girl hesitated. She hadn't encountered this particular perversion before. She was usually asked to spread her legs and expose herself, to get down on all fours and poke various objects into her various orifices, but no one had ever asked her to talk about Russia. But she quickly collected herself, and began searching her memory for tidbits from her school textbooks or training manuals for tour guides and translators. Yes, she had taken English in night school when she'd been planning a career as a tour guide. Her original idea had been to take foreigners on excursions around the Golden Ring . . . But offering tours around her own body had turned out to be far more profitable.

Russia is a great country. We have many forests, lakes, rivers . . .

Yeah, deep rivers. And fields with smooth grass, very smooth, just like my skin . . .

Tanya started to improvise, running her hand up and down her breasts as she spoke. Peter's grip on his cock tightened and he began to stroke it slowly.

And what about people?

People are nice and friendly. But you are better, I'm sure!

The girl was afraid he'd get jealous of the male Russian population.

Actually, there are not so many people in our country. Most part of territory is a virgin land.

Virgin?

Virgin land. Ever waiting for strong man like you.

To fuck it?

Yeah, to fuck it over! That is our history. In the very beginning, as it is said in ancient chronicle, people of Russia approached men from West and said "Our land is large and plentiful, but without order. Come and possess us." So it is now. We got oil and gas, wood, furs, caviar, and also plenty of lonely girls. We got many resources. But we have lack of fuckers like you.

U got me now, baby!

I feel it! And I'm horny!

Sing! Sing a Russian song, baby!

The apple and pear trees are in bloom,
Mists have come over the river . . .

Oh, yeah! How about poetry? Do you know any Russian poetry?

I think I do . . .

Let me have it!

Tatyana's Letter to Onegin:
I'm writing you this declaration—
What more can I in candor say?
It may be now your inclination
To scorn me and to turn away . . .

Ah, shit! I'm coming! Who's your daddy?

My daddy?

Who is your daddy, fucking Russia?
You. U R my daddy!!!
Peter came into a napkin he had had the foresight to stick
into his pants and immediately clicked exit. The session was over.
Nine minutes and change.

Nils tossed the napkin with his slimy unborn offspring into
the trash can. Then he took a second napkin from the desk,
carefully wiped his hands, and tossed it away after the first one.
He sat limply at his desk for a couple of minutes, eyes closed.
Visions arose into his consciousness: golden fields of wheat, oil
rigs, mountains of diamonds, piles of bearskins, a castle with
rows of severed heads adorning its walls, and, of course, forestfuls
of graceful, supple birches. He pictured himself riding along a
cobblestone road through Russian pastoral landscapes, encased
in glittering steel armor and wearing a helmet with a splendid
plume on top. Russian serfs, notably female, lined both sides of
the roadway, all of them on their hands and knees, and one of
them, a maiden of striking beauty, came out into the middle of
the road to greet him, her master, with a silver tray bearing a loaf
of fragrant, freshly baked bread, a salt cellar, and a small bowl
filled with pure cocaine.

Peter took a moment to savor his dream, then turned back to
his work.

He had to deal with a Russian complaint that had come in the
night before concerning the quality of a shipment of frozen potatoes. The Russians had gotten picky lately. They used to accept anything, so long as the label said "Product of the Netherlands," and
never used to complain. Now they'd started spelling everything out
meticulously in their contracts, and when the shipments arrived
they would bring a surveyor along; they would fish around in the
cartons, break the seals, and would call in some expert at the slightest suspicion; before you knew it, they'd be lodging a complaint.

It was the oil that had spoiled them. First oil, then gas. And the throngs of beautiful girls whom the Russians themselves could screw for nothing, but who would charge foreigners just for looking. It wouldn't last forever, though. Their own Russian expert, a member of the Academy of Sciences, said that the known oil reserves would only last five or six more years. And, in the meantime, the Russians had forgotten how to plow their land and grow their own food. The time would come, he said, when they would crawl to the Netherlands on their knees for a piece of rotten potato and would beg the Dutch to buy their own daughters.

But all that was just poetry. Prose required that the complaint be forwarded to the supplier, in China. Triple F actually purchased its Dutch potatoes from a different Dutch company, but they were still delivered directly from the Chinese port of Qingdao.

Nils had long suspected that the unscrupulous Asians had been pasting fake labels on their own low-grade potatoes, substituting them for the name-brand product, licensed and monitored by a European company, that they had been contracted to supply. Nils had already written his Dutch partner about the complaint. But today he decided to speak directly with the Chinese export manager, a guy named Ni Guan. This Ni Guan dealt with direct exports to Russia, apparently through that same company, Cold Plus. The Chinese sold frozen fish straight to the Russians, but their potatoes went through European packaging plants. Russia was the ultimate purchaser, and Ni also handled the potatoes accounts. And, really, they didn't devote sufficient attention to the quality of their deliveries, figuring—based on their previous experience with the Russian consumer—that Russians weren't picky and would eat anything. But the times were a-changing. The Russian purchasers were bringing their European partners to heel; in their turn the Europeans would have to train the Asians.

The time difference between Qingdao and St. Petersburg is five hours. Between Qingdao and Drachten, seven hours. Ni Guan was about ready to leave work when the phone on his desk rang. The secretary reported that Peter Nils from the Frozen French Fries company was on the line, and she connected them.

His European customer had a complaint about potatoes; the official version had arrived by fax an hour before. Ni listened patiently without interrupting, taking notes on a scrap of paper, as the Dutch representative berated him. Ni promised that the problem would be solved to their satisfaction, and that in the future his company would pay special attention to the quality of goods being sent to the Netherlands.

Ni-Eddie hung up, gathered his cell phone, apartment keys, and wallet into a plastic bag and left the office. On the way down in the elevator, all he could think about was some hot rice or noodles. It had been another busy day at work; Eddie hadn't even had time for lunch.

On the first floor, he was surprised to see his young colleague Tsin Chi—Cindy—waiting for him at the door to the elevator. Ni gave her a polite smile and bowed his head slightly to convey *bye, see you tomorrow, poka*. In addition to a couple of Chinese dialects, Ni also knew English well, could communicate tolerably in Russian, and had recently started learning German.

But Cindy blocked his way. She stared directly into her boss's eyes and didn't say a word.

"Comrade Tsin?"

"Yes, my lord?"

"Did . . . you have something you wanted to ask me?"

"Yes, sir, I did. I wanted to ask why you've been avoiding me. Maybe I'm not pretty enough for you? Maybe you're holding out for a supermodel off the cover of *Playboy*, and nothing less will do? Maybe

I should sign up for a photo session and bring you a dirty magazine with my photos in it, so that you'll notice me as a woman?"

Tsin's voice was a little too loud for the lobby, and Ni glanced around uneasily. The elevator doors parted and a crowd of coworkers poured out. Comrade Luan, the department head, walked by. Ni bowed to him, and his boss gave a barely detectable nod in return.

"Let's talk somewhere else. I'm starving—you must have seen that I didn't have time for lunch. We can have dinner together. Follow me."

Eddie made for the exit. Cindy waited a moment, then followed him out.

There were a number of restaurants around the business complex, but Eddie didn't want to run into anyone from the company. Why fuel gossip? He crossed the street to the bus stop and boarded one headed for the entertainment district by the shore. Cindy got on after him. The bus started off and merged into the heavy traffic creeping out of town.

A half-hour later the high-tech buildings of the business district were behind them, and they found themselves in a little Chinese version of Europe, complete with red-tile-roofed houses and neatly kept gardens.

Qingdao, translated from Chinese, means "green island." Indeed, this part of the city, viewed from the ocean side, looks like one big park, with German-style mansions scattered about. In 1898 China sold Qingdao to Germany, along with the right to build a railroad and develop mineral deposits within a fifteen-kilometer zone on both sides of the tracks. Coal-mining activity and the port spurred development, and the town grew and flourished. The Europeans introduced electricity and founded a university—the one where Ni Guan got his degree.

After the Germans left, history hurled Qingdao into chaos: The Japanese occupied the city, then Chinese revolutionaries took over, then the Japanese occupied it again, and then China again, the Kuomintang, and again Chinese revolutionaries.

With the Chinese industrial boom, Qingdao became the major shipping port of the eastern province of Shandun, with an annual turnover of over two hundred million tons. Skyscrapers rose and filled with businesses. In the free economic zone of Qingdao, capitalism began to develop at a fantastic pace, under sensitive supervision by communist warships with large-caliber weaponry: The port of Qingdao is the home base for the People's Republic of China's North Sea Fleet.

The German colonists were gone, but they left behind those red-tile-roofed mansions and the best beer in all of China: Qingdao (Tsingtao). Ni was giving this beer some serious consideration.

They got off the bus and went into a small establishment that served German food—that is to say, Bavarian sausages and Chinese beer. Ni and Tsin sat down and gave their order to a deferential young waiter, then lit up a couple of Great Wall cigarettes—made in China from Chinese tobacco at a factory licensed by a multinational corporation. Ni smoked the strong kind; Tsin's were light, thin, menthol cigarettes, made for ladies.

The restaurant's radio played gently in the background, Chinese pop. The song was about a girl's love for her fiancé, a sailor who was heading out to sea. Despite the melancholy lyrics, the melody and rhythm were fairly upbeat, as though the girl had no real intention of pacing the shore in solitude while her betrothed plowed the briny depths.

Ni sat silently; only after he'd finished off a couple of sausages and a half liter of cold Qingdao did he finally speak:

"Tsin, for a long time now I have been wanting to tell you what a wonderful girl you are, and how much I like you, but . . ."

"But what? Is there someone else?"

Tsin hadn't touched her sausages and had just been staring

at Ni the whole time, which made it a little awkward for him to eat.

"No, I don't have anyone else."

"So, what, you're gay?"

Ni nearly spit out his mouthful of beer. His face flushed bright red.

"Comrade Tsin! What are you talking about?"

"Don't call me comrade, here. Here I'm just a girl who wants to find her way into your bed. So the question, given the circumstances, is perfectly normal."

Her candor shocked Eddie. Though he himself had been wanting to have this conversation, in a sense.

"No, that's not it. That is, it's not that I'm gay . . . it's something else . . . I'm not gay . . . *shit!*"

Cindy brightened and slapped Eddie gently on the arm.

"Right, boss, I get it. You're not gay. So wouldn't this be a good time for us to drink out of the same glass like they do in Europe, so we can officially be friends?"

Without waiting for an answer, Tsin took her glass and entwined her arm with Ni's. They drank and Tsin leaned across the table for a kiss.

"No!"

Ni put his empty glass down on the table, leaned away, and looked around to see if there was anyone nearby who might know him.

"You see, Tsin," he said, "there are certain things that I just can't tell you about. It's about my family. I couldn't get married just now."

"What did you say?"

"I'm not free. For the next few years I can't allow myself to marry and have children, I mean, a child. That's what I've been trying to tell you."

Ni's confession made no impression on Tsin.

"So?"

"What do you mean, 'so'?"

"What do you mean, 'what do I mean'?"

Eddie was confused. He would have thought it would all be obvious to Cindy, who was, after all, a clever young lady.

"I can't marry you, so we can't date, or be together."

"Who told you that?"

Ni was utterly and sincerely baffled at this. Then Tsin's shoulders began to quiver. She covered her mouth with her hand and laughed silently.

When she recovered, she bent her head over the table and said, a little too loudly:

"Eddie, I don't want to marry you. I don't want to marry anyone right now, if you must know. I just want someone to sleep with. That's all, get it? *Tingi-tingi, chpok-chpok*, like in the movies. You watch porn, don't you? Of course you do, everyone does. Or even better, like in Japanese anime. I want you to lay me out on your bed, spread my legs out wide, and fuck me hard. I want you to lean me up against the windowsill and screw me there. I want you to screw me on the floor, pressing my head into the tatami. I want you to flatten me up against the wall and lift up my left leg. I want . . ."

"Enough!"

With trembling hands, Ni got out his wallet, counted out some bills, tossed them on the table, and stood up. But Tsin took his hand and stared into his eyes.

Ni Guan felt his resolve weaken. He was going to have to give in.

"I live alone." Cindy raised her hand. The waiter appeared.

"Call us a cab, please."

The Qingdao weather report came on the radio: 23.5 degrees Celsius, overcast, a north wind, four meters per second, humidity 94.1%. When Eddie and Cindy left the café, a light rain was falling. The cab arrived. Cindy tipped the waiter, who had accompanied them out, and gave the driver her address.

They rode the whole way without a word. Cindy pressed up against Eddie but refrained from any improper touching. She sat demurely with her hip pressed against his, holding his hand. Ni's eyes clouded over. The mere touch of the girl's narrow, warm palm filled him with desire.

The taxi took its time, driving through the entertainment district and the residential area of the city with its blocks of nondescript, identical high-rise apartment buildings. The driver honked apathetically, steering through the thick crowd of cars, motorcycles, bikes, and pedestrians.

At the entrance to Cindy's building a gray-haired woman stared mutely at them as they walked in. "From the apartment executive committee, no doubt," thought Ni. "She'll file a report. To hell with her!"

Tsin unlocked her door and they tumbled into a tiny room. The only furnishings were a small sofa bed, a nightstand, and a wooden bookshelf nailed into the wall.

Ni picked up a book at random. Lyrics by Wang Wei, a Chinese poet from the Tang dynasty period.

Ni opened the book and read aloud:

Two hundred thousand concubines
Had in his harem
The Yellow Emperor.
He knew the secret
Of coupling
That gives a man
A woman's life force.
The Yellow Emperor
Took in the life force
Of all his concubines.

And, attaining immortality,
He soared up to the heavens
Astride a yellow dragon.

Tsin continued, reciting from memory:

The emperor's sister
Then said to her brother:
"In our veins flows
Royal blood.
But Your Majesty
Has ten thousand concubines,
And I only have one husband."
Then the emperor gave Shan-in
Thirty young men for her bed,
And though they labored day and night,
Working in shifts,
Still they had to be replaced every six months.
And Shan-in grew more beautiful
With every year,
Filling with the life force
Of her thirty concubines.

Ni Guan continued:

He holds up
The Earth and Sky.
He penetrates the shell's crevasse
He enters the jasper cave.
He moves back and forth,
He is like unto a golden hammer
Beating against an anvil
He spews forth

A pearly stream;
He irrigates
The sacred field of life.
He himself is a mighty tree
On this field.

He is Man
He is White Tiger.
He is Lead.
He is Fire.
He is West.

Tsin Chi continued:

She is Woman.
She is Yellow Dragon.
She is Cinnabar.
She is Water.
She is East.

When they flow together
Quicksilver is born,
Eternal beginning.

. . . Outside the window, the rain stopped, then started again, and the northern wind hurled handfuls of ocean water against the glass. Ni and Tsin lay naked on the narrow sofa bed, clinging to each other and smoking Great Wall cigarettes, tossing the butts into an empty Pepsi can.

"Ni!"

"Tsin?"

"Those things you couldn't tell me about, why you can't get married, do they have to do with some violation of the Party's demographic program?"

"Yes."

"Do you have an illegitimate child? Maybe two or three?"

"Ten. Like a sailor with a girl and a baby in every port. No, of course not."

"So there's no kid?"

"There is one, but it's not mine."

"Oh!"

Tsin asked no more questions. She snuffed out her half-smoked cigarette, propped herself up onto her onto her elbow, and looked out the window.

"When I was a kid I lived out in the country. There was a poster on the biggest building in the town, which was the school: 'Fewer children—more pigs!' I saw that poster every day. And when I learned to read it was the first thing that I read all by myself. It scared me. I'm still scared. Sometimes I have nightmares: I'm in labor, surrounded by doctors. I'm screaming and straining, but then it's over. The baby cries, but something's wrong. The doctor in his white coat holds the baby up for me to see, and it's a piglet. It just gets worse from there. Everyone congratulates me—it turns out there are sixteen piglets in my farrow and that they're going to send me to Beijing and put me on exhibit at the big agricultural exposition. I also have this other recurring dream: I'm in the maternity hospital, and there are rows of basinets with babies in them, and then these butchers come in with knives, and they chop the babies into pieces and throw them into a big plastic bag, and I see that the babies are pigs. And one of the butchers says that suckling pig is really tasty with sweet-and-sour sauce. It was only when I got older that I wondered what the slogan meant. People think that it means you need to have fewer babies and work harder on the farm, raising pigs and other animals for meat. But it could mean something else, that it's the babies who eat up the pigs—all those babies will grow up and eat meat, or else eat all the food meant for the pigs, which means, either way, that the more children there are, the fewer pigs. Which means that the Party and the country need pigs more than they need children."

"You're quite an impressionable girl," said Ni.

But said nothing about the big poster in his own hometown that read "One more baby, one more grave!" He'd had nightmares too. One where all the children in his class are lined up a row, holding shovels, digging their own graves. And when they look up he sees that their eyes are glazed over, that they're already dead. And the skin peels off their bodies in long strips that fall to the ground and mix with the dirt. And he realizes that he is also one of those children digging their graves, and that he, too, is dead.

LOVE, RUSSIAN STYLE

Semipyatnitsky had lunch in a café on the first floor of his office building, a place he called the Barf Bar. A plate of dubious-looking beef with undercooked rice. He didn't go to the Harbin today; too hot—24 degrees Celsius!—to drag himself all that way. The heat was unusual for St. Petersburg, and particularly unbearable due to high humidity and all the fumes and automobile exhaust filling the air. Anyway, the mere thought of sweet-and-sour pork made him sick.

He spent the second half of his lunch hour at his desk. To avoid work-related distractions, Maximus cranked up his MP3 player and put on his earphones. B.G.—Boris Grebenshikov.

> *Where I'm from, everyone knew Kolya*
> *Kolya, everyone's best friend and pal.*
> *He taught us to drink,*
> *And drinking took the place*
> *of freedom,*
> *And the jasper root took the place*
> *Of the compass and life vest.*

In Chinese erotic poetry the "jasper root" served as the conventional metaphor for the male organ. Maximus could have written entire volumes of hermeneutics, interpreting the songs of Grebenshikov's band Aquarium. Though there's already a commentary along these lines in Ilya Stogoff's novel *Macho Men Don't Cry*, which hit the seventies generation with the force of revelation.

> *And on Sunday morning we go again to the flock*
> *And receive our blessing:*
> *Be fruitful and multiply in the dark.*

It's about life in our day and age, though the meaning is eternal, as always with B.G. To live and strive . . . for what? For whom? For the children. But what will those children be striving for? Where will they be going? And what could be more cruel: to be fruitful and multiply, to create a new being who will not be able to find his own way, and to abandon him without a single indicator of the right path? Just a stone where three roads meet: Whichever way you choose will cost you dearly . . .

The song went on, and Maximus listened. Then lunch break was over, and Semipyatnitsky tuned back in to his work.

The warehouse was refusing to accept two containers of shrimp from Canada.

Maximus listened patiently to fifteen minutes of telephone hysterics from the warehouse director: There's no place to put the shrimp, the warehouse is already crammed full of shrimp. Then he hung up and issued an order to his assistant:

"Sasha, have the containers sent from the port to the warehouse. Today."

"But how? There's no space at the warehouse!"

"There's plenty of space. They probably took too many shrimp pills and started hallucinating."

"Meaning?"

"Forget about it. They'll figure something out—they'll find a place and unload them there. It's not the first time."

Maximus never indulged the warehouse workers. So they always wanted to rough him up when they ran into him at company get-togethers. They would come at him foaming at the mouth, fists clenched, but their aggression would dissipate when it came into contact with his indifference. And this time Semipyatnitsky recalled vividly what he had seen during his unannounced visit, when he'd gone to retrieve the Dutch pills. This relieved him of the last shreds of whatever sympathy he might have had for the blue-collar Cold Plus employees.

The working day began to wane. Maximus ducked into the restroom and gulped down a couple of the pink pills. There were still a few left in his jacket pocket. It wasn't that he particularly needed to get high; rather, a sort of spirit of adventure had come over him, an irresistible desire to test their effects one more time, to see how they would work with another person. That is, how they would work *on* another person.

All things considered, and given the way things had been going lately, he was surprised *not* to find the goddess of sex from the next office over in the elevator waiting for him. She wasn't in the lobby on the first floor either. Maximus went outside and lit a cigarette near the front door. He was sure that she would turn up.

Sure enough, five minutes later, there she was, coming out the door. She had a preoccupied air about her, a look of distress, which in no way diminished her allure.

"Greetings, Sweetie!"

Maximus was startled by his own lack of self-consciousness. The drug hadn't had time to take effect yet. It had to be psychosomatic: The mere thought of the pills' imminent effect dissolved all his inhibitions.

That was how he used to pick up girls, in his distant, lost youth. Maximus had only two phrases in his repertoire: "Greetings, Sweetie!" and "Got any plans for tonight?" But as he had pointed out at the time, when a friend made fun of his tactics, why bother to think up anything original when these worked just fine? Not every time, objected his friend. Maximus responded that there's only one absolutely guaranteed method to get a woman into your bed—just grab her and give her the cross-thigh flip.

The girl gave Semipyatnitsky a surprised look and smiled oh so slightly.

"Greetings yourself."

"Not feeling so well today?"

"I have a headache."

Maximus reached into his pocket, got out a couple of the pills, and held them out to her.

"These work pretty well. I use them myself."

The girl hesitated, but took one nonetheless.

"Take two. The dose is two. Go ahead—you can take them without water."

The goddess complied.

"My car is over there. Let's go."

"I live pretty far away, in Prosvet, on Enlightenment Prospect."

"You're right, that's pretty far. Let's find some place closer."

When a man has absolute confidence in what he's saying and doing, Maximus reflected, there isn't a woman alive who won't give in. The goddess climbed into the car. Maximus started the engine and backed out of his parking space.

"What's your name, my beauty?"

"Maya."

Maximus gave an approving nod. That's about what he'd been expecting. Maya had been the name of his first, unrequited love, a girl he'd met in Young Pioneer Camp, when he was little. Not that little, actually. Meaning, if things had worked out differently and if he had been a bit surer of himself at the time, something might have come of it. So this love of his had remained in his memory as an unrealized desire, along with the sensation of his first fully conscious erection.

Maya is also the name of the Hindu goddess of material nature, of illusion embodied.

"Maximus Semipyatnitsky. Descendent of the ancient Khazar race, heir of the Great Khagans. Writer of genius. And leading specialist in the Import Department of Cold Plus Company. Though the latter is nothing more than an embarrassing stumble along my world-historical path."

"What an honor for a girl as simple and modest as myself!"

The goddess had perked up, and it showed. Girls like to be amused.

"Are you from Barnaul?"

"No, from Karaganda."

"I thought it was something like that."

"Why? Do I look like some simple country girl?"

"No. You look beautiful. And only girls from the country are beautiful anymore. Have you ever been to Ireland?"

"No."

"Me neither. So let's go to an Irish pub."

Maximus parked in a cozy alley near the pub he had in mind. He figured he could drink his fill and then call a cab.

"The best cocktail here is called the Irish Flag. See, it's got three different-colored layers. No, don't stir it. Just drink."

Five pairs of cocktails made their way down the hatch smoothly, encountering no obstacles.

"Now tell me a story!"

"What can I tell you, O Khazar writer of genius?"

"Whatever suits the occasion. How about how your stepfather raped you? We wouldn't want to violate the conventions of pseudo-psychological novels and movies."

"But my stepfather didn't rape me! I don't even have a stepfather! Just a mom and a dad, and, sorry to disappoint you, they were absolutely normal people."

"The main thing is to not disappoint the reader."

"What reader?"

"Hasn't it ever seemed to you that your life is being narrated, bit by bit? Don't you ever see a computer monitor inside your head full of sentences lighting up all by themselves?"

"Oh, I get it . . . I can see there's no fooling you. It was my grandfather."

"It was your grandfather what?"

"My grandfather was my first lover, if you can call it that."

"Details. We need details. Every last one."

"I know. That's where the devil is, in the details."

"How'd you know?"

"I read it somewhere."

The girl adopted an appropriately reflective pose, lit a cigarette, affected a nervous air, and began her story:

"When I was really little, I used to spend a lot of time with my grandpa. My parents worked. My grandpa really loved me and used to spoil me. He used to take me in his lap and kiss me. At first there was nothing unusual about it—it was just a kid and her grandfather, like all children and their grandparents: He'd kiss me on the forehead or the cheeks. Sometimes on my tummy. But later, when I was seven or eight, he started to kiss me down there, lower. A lot lower. And it wasn't just simple kissing. He tried to poke his tongue in, as far as it would go. And his rough cheeks and chin used to scratch the insides of my thighs. But I put up with it. I really loved my grandpa. He never asked me not to tell, but I knew that it wasn't the kind of thing you talked about. So it was our little secret. I got older, started going through puberty. And our one-on-one sessions continued. We came up with our own special code names for it. Not the usual stuff—honeybees and flowers and other clichés. No, he would say: 'I'm most inclined to partake of water from the crystal spring.' Or: 'A ray of moonlight is thrusting through the clouds.' He was an artist at heart, my grandfather—he had a thing for classical Chinese poetry. For the first few years I was only putting up with it all, but with time I began to experience certain sensations, and came to enjoy our sessions. I was fairly shy as a child, didn't have a lot of friends. I would just hurry home from school and go to Grandpa's. I'd come in without a word and curl up in a threadbare old armchair. And he would cheerfully ask me about how my day at school had gone, and would sit down on the floor in front of me, lift my skirt, and lower my panties and toss them on the floor. Then he would direct his attention to the 'spring.' He would spend a long time down there, a half hour, sometimes a whole hour. If no one interrupted us. And no one would. My parents came back late from work, and my grandmother had died long before—I don't remember her at all. He would lick his way around my inner parts, which were as yet completely hairless, and I would stroke his gray head. Just like a grownup. He never did anything else with me. I don't know why—maybe he couldn't get it up, or maybe he was afraid to hurt or frighten me. But he never asked me to . . . well, you know."

"So how did it all end?"

"It didn't, really. He just died. For me this was, and remains, the greatest loss of my life. I remember his body in the coffin in our apartment, in the same room that used to be his, and where the two of us used to do what we did together . . . The hearse came—they closed the coffin and took my grandfather to the cemetery. There, in front of the freshly dug grave, they lifted the coffin lid so that his relatives could say their last good-byes. But apparently they'd done a bad job of securing his chin . . . they'd had to bring the coffin down four flights of stairs . . . and the ride in the hearse had involved a fair bit of jostling. Anyway, when they opened the coffin, I saw his face—I was standing right there, closer than anyone else . . . his jaw had shifted to one side, and his long, violet-colored tongue was dangling out of his mouth. The same tongue that . . . well. My legs gave way under me and I fainted. Everyone thought that it was from grief or from horror at the sight of him, but that wasn't it at all."

The air over their table filled with silence. The goddess lifted her glass and downed her sixth cocktail in a single swig.

"So, you think I'm some kind of pervert?" she asked after a minute.

"I think that the worst perversion is to be what they call a 'normal person,'" Maximus replied. "To get up every morning, shave or put on your makeup, go to the office, work all day long, fill your refrigerator and empty it again, spend your nights in front of the TV. People who live that way are the real sickos. That is what I think."

Maximus lifted his own sixth cocktail and, like the goddess, downed it in one swig.

Outside the bar, Maximus embraced Maya tenderly, and she laid her head trustfully on his shoulder. The excess of emotion overflowing inside him brought Maximus close to tears. It occurred to him that in Russia, true love was actually pity. Perhaps that's where the Russian soul most reveals its essentially feminine nature. They say that it's when a woman feels pity that she truly loves. Though admittedly it's only Russians who say that. Or maybe all love is really made up of pity, compassion. What else can a single, lonely soul, trapped in the cage of the material world and suffering a multitude of sorrows, feel toward another soul like itself? And don't the Hindus say that all souls are by nature female?

Then, out of the middle of nowhere, he remembered the classic anecdote about Lieutenant Rzhevsky.

Lieutenant Rzhevsky goes into the officers' club and says: "Gentlemen! What has Russia come to? I was walking down the street just now, and this little girl comes up to me, age twelve or so, a perfect little blue-eyed angel, but skinny as a toothpick and all in rags, and she says: 'Uncle, give me a piece of bread, and I'll do anything you want me to!' And just imagine, gentlemen, I did—I fucked her and cried, fucked her and cried!"

That's so disgusting, thought Semipyatnitsky. But it's still pity, isn't it. Pity and love. Love, Russian style.

FOREIGN POLICY

And Saat began his new life as the Khagan. First, as the Great Bek had instructed, he had to visit the harem. And in the harem there were ten sevens of women, one from each of seventy different tribes, the seventy peoples that Great Khazaria had united together on the bright path, just as it says in the Khazar national anthem. The Khagan's couriers had gone out into the towns and villages, the forests and encampments, and requisitioned these women, selecting them in accordance with the ideal anthropological standard that had been set for each tribe. Only the most beautiful were brought to the Khagan's palace.

At first Saat thought that he would try out a different bedroom each night: that is, one wife per night. But when he sat down and clicked the pearly beads of his silver abacus, he realized that that this wasn't going to work. At that rate each noble princess would experience the bliss of love only four times a year. Or maybe five, for the ones early in the rotation, and if it was a leap year. The girls would get lonely. So he would have to steel his flesh and sacrifice himself on the altar of the state. Saat resolved to visit four wives every night.

A monumental labor. Every third night or so, of course, the demon in him would fully savor the pleasures of the flesh. But then he wouldn't be able to stand any more, could not bear to look upon any more, any more breasts or thighs, any more heavy-lidded eyes! And when he again smelled their perfume, or that fishy smell between their legs, he would just get disgusted and feel like throwing up.

But this wasn't about his pleasure: It was a matter of state. This much Saat learned on the first morning. He dragged himself on rubbery legs back to his gilded bed with its swan-down mattress, hoping to sleep it off until sunset. But a delegation appeared in his room unbidden, four scribes holding waxed slates, and the Bek himself at their head. They arranged themselves around the room, each on a special seat that had been prepared for him, styluses at ready, all ears. And the Great Bek spoke:

"Tell me, O Khagan, how it went with your wives. State first their name, then their tribe of origin and ID number. And spare us no detail!"

Saat hesitated, but the Great Bek encouraged him: "Bear in mind this is not an intimate, personal matter. These are noble maidens serving the welfare of the realm."

So Saat then told them everything, keeping no secrets; he told how and how many; he told of contortions and positions, of breasts and thighs, of loud moans and passionate climaxes; he told of women who lay still and unresponsive like logs, and of those who craved all manner of debauchery or asked to be whipped, who summoned maidservants to watch, who ordered him to crawl about on all fours and to drink amber-colored urine; he told of the one who said she wanted the stag to drink deeply of her spring, who stroked his hair and called him Grandpa.

Saat told them everything, and the scribes wrote it all down, scratching it into their slates, and the Great Bek rested his head in his hand and thought various thoughts.

Afterward the Great Bek studied the scribes' slates. He then summoned his ministers and warriors and issued instructions:

"Number One's people are restless, they must be tamed. Take away their bread and beer—that will make them scrawnier and less likely to cause trouble. Number Two's people are strong and hostile—bring in some border troops and have them needle away at them with small-scale banditry: Have them beat the men and ravish the maidens, though not so much as to cause any harm to the economy or to the glory of Khazaria in the land beyond the hills. Number Three's people are lethargic, sleeping even when awake—send our musicians and actors forth to the bazaars, have them play loudly on their flutes and entertain the masses day and night. That may awaken them. As for Number Four's people: Leave everything as it is. It's best not to touch them—or you'll cause a stink on both sides from the River Itil all the way to the Khazar Sea."

The Bek departed with the scribes and the new Khagan collapsed on his bed, deeply moved: Great is the wisdom of tradition! What better way to get to know a country than by fucking all its crevasses? And to use for that purpose a sweet, noble girl. And by knowing the peoples of the realm in this way, it is easy to maintain power, and to preserve the unity of the mighty Khaganate.

PROSPECT OF ENLIGHTENMENT

Early the next morning Maximus sat at the open window of an apartment on Enlightenment Prospect, greedily gulping in the fresh air, which hadn't yet become saturated with poisonous exhaust. Maya lay on the sofa bed, having kicked off the covers, with her arms, legs, hair, and breasts splayed every which way across the sheets.

Maximus looked over at her and felt that he no longer felt anything. Not love, not passion, not even pity. Well, maybe a touch of pity remained, but it was mixed with scorn, not love.

So, thought Maximus, does this mean that there's no such thing as love? It's all just pills?

How did we survive before, before the Dutch came up with their drug?

Or were the pills something like insulin—get hooked on them, and before you know it your heart loses the ability to process its own emotions without a fresh dose?

Or have the pills always been with us, just in some other form?

Maybe the girl was in fact beautiful. Yes, sure she was, even very much so. But it was a strange, deathly beauty! The beauty of a corpse. For she would be just as beautiful if she were to die right this minute. Maybe even more beautiful—a little pallor would add the perfect finishing touch.

Beauty is the promise of happiness. Semipyatnitsky had long known this maxim, and had even quoted it somewhere in one of his stories. But now he saw that the promise had become a lie. Everything is mere illusion, and beauty is the delusion that there is happiness to be had tomorrow, when you make it your own. But once you do, it all empties out. And you understand that possessing it wasn't the point; that it's impossible, in fact. The girl, fine; you can possess her in a social or physical sense, but not her beauty. Because beauty isn't something that belongs to her alone. Beauty is from some other, celestial plane. Only there can beauty, and perfection, and happiness be realized.

Four used condoms, full of semen, lay in a little pile on the doily on the table. And all the temptations of the flesh, all possible aesthetic achievements, even the great works of art from the portrait of Mona Lisa to the verses of Igor Severianin, from the architecture of Versailles to the music of the Beatles, appeared to Maximus in his present state like just so many used rubbers.

Maya's head slipped off the pillow and gave out a refined, whistling snore. Maximus dressed and left the apartment. The door slammed behind him.

When he came out the front of the building, he found himself surrounded on all sides by identical concrete towers, rising like great cliffs pitted with rows and rows of identical, nest-like apartments. Whenever he found himself in the northern suburbs, Maximus felt as though he'd landed in some strange and alien place—if not a different planet, then at least an unfamiliar city.

Yes, the Cyclopean hulks of the buildings loomed up and blocked the sky. People emerged from the front doors of the towers and merged together to form a great stream, flowing toward the only point of egress, *prosvet*, sliver of light, sliver of dawn, Prospect of Enlightenment. They resembled the throngs of souls on Judgment Day, destined either to be borne up to Paradise or hurled on a downward spiral through the circles of Hell.

Must be heading for the metro.

Maximus lit up a cigarette and joined the crowd.

PART III

Serkel

HAKAN

Maximus had acquired a new hobby. During the day he obediently carried out his duties at the office: verified accounts, argued with brokers and shippers, persuaded suppliers to extend deadlines and raise credit limits, read e-mail, wrote messages, and drafted contracts and reports for the management. Then, after work, he frequented used bookstores or sat at home at the computer, searching the Internet for information about the history of the Khazar Khaganate. Before long he considered himself to be an expert on the matter and even toyed with the idea of writing an essay on the Khazars.

And there were no repercussions as far as Maya went. Nobody could have been more surprised than she herself at her precipitous decision to sleep with a mid-level manager from the next office over. Her social position, her tactical, technological, and physical specifications—they all made demands Semipyatnitsky couldn't hope to meet, as a suitor. He'd gone out to dinner with her a couple of times since that night: once at the Barf Bar, another time at the Harbin. They had indulged in empty chatter about trivialities: just friends.

Before long Maximus saw her being picked up from work in a Porsche Cayenne with a conspicuous tricolored government pass on the windshield.

But this didn't really bother him. He had become preoccupied with Khazaria. He felt that the secrets of that ancient land would hold the key to both his own fate and that of the Fatherland, as well as to a whole range of geopolitical and national problems. At times he would feel that the truth was close at hand, but soon this discovery would get caught up in a mass of contradictory historical facts and interpretations, and slip from his grasp.

Maximus wasted no time over lunch. He could take the elevator down to the first floor, put "today's special" on a tray, pay, eat, have a smoke, and ride the elevator back up to the office all within the space of a half hour. That left the other half of his lunch hour open.

Semipyatnitsky considered it his right to be idle during that time. He surfed the web, beginning with news sites and gradually switching to chat sites and forums, following links further and further up the Internet's esoteric asshole.

So it happened that one time he stumbled onto a blog post by someone who signed himself Hakan, with a bearded cartoon avatar instead of a photograph.

From then on Maximus even gave up TV. He could keep up with current events by reading Hakan's blog: a never-ending flow of opinions on all the most striking and ludicrous events in Russian public life.

When pogroms occurred in the Karelian village of Kondopoga, Hakan posted a stirring manifesto:

Russians Out of Karelia!

The patience of the Karelian nation has reached its limit. The uninvited guests of this beneficent northern land interpret our inherent goodness and our gentle and kind natures as weakness and timidity. Hospitality is a good thing, but when the guest forgets his place and begins to act like the host, and even attempts to crowd the homeowner out of his own space, it's time to send him packing!

Karelia, of course, is a vast and spacious land, but even here, space is finite. Tens of thousands of strangers have inundated us from the south. And of all the immigrants in Karelia, the Russian diaspora represents the most populous, disrespectful, criminal, and dangerous group.

Wherever we go, schools, workplaces, institutions of all

kinds, everywhere we see the same old faces. I'm sick and tired of them, these ugly Slavic faces. These newcomers have infested all of Karelia! Conniving with the local authorities, who are in the hands of the Russians, these tumbleweeds spread their uncivilized ways across our homeland.

Even as they live on our land, they show no willingness to respect our laws and customs. They make no effort to learn the Karelian language, the beautiful, mellifluous tongue of our great epic Kalevala, *and instead they force us to study their guttural, incomprehensible lingo, an impoverished mongrel tongue cobbled together from words and concepts stolen from other languages.*

Karelia is a land of woods and lakes, a vast virgin wilderness! The indigenous population, the Karelians, always lived in harmony with their environment. In their interactions with nature, they acted with moderation, respecting ancient tradition. Karelians of all walks of life—fishermen, hunters, foresters—took from nature only what they needed, claiming no excess; instead of seeking quick profits, they ensured the preservation and renewal of the natural resources of the land.

Then the aliens, the greedy Russians, came and disfigured the pristine shorelines of our crystal lakes, building cellulose and paper processing plants that spew toxins into the air and water. The Russian timber industries are destroying our precious Karelian forests. These squatters show no inclination or ability to preserve even their own land, so why should they care about anyone else's? Having long ago poisoned and sold off everything of any value in their own habitat, they now extend their greedy paws toward the riches of the north.

The immigrants' predatory appetites know no bounds, great or small. And now the original natives of the Republic of Karelia can no longer can find work in their own country; all the jobs have been taken over by Russian gastarbeiter. The immigrants have taken over our stores and markets, so we Karelians can no longer practice our own traditional crafts. As a result, the ancient ways of our native people are falling into wrack and ruin.

Long ago, that great northern race, the Varangians, generously offered their protection to the slumbering Slavic tribes, created a state for them, and brought them into contact with European culture. The savages even took their name from the Varangians' language, which identified the noble northern race that ruled the backward eastern territories as "Rus." As such, the word "Russian" answers not the question "who" but rather "whose." The peoples of Europe called these Slavs the slaves of Rus, of the Varangians. But now they have taken that name for themselves.

Today's Russians haven't even preserved the Slavic bloodline, which was improved and enhanced by its contact with the northern gene bank. The real Russians were exterminated during the Mongol invasion, the reign of the Oprichniks, and the Time of Troubles. Thereafter, all the Russian lands were overrun by the survivors, Muscovites, a bastardized mix of Tatars and Jews. And these are the Russians of today: nomads and money-grubbers, lacking any roots to the land.

And they display the most blatant historical ingratitude. Instead of meekly yielding before the superior northern race, who had first made human beings out of these bears and peasants, instead of kneeling before the Karelians, who preserved the purity of the true Rus bloodline, these bastard crossbreeds are now trying to take over our territory!

Their insolence surpasses all reason: First they incite bloody violence against other immigrants, whose diasporas just happen to be more sparsely dispersed, and then they divide our land, our markets, and our natural resources into "spheres of influence"! It's as though the aliens have completely forgotten where they are—who is the host here, and who the guest.

Herewith I declare the establishment of the People's Front for the Liberation of Karelia, whose goal it is to cleanse our native land of undesirable immigrants, to establish justice and order, and to improve the welfare of the working people of Karelia, who for centuries have been robbed and oppressed by these foreigners.

The People's Front for the Liberation of Karelia hereby establishes lateral ties with the Fronts of the fraternal peoples of the republics of Sakha-Yakutia, of Tuva, and of Chuvashia, among others, and stands ready to coordinate its efforts to liberate these neighboring lands. There is no place here for the Russian plunderers!

We will not emulate the ignorant Asiatics and Russians and imitate their savage customs, will not instigate bloody brawls and pogroms or commit acts of arson. We Karelians are a civilized European nation, belonging to the sophisticated northern race. And we will solve our problems in a civilized manner.

All Russians are hereby invited to gather all their belongings and quit the territory of Karelia within forty-eight hours to return to their historical homeland. We know that entire villages in central Russia are dying out; fields stand fallow and vacant. Why shouldn't the Russians go back where they came from, and plant potatoes and parsley? We will no longer permit them to cut down our forests and poison our lakes!

All material property and businesses on the territory of the Republic of Karelia are hereby declared the property of the Karelian people and will be distributed to native representatives of the republic according to the principles of social equality.

We guarantee that during the course of these forty-eight hours the people undergoing resettlement will not be subjected to any violence or intimidation; all Russians will be ensured a

*safe and unencumbered departure. Any deportees lacking suffi-
cient funds may apply to district offices of the Front, where they
will be provided with reserved-seat tickets to Ryazan, free of
charge.*

*Thus will the Russians be assured of the nobility and gener-
osity of the Karelian people, whose virtues they were unable to
appreciate when they were guests in our land.*

*If any Russians do not quit the territory of Karelia, the
Front assumes no responsibility for any acts of vengeance or
attempts to restore justice that may inevitably and spontaneously spread through the republic upon the expiration of the
grace period.*

*The Karelians are a generous and peace-loving people, but
when an occupying nation shows contempt for their will, they
are capable of a great and terrible wrath. The Russian thieves
and drunkards will face real men, marksmen who can aim and
hit a squirrel in the eye and can fell an ancient spruce with
three mighty blows. The Karelian huntsmen will emerge from
the forests bearing hunting rifles and axes, and when they do,
the squatters who remain will envy the dead!*

Consider this a warning. Your time is at hand.

Hakan

Best friend and protector of all Karelians.

Maximus guffawed, startling his coworkers, when he read the
above during the second half of his lunch break. But judging from
the serious discussion that ensued subsequently in the comments
section, the author's readers had completely missed the article's
sardonic humor.

The indefatigable Hakan also took it upon himself to comment on a bill that had been passed allowing oil and gas mo-
nopolies to maintain their own armed security services for the
defense of their facilities. Immediately after this news made its

way through the media, Hakan posted another tongue-in-cheek composition on his blog, which Maximus read during his next lunch hour:

I Serve Gazprom!

Someone is stealing my ideas. No, I do not publicize them on-line; that would make it too easy for the criminals. I do not share them with my friends; you can't trust anyone! But I do jot things down in a notebook that I carry around with me, so as not to miss anything. Anyway, I must have been careless and left my notebook unguarded at some point for an hour or two, say, during my lunch hour. And someone copied my notes and stole my ideas! An act of espionage. There's no other way to put it.

The subject in today's entry is the army. Recently I was at one of those free public events for plebeians, some Day of Something or Other, and when I saw the logo of an oil rig depicted in silhouette on all the posters and banners advertising this government-supported Bacchanalia, I was inspired. Right then and there I composed a series of appeals, slogans, and mottos, and even started outlining some ideas for uniforms. So here you go: Today I look at the news and I see that "The Gazprom and Transneft Corporations are forming their own military units." The most insane predictions of our pessimistic and depressive novelists and screenwriters, produced under the influence of a continual narcotic haze, pale in comparison with reality.

But might it have been a joke? Some journalistic canard? An exaggeration? Maybe these organizations are simply attempting to beef up their on-site security by hiring more military veterans, or by stocking up on pepper spray.

But no, alas. It's for real! Official government legislation, no less, and I quote: "A legislative initiative to grant the compa-

nies Gazprom and Transneft the authority to form their own internal structures to ensure the security of their operations associated with the extraction, refinement, and transportation of energy resources was adopted in the third reading."

Initiative! The third reading! How did this happen? Who sponsored this bill? "Representatives of all parties introduced the proposal to amend the weapons law with the support of the current administration."

All parties! All at once!! Unanimously! And naturally, "with the support of . . ." How can you not support something like that? Here it is at last, the long-awaited orgasm, the moment of the great coupling between big business, our political parties, and the current administration. Not the most traditional sexual configuration, but this only intensifies the climax.

Maybe it's because I'm only an amateur connoisseur of state porn, but allow me to ask a stupid question: Why? Who are this new army's presumed enemies? The explanation is as follows: "In accordance with the new law, the Gazprom and Transneft corporations, along with their subsidiaries, are granted the right to acquire special equipment and military armaments for the defense of oil pipelines and other facilities whose purpose is to obtain, refine, and transport materials through government contract."

Seems to make sense. This army's purpose is to protect the pipeline.

But . . . what is there left for our, allow me to say, constitutionally based institutions of law and order to do? We already have so many, I can't even begin to list them all, I might forget one or get mixed up, and some smart-aleck troll will post a sarcastic comment: "Go back and learn the basics before you start bitching!"

For is it not those very institutions that, according to Russian law, are tasked to defend all property, including pipelines, from being damaged, vandalized, or stolen? Or is the term "all property" just a distraction in this context? And who's going to pay for this militia, anyway (or, sorry, correct me if I slept through it and they've already been labeled "police" instead)? Wouldn't it just make more sense to create a special militarized unit of "real," governmental police for the defense of the pipeline? But . . . defense against whom, exactly? . . .

Against our own people, maybe? After all, an ordinary policeman, hungry and therefore himself by necessity a thief, is also one of the people. So what if he refuses to shoot at his own countrymen? Naturally, in that case it makes more sense for Gazprom to have its own units, to ensure that they have no other priorities.

The article says: "This decision, experts believe, is primarily justified in that it addresses the potential breakdowns and risks associated with the human factor." Understood. Everything would be fine if it weren't for the human factor; you simply can't trust people. Especially your own citizens—workers as well as the general public. They might, for example, go on strike. Or launch some kind of public protest—march in the streets or something. And that's the last thing the pipeline needs; it must function reliably, without interruption.

May I make a suggestion? Let Gazprom and Transneft recruit their regiments from among the native warriors of the savage Tulgandyr tribe. That will take care of any potential problems. The Tulgandyrs speak no Russian, are illiterate, have no trade unions, and are good marksmen! I happen to be one of the few people who know how to get them a message, and I would be willing to undertake the task of recruiting them myself, for a small commission.

And here's another flash of insight: The pipeline defense army isn't actually a part of the Russian Federation military, right? Right. It's a separate army, commercial in nature.

Conveniently, then, it isn't bound by Russia's responsibilities, isn't constrained by local or international law. And why not? Why shouldn't it declare itself exterritorial? To wit: Its task is to defend the pipeline, wherever the pipeline might lie. Let's say someone tries to siphon off gas from somewhere, say, in Ukraine. Gazprom tank divisions are deployed onto Ukrainian territory, which is independent from Russia. The President of Ukraine attempts to call the Russian President, but can't get through: "We're sorry, the subscriber you have dialed cannot be reached." Three days later the subscriber shows up in person and explains that his cell battery had died. He explains to the President of Ukraine that Gazprom is a commercial organization and has to defend its interests, but he is a government official and lacks the authority to get involved in the case. Then to Europe he will explain that they don't understand, that we have to do this in order to guarantee uninterrupted gas deliveries and the fulfillment of our obligations to them. And Europe will remain silent.

So you see, there is a wealth of geopolitical implication to all this. It's not the first time. Take the East India Company. It wasn't Britain that occupied India, as I recall, but this corporation, which had its own troops and paid taxes like any business. The legislators and administrators who supported them serve as an instructive example that is relevant to us today!

That said, let us not neglect the potential value of our own standing Russian army in this context. All it would take would be some minor changes to its symbols, rituals, and insignias, and a revision of the methodology and the political priorities applied in training new recruits.

Their banners are first on the list. All those hammers and sickles are long gone, of course, and we have no need for stars now either. So why not use the silhouette of an oil rig? The rig can go on the state's highest medal of honor, too: Call it the

"Golden Gusher" and bestow an honorary title upon its recipients: "Hero of Gazprom." Awardees will be expected to express their gratitude with the words "I serve Gazprom!"
And don't forget about the youth demographic. We'll need a new organization: "The Young Pioneers of the Oil Deposits." Black neckerchiefs. Badges with little oil rigs on them. And slogans: "Be prepared—for the struggle for Transneft!"

The blog was very popular. It was taken up by a couple of professional Internet publications, which posted the text under bold headlines: "Pipeline Defense Force" and "Gazprom Tanks Enter Ukraine!"

When Ramzan Kadyrov was inaugurated as president of the Republic of Chechnya, Hakan posted a joke: "Ramzan Kadyrov, the new President of the Republic of Chechnya, took his oath of office on the Holy Koran, the Constitution of the Republic of Chechnya, and the Constitution of the Russian Federation—all at the same time. If the President of the Republic of Chechnya, when taking the oath of office, placed his right hand on the Holy Koran, and his left hand on the Constitution of the Republic of Chechnya, then what did he place on the Constitution of the Russian Federation?"

Maximus read the joke, leaned back in his office chair, and heaved with silent laughter. His colleagues, engrossed in their work, cast uneasy glances in his direction. Was he losing it?

But Maximus didn't mind seeming a bit of an oddball. When he got home at night he would turn on his computer, pull up the file with his essay on Khazaria, and enter corrections and revisions. In a couple of weeks it was finished.

We quote it here in its entirety, in the original Semipyatnitsky version, uncut, with all its long quotations intact, so as to give the reader a sense of what was brewing in the kettle of our hero's mind during those fateful days.

TRACES OF KHAZARIA

Khazaria is a mythological, nonexistent land, a country that might never have actually existed, or if it did, then in a form we cannot conceive of today, as this was a land that left behind no unambiguous historical documentation and very little in the way of archeological evidence, only contradictory comments in the chronicles, and not a single deciphered text. Therefore, any attempt at writing its history must begin with a survey of the most applicable extant sources, all of which happen to be of a fantastical and imaginative nature—though these qualities, given our intentions, can't be seen as defects. I speak, of course, of the references to Khazaria in literature and fiction, which are no less valuable than facts, and best capture the otherworldly flavor of this vanished nation.

I will cite just one example, for the time being. We know it from elementary school: Alexander Pushkin's poem "The Song of the Wise Oleg." As we all (?) recall, it begins with the lines:

> *As now wise Oleg prepares*
> *His revenge against the dull-witted Khozars:*
> *For their fierce raid, he dooms*
> *Their settlements and fields*
> *To sword and flame . . .*

Judging by these lines, Khazaria was not considered a nomadic horde: The enemy had settlements and fields, that is, plots of land cultivated with grain that had caught the eye of Prince Oleg and aroused in him these thoughts of plunder.

As for Prince Oleg himself, his real name was Helgi, and he was a full-blooded Scandinavian. The first mention of him in *The Tale of Bygone Years* reads as follows: "In the year 6387, Rurik died, having turned over his princedom to his kinsman Oleg, entrusting to him his son Igor's care, for the heir was still very small."

In the Scandinavian original, Igor's name is Ingvar; he was a Swede as well. By all accounts Helgi governed Rurik's princedom as a regent for the underage heir Ingvar, and in his name he made many conquests, including the capture of Kiev in the year 6390 from the Creation of the World, or 882 in the new reckoning, counting from the birth of Christ. *The Tale of Bygone Years* confirms Helgi's regency during the reign of Ingvar as follows: " ... and Oleg said to Askold and Dir: 'You are not princes and not of princely blood, but I am of princely blood,' and he showed them Igor: 'This is the son of Rurik.' And they slew Askold and Dir ... "

It is difficult for us to understand it today, but in those distant times the legitimacy of government in the people's consciousness was firmly based on heredity, and succession was almost always determined by reference to the dynastic bloodline. If it was difficult to prove a direct line of descent from the great ancestors, then the system required that such a connection be invented.

From almost the very beginning of his reign, Helgi was involved in a conflict with the Khazar state, under whose protection the majority of Slavic tribes found themselves during that time.

"In the year 6392 [884], Oleg marched against the Northerners, and conquered the Northerners, and imposed a light tribute, and assured them that they need not pay tribute to the Khazars, saying: 'I am their enemy, and there is no reason for you [to pay them].'"

"In the year 6393 [885], [Oleg] sent word to the Radimiches, asking them, 'To whom do you pay tribute?' And they answered, 'to the Khazars.' And Oleg said to them: 'Do not give tribute to the Khazars, pay me instead.' And they each gave Oleg a *shcheliag*, as they had given to the Khazars. And Oleg ruled over the Polians, and the Drevlians, and the Northerners, and the Radimiches, and waged war against the Uliches and Tivertses."

What is important here is that Helgi imposed a light tribute on the Northerners, and demanded no more from the Radimiches than they had been paying to the Khazars. Evidently he pursued goals that were less military in nature than political: He aimed to constrain the Khazars and undercut their influence in the region.

The Tale of Bygone Years describes Oleg's death, which gave Pushkin the plot for his poem, as follows: "And Oleg lived, ruling in Kiev, keeping peace between all the lands. And autumn came, and Oleg remembered his horse, whom he had put out to pasture, having decided never to mount him, for he had asked the soothsayers and sorcerers: 'What will be the cause of my death?' And one sorcerer had foretold: 'Prince! Your beloved horse, whom you ride, will be the cause.' Oleg took these words to heart, and he said: 'I will never mount him, nor set eyes on him, ever again.' And he ordered him to be fed and henceforth never to be brought to him, and he lived for several years afterward without seeing him, while he waged war against the Greeks. And when he returned to Kiev, and four years had passed, in the fifth year he remembered his horse, whom the soothsayers had prophesied would cause his death. And he summoned the master of the stables and said to him: 'Where is my horse, whom I ordered to be fed and cared for?' And he answered: 'He died.' Oleg laughed and belittled those sorcerers of old, saying: 'The soothsayers speak falsely; it did not come to pass: The horse died, but I am alive.' And he ordered a horse to be saddled: 'Let me see his bones.' And he came to the place in the field where his old steed's bare bones and skull lay, and he dismounted, laughed, and said: 'So this skull was to cause my death?' And he stepped on the skull, and out of the skull crawled a snake, and bit him on the foot. And from the snakebite he took ill and died. All the people mourned for him with great laments, and bore him off, and buried him on a mountain called Shchekovitsa; and his grave is there to this day, it is known as the Grave of Oleg."

Pushkin describes Oleg's death similarly in his poem. So why, in considering "The Song of the Wise Oleg," do I cite detailed passages from *The Tale of Bygone Years*? With good reason, reader.

The chronicler doesn't say a word about when, exactly, and in what circumstances, the soothsayers had spoken their prophecy about Oleg's death. But Pushkin's poem begins with this episode. During his eventful life, Helgi went on many campaigns, even against Byzantium. So it's no mere whim that the chronicler situates the story of his death after the war with the Greek Christians—which was, though a glorious campaign, according to the author of the chronicle (a monk of the Kievan Cave Monastery), a sin nonetheless. But the poet, on the other hand, brings the soothsayers to Oleg before his plunderous campaign against Khazaria, which the prince justifies as an act of vengeance. Why so? The explanation lies on the surface, and it's strange that philology hasn't offered such an interpretation of Pushkin's poem, at least to my knowledge.

Oleg's death fulfills a curse; it comes as retribution for his destruction of the Khazar lands. Such is the secret message of Pushkin's poem.

Let us now move from the episode of Oleg/Helgi's death to the site of his grave. *The Tale of Bygone Years* situates it on a mountain called Shchekovitsa, which was most likely on the shore of the Dneiper River. Scholars have determined its location to be near Kiev and indeed the mountain has preserved its original name.

Popular legend, however, insists that Oleg's grave is located in one of the mounds of Staraya Ladoga, the original historical capital of Varangian Rus. And a different ancient Russian chronicle states: "Oleg went to Novgorod and then to Ladoga . . . and a snake bit him in the foot, and from that he died; his grave is in Ladoga."

On 17 July 2003, commemorating the anniversary marking 1,250 years from the founding of Staraya Ladoga, the president of Russia visited the settlement. The press reported that the president did not enter the excavation site near the grave of Oleg because it was full of snakes (!). Putin stood nearby on the riverbank for a long time, staring into the distance. The landscape in that area is indeed marvelous; well worth looking at. I have been on that *kurgan*, at night in fact. And there were no snakes in sight.

Apparently the snakes at the *kurgans* of Staraya Ladoga are discriminating in their tastes . . .

The news reports cited "local residents who cautioned the President's security service about snakes," but these reports are unconvincing. It is more likely that the sorcerers in his entourage consider Putin to be the descendent of the Varangian princes, and as such he has inherited the ancient curse that was placed upon them for destroying Khazaria. And to this day the snakes of Staraya Ladoga preserve this legacy of revenge.

Many interesting facts are associated with Staraya Ladoga and with this ancient town's role in the history of Rus. Professor A. N. Kirpichnikov, Director of the Staraya Ladoga Archeological Expedition of the Russian Academy of Science's Institute of the History of Material Culture, writes:

Our excavations revealed a multitude of beads, including an intact set of 2,500 beads, most likely intended for sale, and a mold for casting silver ingots, the second international currency of that time after the *dirkhem*. The ingots were cast in cylindrical form. Here too was discovered a ring with an Arabian design on the setting, and a gem of mountainous crystal. The inscription is from a sura in the Koran: "May Allah's aid be with me, and on that aid alone do I place my hope and trust." The ring had served as a seal (for marking shipments, goods, and documents) and, judging from the Arabic design, could have only belonged to a merchant from the East—evidence that traders from distant lands had visited Ladoga . . . From Scandinavia to the eastern lands travelers most likely would have made their way along the Great Volga route. The ring with the Arabic inscription and the other discoveries are significant indicators confirming Ladoga's ties with distant countries, and evidencing its international economic significance in the tenth century.

In those days in Ladoga there were guilds of shipowners and sailors who came by way of the Volkhov River, from the Caspian Sea in the south, and from Scandinavia in the north. Ladoga itself also served as an assembly point for ship crews. These traders were attracted to the local market, especially to the furs from the northern forests that were on sale there, and which were considered the best in the world, and were paid for in silver.

. . . About the origins of the Rus people, opinions among scholars differ widely. The documentary sources situate the Rus people only on the territory of Eastern Europe; they are mentioned together with the Slavs. A chronicle entry notes that the Slavs and the Rus, the most important settlers in the area, spoke a common language. It seems to me that the difference between the Rus and the Slavs was not ethnic, but social. The Rus comprised an elite, an upper stratum of society. They engaged in trade, purchased concubines, and so forth. The social function of the Slavs was to serve this elite.

Many scholars hold to the opinion that the Rus were Scandinavians. This is not necessarily so. Most likely the Rus comprised international merchant communities and ships' crews. Such groups may have included Scandinavians, as well as Finns and Slavs. Scandinavian sources do not identify the Rus as a people with a single distinct ethnicity.

The Rus are mentioned in the chronicles during the
tenth and eleventh centuries, after which the concept ex-
pands and evolves: the Russian land, Rus, Russia. Who the
initial Rus were remains an open question . . . But in the
era of trade revolution the division of people into Rus and
Slavs, in my opinion, is of broad sociological importance.

Even more interesting is the fact that Arabic, Byzantine, and
European sources use the title "Hakan" (Khagan) to identify the
rulers of Rus during the time when Staraya Ladoga was its capital. Ibn Rustah writes:

Ar-Rusiyi is located on an island in the middle of a lake.
The island on which they live is a three-day's journey
in length, is covered with forests and swamps, and is so
unhealthy and damp that the earth squishes underfoot
with every step. They have a tsar, called the Hakan of
the Rus. They come up by river, by ship, attack the Slavs
and take them prisoner, transport them to Khazaran and
Bulkar, and sell them there. They do not cultivate the
land; they eat only what is brought in from the land of
the Slavs . . . They do not claim ownership of land or
villages. Their only occupation is trading sable, squirrel,
and other furs, which they sell to buyers. They receive
payment in coins that they keep in the folds of their
belts . . . They treat their slaves well and clothe them well,
for they are objects of trade. They have many towns, and
they lead an unconstrained life. They treat guests with
respect, including travelers who come from foreign lands
and seek their protection . . . And if one of them raises a
complaint against another, he is summoned to the tsar's
court, where they argue their cases. When the tsar pro-
nounces his sentence, what he has commanded is car-

ried out. And if both sides are dissatisfied with the tsar's decision, then the issue is resolved by his command with weapons, and whichever one of them has the sharper sword is victorious . . . They have sorcerers, *znakhary*, some of whom issue orders to the tsar as though they were the rulers.

The same Arab author wrote that there were a hundred thousand people—Rus—on this island (Novgorod or Staraya Ladoga). And they all lived by preying upon the Slavic population. You might be curious to know how many Slavs there were at that time. It turns out that during the centuries after Rus, the northern lands went into decline. The desolation of the Russian lands might also have come as a result of the Khazar curse.

With the above erudite citations I hereby conclude my commentary on Pushkin's poem.

Now let us move on to a survey of the purely historical works concerning Khazaria—though due to the dearth of reliable factual material they differ very little from the literary sources; the only difference is in their purported genre and in the ambitions of their authors, who claim to be providing reliable historical accounts. Nonetheless, an impressive number of books and articles have been written on the subject. A. A. Astaikin has compiled a bibliography of works on the history of Khazaria. I counted two hundred titles and then gave up.

According to A. P. Novoseltsev, the beginning of Khazar studies in Europe is may be traced to the well-known seventeenth-century scholar I. Burksdorf, who published a bilingual edition—the original along with a Latin translation—of the famous Khazar Correspondence. The first purely scholarly Russian (Soviet) work on the history of Khazaria was written by academician M. I. Artamonov. Abroad, the most famous work is D. M. Danlop's *The History of the Jewish Khazars*.

Lev Nikolaevich Gumilyov, the great Eurasian scholar and Turkophile, penned his own history of Khazaria. Along with his many other historical and theoretical achievements, he discovered Samandar, the ancient capital of Khazaria that predated even Itil. He published an account of his expedition to the area, which goes roughly as follows: The research expedition traveled in the area around the Terek, through Chechnya and Dagestan, but didn't come across anything promising. At that point the expedition had seemed to run dry, along with its funding and the fuel for their vehicles. Then some hills come into sight, the first they had seen, and Lev Nikolaevich said: "Well look there! There it is! Samandar at last, for sure! Samandar. We will have to come back here."

As far as I know, no one ever did go back; now the hills in those lands are completely different, and no one there has any interest in Samandar.

Actually, I love Gumilyov and respect him as an author; it's just that it makes a lot more sense to read his books as fiction rather than history.

Whatever the case, eminent scholars have come up with a history of Khazaria that reads something like this:

Sixth to seventh centuries: the collapse of the Western-Turkish Khaganate, with Khazaria rising on its ruins, ruled by the Turkish Ashin dynasty.

Eighth to ninth centuries: war between the Khazar Khaganate and Iran; Judaism enters the region. Clashes with Varangians; alliances and divisions of spheres of influence.

Ninth to tenth centuries: Khazaria and Rus at war. The fall of Khazaria.

Eleventh to thirteenth centuries: the disappearance of Khazaria from the political map of Eurasia.

The capitals of the Khazar realm were, in order, Belendzher, Samandar, and Itil. A pattern comparable to that of the Russian capitals: Kiev, Moscow, and St. Petersburg. Other important cities include Savgar and Serkel (Belaya Vezha); the last of these was built by Byzantine engineers.

Among the political customs of Khazaria, the more interesting included: power sharing between the Khagan and the Bek; a distinctive inauguration procedure during which the Khagan was throttled with a silken thread; and the Khagan's harem, made up of princesses taken from conquered lands and allied tribes.

During the early years, when Samandar was presumed to be its capital, the economy of Khazaria was based on agriculture, primarily viticulture, and fishing. Later, when the capital moved to Itil, transit trade began to flourish. Merchants who came from other lands noted with some surprise that the Khazars were able to thrive on trade, though they produced nothing at all in their country except for a suspicious-looking substance they called "fish paste."

As for the appearance of the Khazar people, travelers reported that there were "white" and "black" Khazars. The "whites" were tall, blond, and blue-eyed, resembled Swedes, and represented the elite of their society. They were served by the "blacks," who had dark hair and skin and were short of stature and were of generally unprepossessing appearance. Soviet historians expressed some doubt about this division and conjectured that the differences between the elite and the common people had nothing to do with race: Perhaps, they theorized, the Khazar proletariat just didn't have many opportunities to bathe.

It is also known that when the Khazars besieged the Armenian capital, the latter initiated the world's very first Halloween celebration, setting out in view of the Khazar warriors a huge pumpkin with carved-out eyes and a straw beard stuck on the bottom. They told the Khazars: "This is your Khagan!" For some reason the Khazars took offense, and the episode led to a bloodbath.

The Khazar Khaganate had an active foreign policy. They established alliances and declared wars, spread their influence and participated in the lives of both European and Asian states, leaving traces in many foreign chronicles. For example, the Byzantine emperor Mikhail III once called Photius, the Patriarch of Constantinople, a "Khazar-face." But for all that, Khazaria didn't leave a single written source for its future historians.

Excavation of one Khazar settlement, it's true, unearthed a stone with written inscriptions that are presumed to be Khazar. But despite all their combined efforts, historians and linguists have been unable to decipher them.

Scholars do have access to one source that is conventionally presumed to be Khazar. This is the correspondence between a Spanish Jew known as Hasdai ibn Shaprut and the Khagan Joseph. The authenticity of the correspondence has long been challenged, skeptics arguing that if there had been no letters, then the medieval Jews would have had to invent them. The same thing can be said about the very existence of the Khazar Khaganate.

The most energetic scholars of Khazar history tend to concern themselves with questions related to Judaism, being either Zionists or anti-Zionists. It's clear why. For a people scattered across the face of the earth, the existence of an empire in which their beliefs served as the official state religion (?) was (is) of great significance. After ancient Israel and before modern-day Israel there have been only two such experiments with the Jewish nation as a state, both of them on the territory of what is now Russia: the Khazar Khaganate in the Volga delta and the Jewish Autonomous Region in the Far East, with its capital in the city of Birobidzhan.

Special mention should be made of the book by noted Hungarian and Jewish writer Arthur Koestler entitled *The Thirteenth Tribe: The Khazar Empire and Its Heritage*. The author had an eventful life. Here, in brief, are the highlights of his biography:

Koestler was born on September 5, 1905 in Budapest. From 1926 to 1929 he served as a Near East correspondent for a German publishing concern; he spent 1929–30 working in Paris. In 1931 he flew to the North Pole on the dirigible *Graf Zeppelin*. Subsequently he traveled around Central Asia, and spent a year living in the Soviet Union. At the end of his life he argued on behalf of the Exit movement, which defends the right of people to take their own lives; he put this idea into practice in London on March 1, 1983 by taking a lethal dose of a soporific (?) drug.

Arthur Koestler prefaces *The Thirteenth Tribe* with a quote from the Arab writer Al-Muqadassi: "In Khazaria, sheep, honey, and Jews exist in large quantities."

The Russian translator of Koestler's book includes the entire quotation, not without a certain ridicule: "Al-Khazar is a vast region beyond the Caspian Sea. Impassable mud, great quantities of sheep, honey, and Jews."

One is forced to admit that, with some exceptions, very little has changed since those days. Modern *akyn* bard Boris Grebenshikov has a song about the modern country that occupies the territory of what used to be the Khazan Khaganate:

They make a show of pride;
They seem so debonair;
But when you look inside:
Dirt, mud, and disrepair.

The main thesis of Koestler's book, which he argues very effectively, is that the so-called Western Jews are not even Semitic in origin; they came not from the Near East, but from Khazaria.

Studies on the history of Khazaria provide us with an entire palette of different and often contradictory conclusions. The major axes of the "Khazar polemics" in their present form are as follows:

First axis: Khazaria and Judaism. First: Were they Jewish or not? The majority of scholars agree that they were. In other words, Khazaria adopted Judaism as a state religion. Views differ, though, as to the dates, circumstances and implications of this religious reform. Authors inclining toward Zionism identify the earliest plausible date, arguing that Khazaria adopted Judaism just before it reached its peak as a state, and attributing its success directly to the conversion. Authors inclined toward anti-Semitism argue for a later date, one that immediately precedes the fall of the Khazar Empire. Naturally they consider Judaism the cause for the empire's decline and fall.

Academic historians who are relatively unbiased concerning this question incline toward the view that only the elite converted to Judaism and that this change did not have a major influence on the lives of the masses or on the fate of the state.

Second axis: origins. Distinguished scholar A. A. Tiunyaev offers the least disputable version of the origin of the Khazars: "The Khazars, a nomadic people belonging to a so-called Turkish tribe that initially dwelled between the Caspian and Black Seas, appeared in Eastern Europe in the fourth century after the invasion of the Huns." However, even as scholars repeat this phrase, "appeared . . . after," they maintain an enigmatic silence as to its meaning. Either the Huns who settled in these parts began to be called Khazars, or some other kind of invasion took place. All scholarship on the subject retains this ambiguity: Whenever mentioning the origin of the Khazars, they resort to the phrase: "appeared . . . after."

Third axis: the dispute as to heritage. If the existing scholarship is uniformly unsatisfying regarding the origin of the Khazars, there is a clear surplus of theories about the heirs to that culture's historical glory. The abovementioned Koestler considers all European Jews, the Ashkenazi, to be descendants of the Khazars. Lev Gumilyov, after carefully studying data on the skull shapes and average height of the Terek Kazaks, identified them as heirs to the Khazar ethnicity. God Himself decreed that the Crimean Karaites would succeed the Khazars. But the Altai peoples also claim this legacy, citing common language features. The Russians, too, are in the fray: Some scholars modestly remind their readers that Slavs made up the majority of the Khaganate's population and hence held the rightful claim to Khazaria. Others simply assert that the Khazars were in fact Russians, and that there were no Turks in sight. For my part, I've found quite a bit of evidence that the Khazars were Chechens.

To sum up: According to data gathered and verified by historians, the Khazar Khaganate was a state either of Turks, or Jews, or Slavs, or Caucasians, or, in general, of Swedes. The Khazars appeared from somewhere. Or they always were present, but under a different name. During the Khazar Khaganate or in the sixth, or the eighth, or eleventh century they adopted Judaism. Judaism was adopted either by a small group in the highest social elite, or by the masses; it either influenced the fate and culture of the Khaganate or did not; it either enabled its rise or hastened its collapse, or was never adopted at all. After the disappearance of the Khazar Khaganate, the heirs to its culture and traditions were either Crimean Karaites, or European Jews, or Altais, or there were no heirs whatsoever.

Thus, my research has lead me to three precise and definitive conclusions:

- The Khazar Khaganate existed in the past in some territory or other; or,
- The Khazar Khaganate existed and continues to exist, but in a different dimension, some kind of parallel reality; or,
- The Khazar Khaganate never existed anywhere. It is a model or plan, devised at some point in history, that is destined to, or simply might happen to, come into being sometime in the future.

INAUGURATION

And the time came for the great celebration of the entire Khazar people. In the bazaars entertainers played flutes and told funny stories. Sorcerers kindled fires, sending clouds of heady smoke into the sky. Colorful rags fluttered in the breeze over the roof-tops, frightening the feathered creatures of the air. Crippled veterans of righteous wars were served leftover dead groundhogs for the glory of the Khagan and the Bek—let them, too, rejoice! And the Khagan's palace filled with people; the entire Khazar elite—the *beau monde*—gathered there. Faces white, silks rustling, emeralds and rubies sparkling; if all the lamps in the palace had been extinguished, it would still be full of light from all the precious stones. Brilliant of mind and pure of soul! What are you next to them? The elite has gathered, the elite will feed its face. What a feast! Tables laden with victuals, fine drinks glittering in silver carafes, you could drown in them. The palace buzzed like a nest of wasps, everyone eating and drinking, drinking and eating. Now into the center of the hall strode the Great Bek. His jewel-encrusted platinum staff thundered against the floor and the sound reverberated through the great hall!

All fell silent. A portable throne was brought out and the crowd cried out, summoning the new Khagan:

"Khagan! Khagan! Kha-gan!"

The Great Bek roused the crowd:

"You call that a chant? The Khagan will not come forth, there will be no celebration, unless you let him hear you!"

And they shouted louder:

"Kha-gan! Kha-gan! Kha-gan! Grandfather Kha-gan!"

Someone poked Saat lightly on the back, and he emerged from the secret room into the great hall.

"Hurra-a-a-a-a-a-ah!"

The crowd roared, and loud music filled the hall. And Saat, embarrassed and blushing bright red like a fish from the Itil, approached the throne and took his seat. Oh, it's hot in the hall, so hot! Hot as a skillet!

The Bek spoke:

"Here he is, great Khazars, sovereign people, our new Khagan, Osya the Thirteenth! Let us be loyal to him, as we were loyal to his forebears, ancient Khagans from the beginning of time!"

"We will be loyal!" shouted the people. "We will!"

And again the Great Bek pounded the floor with his crook: silence!

"First we must observe our ancient tradition and test the new Khagan, to determine the duration of his rule."

From behind the Khagan's back emerged an executioner arrayed in camouflage from head to toe, branches sewed onto his clothing, his face covered with a black stocking with holes cut for the eyes. Now this was a surprise! No one had said anything to Saat about this.

The executioner came up behind Saat and wound a fine silken noose around his neck. So this is the end. It wasn't your destiny to fall and rot on the field of battle, nor were you fated to end your days in poverty and starvation; no, Saat, in celebration and revelry are you to perish, in peacetime, amid sweet feasting, to the sound of joyful music. Such is human life: There is no escaping death!

Saat thought this thought, then stood calmly, prepared to meet his eternal rest. But the Great Bek came up before him.

He spoke:

"Tell us, Saat, son of Nattukh, how long will you rule as Khagan of Khazaria? The executioner will begin to strangle you, and you will speak the numbers—count up from one, leaving no number out! And when you can go on no longer, lift your right hand and speak, say you have had enough. Then we will know."

And the Great Bek gave a sign to the executioner, then stepped to one side. The executioner pulled the silken noose lightly toward himself. Saat began counting:

"One, two ..."

The executioner pulled tighter on the silk string, oh, how it hurt!

"Three, four ..."

And now Saat's strength was failing; he couldn't go on, the light went dark, the crowd multiplied and oscillated before his eyes; the people flailed about in a demonic dance. But Saat strained with all his might:

"Five, six, seven ..."

And he felt that he could not possibly go on; he was drained. Death was upon him. He lifted his hand and rasped out: "Enough!"

The executioner immediately released the noose; servants rushed forth to pour water over the Khagan, to fan him, to rub his neck gently with fine oil.

"Glory to the Khagan!" howled the Khazar elite.

And the Great Bek spoke:

"You have spoken, O Khagan! Your time on the throne ruling the land of the Khazars is to be seven terms. And after that your body will be hewed into seven pieces, and into every piece will enter the sins of the Khazar land, one piece for every year of your rule, and we will curse and revile you, and will burn the pieces of your body. Now, though, you are to give no thought to yourself, for it is clear what is to be your fate. Your mind is free for the concerns of the realm!" Touched, the Great Bek shed a tender tear. And Saat rose from the throne and blessed his people. And a sweet fog billowed up and filled the air of the hall. And a ringing sound ... a ringing sound filled every corner ... but where was the sound coming from?

IT'S IN THE WATER

In Saat's . . . uh, Maximus's, apartment, the alarm clock was emitting a metallic ringing sound. Recently an entire delegation of his neighbors in the apartment building had presented him with a formal request that he keep the volume down in the morning. How they had managed to persuade him, Semipyatnitsky would not reveal, but now he had to use an ordinary alarm clock to waken him into this reality so that he could get himself to work on time.

His first order of business every morning was to solve the problem of his identity, that is, to answer two questions: Who was he, and why did he have to get up this exact minute and go out somewhere? The answer to the second question was to flow naturally from the answer to the first.

Maximus said to himself: I am a middle manager in the Import Department of the Cold Plus Company, in St. Petersburg, Russia. Tenant in an apartment located at 6-66 Dybenko Street. Debtor, signatory on three different loans. Hence, whether I want to or not, I must quit my bed now, hasten to the bathroom, and shave. And then get dressed and go to the office. There is no other option.

Semipyatnitsky thought it would make sense to write this mantra down on a piece of paper and simply read it out loud to himself every morning. Or, even better, record it on tape and set it to play . . . wait, a tape player wouldn't work; it would bring on the neighbors again.

The neighbors . . . they were such pests! Not just the neighbors; people everywhere were generally just as bad. But only God is perfectly beautiful, anyway. As it says in the Hadith: "Allah is beautiful and loves beauty." And if that's the case, then He doesn't love people. Why should he? And why should I?

Preoccupied with these and other deep thoughts, Semipyatnitsky somehow made his way to work. He was desperately thirsty. He tossed his briefcase and car keys onto his desk and headed for the break room, where employees who couldn't even afford the Barf Bar could sit and eat the snacks or lunch that they had packed and brought from home.

There was only one person there, a girl nibbling at a thin sandwich, chasing down every piece with a sip of watery instant coffee from the office stash, which was kept in a giant economy-size bag on the counter. This was the very same coffee that was left over in the form of a fine powder after the best beans—according to the ads for this particular brand—were taken from the unfortunate Africans.

Maximus politely initiated a conversation.

"Morning! Still asleep?"

"Yes, I could barely get myself to work this morning. All I wanted to do was stay in bed."

As if anyone actually wanted to come to work! Maximus himself, no matter how he tried, couldn't come up with any convincing arguments for it, except for the threat of being kicked out of his apartment and losing his car and starving to death. On a practical level, these arguments made perfect sense, but philosophically speaking they were inadequate. Maximus launched into a tirade:

"For a man of our day and age the Shakespearian question 'to be or not to be' is no longer of any relevance. To be—of course, what's the alternative? For some extremists, like the skinheads, the question becomes 'to beat or not to beat,' but they got their answer long ago, which is why they decided to shave their heads. But they're the minority. For the majority of people, the key existential question today is: 'to go to the office or to let it all go to hell?' Considering the fact that society won't allow you to live for free, once you've dispensed with office work you're left with the following options: You can become a prostitute on the street, in a salon, or in a virtual chat room. You can become a drug dealer: sit at home in your apartment, aka drug den; poke around on the Internet and the client will show up on his own. You can get into direct sales—Herbalife or vacuum cleaners that cost as much as used cars. Or you can sign a contract with the devil, and he'll make you a rock star, a popular writer, a celebrity, or some other brand of high-profile parasite. And in return you sign over your soul. What your soul is, and why you need it—you don't know yourself. But the devil, well, the devil knows who needs it and why . . . "

The girl hastily gulped down her coffee and muttered nervously, "That's not what I meant. I like my job. It can be very interesting. And the pay isn't bad. It's just that I got to bed a little late last night. Other than that, everything's fine, really. Right, then, gotta go. I've got some . . . data to enter . . . reports, too."

She grabbed her purse and evaporated.

There you have it, yet again. No one understands anything.

Maximus got his yellow mug out of the cupboard and filled it to the brim with water from the big upside-down plastic bottle on the cooler. You know those coolers, there's one in every office now, with a red tab for hot water and a blue one for cold. Office managers everywhere, even the stingiest ones, cover the costs for regular, year-round delivery of drinking water. Transparent twenty-five liter bottles are delivered in special vans and brought up to the office by mute guys in blue uniforms.

Semipyatnitsky downed his water in one long swig and immediately remembered the things he had to do this morning. His mind filled with work-related thoughts, phrases from correspondence, numbers, facts, and figures. He even felt a sudden zeal for accomplishing these tasks.

Still holding the empty cup, Maximus reflected briefly on this sudden change in his consciousness, and, rooted to the spot, erupted in wild, demonic laughter:

"But of course! How could I not have guessed? The pills!
They dissolve the Dutch pills into the office water supply: PTH,
Positive Thinking! Of course, it's chemistry! Otherwise, why
would anyone bother to come to work? All of the pills must have
the same basic ingredients, but the formula can be modified for
each individual office, based on employers' requests. Or maybe
not, maybe it's all one standard formula that adapts to the specif-
ics of each individual brain. The effect varies depending on the
interaction between the chemicals and the neurons of the manager in question, which are configured for the needs of his company's business and his own particular job. It's cheaper that way,
of course!"

Praise be to Allah, no one else came into the break room, and
so Semipyatnitsky's moment of enlightenment went unheard.

ESCAPE

Maximus went back to his desk and settled into his work. Whatever task you take on, you should do well. This simple maxim was one of the few principles that he adhered to in his life. There's no need to burn with childish enthusiasm or demonstrate excessive passion for your work. In fact, that approach isn't very conducive to quality results. Simply fulfilling your duties calmly, whether you like them or not, is quite a different matter; that *does* produce results, and without causing any extra trouble. Karma yoga, pure and simple! Purposeful activity undertaken in an enlightened state of mind, combined with a renunciation of the fruits of such labor.

If you want to partake of the fruits of your efforts, even the tiniest little morsel, be aware that every company has its own security department, every country has an economic police service, and hell has demons waiting for you. They're down there brandishing hot frying pans, or whatever they use these days, undoubtedly something more technologically advanced—microwave ovens, maybe. They'll grab you by the arm and give you what you deserve. They'll rip those fruits out of your mouth and jam them up a different orifice.

Maximus knew, as everyone did, that the buyers for the stores that carried Cold Plus products operated through bribery. Nowadays there are more eloquent words for it: bonus, incentives. In an extreme case—kickbacks. The Criminal Code, though, still defines it as "commercial bribery."

They were driving past Maximus's office window this very moment, in their Audis and Nissans paid for with cash, not credit. They can even afford to own their own apartments. Girls fall in love with them; simple office workers envy them. Books are published about their lives, and in those books they are so sensitive, so spiritual, and they have such good taste. Even their cynicism is endearing.

Blue-collar workers from the company's warehouses regularly spewed angry accusations at Maximus and his colleagues at the office, calling them bastards and thieves. But Maximus only snickered in response. Compared with the other contract he'd been offered and had rejected multiple times, all of this was petty stuff.

The devil takes no kickbacks. Hell doesn't work on commission. The managers of sin and perdition have only one bonus, one incentive system: your eternal soul, all of it, along with its complete set of transcendental viscera.

Just keep on doing what you're doing, Maximus told himself, just do your job. Give no thought to success or victory, expect no rewards.

Plus, can you really call this work?

Maximus understood that he wasn't really doing anything. Not creating anything, not changing anything. At least in the real world. All his manipulations of the keyboard weren't going to increase the number of frozen crab-paste claws in the universe, not by one measly package. Only the hands of Chinese women, earning a dollar an hour, could accomplish that. Though actually it was considerably less than a dollar an hour.

Maximus earned his keep on a completely different order of magnitude. All he did was stare into a computer monitor, occasionally tapping something on his keyboard as though playing some kind of computer game, never having to leave his comfortable office or hoist his ever-widening backside up out of his chair. That's how his job would look to those Chinese women as they labored away, crouching in rows by a shipping container, or to the dockworkers as they those dragged frost-covered cartons back and forth day in, day out.

Like millions of others of his kind, Maximus performed his

sacred rituals in the World of Information. But that is the way, in fact the only way, surplus value is created in today's world. Because the price of a crab-paste claw, assembled out of fish-processing waste products, chemical additives, and other shit, was practically the same as the price of the initial raw material, that same shit before it was mixed together. And only by dispatching the product through all the circles of the information inferno, from the exporting country's customs service to the importing country's customs service, through the veterinary inspection, marketing analysis, and all the incentive systems designed to motivate workers at home and abroad, could that very same shit end up in the form of a food product on a supermarket shelf, with a price exceeding its initial shitty value many times over.

So Maximus avoided thinking about the fact that he was eating his own yeast-free healthy vitamin-fortified bread on the backs of others. Though he was fully aware of the cost to himself. Maximus had long ago realized that he wasn't being paid for work; it wasn't really work, after all. Rather, his salary represented rent that he was paid for his individual consciousness, for allowing himself to be turned into a computer chip in the great processor of commercial information.

Semipyatnitsky recalled a movie where the handsome actor Keanu Reaves had allowed his brain to be used as a vehicle for smuggling pirated programs. In order to avoid paying customs duties, some businessmen had loaded this program in Reaves's head and had sent him across the border, where other businessmen downloaded the program. Pure fantasy of course. But an office worker lives in a far worse nightmare: His brain isn't merely a chip for storing information; it actually processes it as well, on an ongoing basis, like a computer. So Reaves's mission as a courier in some anti-utopia was trivial in comparison with the daily ordeal of a mid-level manager.

Whatever he does—eat, sleep, walk down the street, watch

TV, or screw his girlfriend—through it all, the processor hums and works. Assessing the status of the system. Making adjustments. Wake a mid-level manager up in the middle of the night, and he will tell you how many containers are scheduled to be unloaded this week at the transit port, what paperwork needs to be completed, and what still has to be done to initiate the letter of credit.

Even your average, clueless CEO spends all his time thinking about this stuff. A clever business owner, though, even as he signs his annual contract with a major client, is only thinking about how he's going to get fellated tonight by some glamorous new whore. There's no reason for him to worry about the details of his business deals. All the necessary programs have been loaded into the brains of mid-level managers specially hired for that purpose. It's called "delegating authority."

It is quite convenient, really. The new-generation "Mid-Level Manager Processor IV" comes in on his own accord, hooks himself into the system, connects to the other processors, disconnects as necessary, maintains himself at his own expense during his free time, and at the end of his life, when he's all used up, removes himself from the system. The ideal device!

All the corporation needs to do is protect him from viruses.

Because although innumerable resources exist to keep the system functioning smoothly—magazines, books, and TV shows that provide processors with useful information about how to keep themselves in working order, how to improve their productivity and even how to find meaning and take satisfaction in their work—you never know when some dangerous new malware might pop up out of nowhere, making your processor suddenly start thinking about itself, about the server through which he works, about his ISP, and other matters that ought not trouble anyone beneath the rank of SysAdmin.

But even then, countermeasures exist to combat that eventuality: the Security Service, the Institute for Family Values, and the Holy Sanhedrin.

Maximus understood all of this, but he was powerless to change the system. He could only allow himself one little act of deceit: Given the fact that his individual operating system allowed for multitasking, he was able to launch several programs at once, some of them performing the operations for which he was being paid, and others—or, say, just one—allowing him to meditate upon forbidden topics.

Everything is fine so long as you can close the subversive windows in time.

Maximus had already figured out the Khazar problem, more or less. But his study of the history of the Khaganate had spawned another problem for his inquisitive mind: the problem of the elites, how they replenished their ranks, and the basis for their legitimacy. He would have written an essay on this topic as well, but his new virtual friend Hakan spared him the unnecessary labor. On Hakan's site Semipyatnitsky discovered a lengthy manifesto that answered all his questions about the secrets of the elect.

This manifesto was so much like Maximus's own thoughts on the subject that it even seemed to him that he could have written it himself.

And maybe he had.

Iron Balls and Elven Magic

Ever since Jason's quest for the Golden Fleece and Robinson Crusoe's journey to that uninhabited island lo those many years ago, all possible variants of the sea-odyssey plot have been repeated over and over in world literature. And even the plot of repeated plots has been exploited by the genius librarian Jorge Luis Borges.

The third millennium after the birth of Christ holds no new themes, heroes, or plots. All we can do is write about what's already been written and about what's been written about what's been written. Our books no longer contain people, things, and places. We are now writing books about books.

But books themselves have become heroes, plots, and settings in our lives. We are no longer interested in criticism. Texts, ancient or modern, have become parts of our contemporary reality and thus have entered the virtual world; we now judge texts based upon the validity of their premises more than their other qualities: That is, we judge them based upon whether they're able to create a more complete sort of reality than the one on this side of the screen . . .

Where we're currently located.

The only fantasy novels I can get through are by Terry Pratchett. I think he's British. The back cover of the one I have here bears a photograph of the author surrounded by drawings of his heroes: He's a jolly-looking fellow with a bushy white beard. If the bio is accurate, he quit his job in an office ten years ago and devoted himself exclusively to writing fantasy novels about this Discworld that he dreamed up.

Unlike our world, which has any number of different theories purporting to explain it, everything is much clearer with Discworld. It's a disk resting on the backs of four elephants, who themselves stand on the back of the Giant Star Turtle A'Tuin. The dirtiest and most densely populated city on the Disc is called Ankh-Morpork. The Disc is populated, along with people, by gnomes, trolls, elves, werewolves, and a whole bunch of other creatures traditionally found in fantasy novels.

There are writers who seem to be describing our own reality, but in fact are creating a completely impossible world. A world in which Cinderellas inevitably marry princes, where savvy and noble investigators always catch criminals, and where the chaste supermodel Maria spends her whole life waiting for Juan, the noble stockbroker . . .

Terry Pratchett created what would seem to be a completely alien world, floating on a tortoise's back, but in fact he's describing our own reality. In his Ankh-Morpork (New York, of course), speciesism (racism) is rampant and the gnomes hate the trolls, which feeling the trolls fully reciprocate. Cinderellas here do NOT marry princes, though this fact causes them a great deal of suffering; modest tailors do not instantaneously become successful businessmen, but remain just what they are, modest tailors; in this world, professional hit men have the right to take anyone's life with impunity so long as there's a contract involved (and presuming they're up to date on their Murderers' Guild dues), and those who don't have someone out there trying to kill them scrupulously pay a special tax supporting the Murderers' Guild to keep it that way. So Terry Pratchett's world is no more fantastical than Saltykov-Shchedrin's Foolsville with its seats of power occupied by bears.

One of Terry's novels, Lords and Ladies, *tells the story of an attempt by elves from a parallel universe to invade a provincial town in Discworld. These elves are not like those cute storybook elves that we're used to. They are cruel and bloodthirsty, power-hungry, envious, greedy, and heartless. Ugly, too.*

They strut around looking like improbably beautiful, elegantly dressed, mythological heroes with perfect physiques, astride fierce warhorses that instill dread and respect in all who see them—but occasionally their spell weakens, and people see them as they really are, with their ugly triangular faces, their awkward bodies clothed in gaudy, tasteless garments, and their scrawny nags. But then the spell kicks in again, and again the mortals are cowed.

What makes elves so powerful is their ability to make people feel weak in their presence. The elves slaughter everyone in their path, and the people can't raise their weapons and resist. The mere sight of the elves renders people utterly powerless.

Yes, we the people are absolutely nothing. We are losers. We are pathetic, lowly creatures; nothing ever works out for us. And that's as it should be. It's fate. Whereas they, they are great and beautiful; they are on top of the world, and so on top of us. They're free to do whatever they want, and we have no right to resist. For they are successful, and we are losers. So it has been, is, and always shall be. O how beautiful they are, how worthy of our adoration! What are we by comparison? No, give in, submit, endure; nail horseshoes on your door, abase yourself, go outside at night with a bowl of your finest, most delicious cream, and stand there by the doorway waiting to give it to the first elf who comes along. Stand by quietly while they deign to ravish your wives and daughters. Afterward, should they choose to bestow on you their unbearable mercy, they will put you out of your misery and kill you.

This is how people think.

This is the secret of the elves' magic.

Yes, the elves' magic takes different forms. Tales of their divine origin, of the supposedly completely different, even "blue," blood of those in power. Silks and satins, velvet, gold, diamonds, pomp and circumstance. All for our benefit. A spectacle for the losers to watch. Lest there be any doubt. We are the losers; they are the elves. They are different. It's their destiny to be on top.

They make history; the press reports all the details of their lives (and in their lives, as opposed to ours, everything that they do—what they eat, who they sleep with, how they defecate—is vital and full of significance); they appear on TV. Their tastes are an example for us to emulate; their life stories excite and entertain us; their actions are above reproach. We are different.

Because if we weren't, we would be who they are; so instead we are who we are, and they are who they are. What other proof do we need that they are the salt of the earth, and we are the losers?

Every once in a while the system breaks down. System error. The elves are seized and dragged to the scaffold. And to our surprise we learn that their blood is the same color as ours—just plain red. And they soil themselves on the electric chair, and when they do, their shit does not smell of roses. It stinks.

King Charles I of England's last word before his death was supposedly this: "Remember." Who was he talking to? Was he instructing new generations of elves to work with systems administrators and purge dangerous viruses from the network? I don't know. All I know is that the system does get overloaded from time to time, and when that happens, those standing closest to the scaffold are the next to put on the bright-colored garments and proclaim themselves elves. And it all starts up again.

To survive in this world you need iron balls. Otherwise there's nothing for you here. Your self-confidence, your arrogance and cruelty have to be stronger than the elves' magic. If they are, you'll be able to look them in the eye and not give in. If you hit an elf in the face, blood will pour out of his nose; if you shoot him in the head, gray, viscous brains will spatter out onto the ceiling.

But when you do . . .

When you do, the elves will launch "Plan B."

When you resisted, you showed that you were different from the others. You're special. You really do have iron balls. Take a look around: Can all those losers, that common herd, really be your equals? You've proven that you are one of us. Now you're an elf too. Hold your head high.

This is why the elves are invincible.

If you're going to stand a chance, you need to learn everything you can about them. First, as you know from fairy tales, they have long pointy ears. And they're afraid of iron. Not gold. Gold is a very soft metal. But iron interferes with the elves' sorcery; iron shreds their innards and exposes what they're really made of to the world.

Elves are diamonds set in gold, if you put your faith in gold. But if you put your faith in iron, then you discover that elves are made of shit.

One more thing. Just one word. One word, but it's the most important one, the key to the elves' psychology, their energy source, their heart of hearts. That word is TERROR.

Elves are afraid; that is their essence. And they base their sorcery on that same terror. They surround themselves with luxury, come up with strange principles and rules: why certain clothing brands are better than others; how a man's car determines his social status; where a true elf should spend his vacation; which other elves he should associate with—all this because they're afraid. Elves aren't stupid, no, not at all; otherwise they couldn't have become elves. And they understand that they have nothing, nothing at all that makes them REALLY different from the rest of us. A simple inventory would expose their inner bankruptcy. So they need to publish glossy magazines, host talk shows, win elections. The show must go on. They can't ever let up, can't stop for a single second. If they did, the first person who came along could brush off the elves' sorcery like a sticky spiderweb dangling from the ceiling in some damp, fetid cellar.

And values are very important. The elves must instill "values" in the masses. They keep the real values for themselves, but for everyone else, they offer flimsy concepts. Family. Country. Honor. Conscience. Diligence. Obedience. The elves believe that the people have nothing of any real value, so they have to be provided with a substitute. Otherwise the people could get very dangerous.

People like me don't believe in anything. We have no roots, no foundation in this world. Undoubtedly, because we have feelings, we sense that things aren't as they should be in this game. Everything is Maya, illusion. Samsara. We don't really believe in the sanctity of those "family values" being preached by overweight, complacent men whose own parents are tucked away in some distant, out-of-the-way village, while they run through a succession of nubile young lovers—and when that gets monotonous, they find some cute boys to screw in the ass or indulge in a little pay-per-view bestiality porn involving burly English Great Danes and little girls. We don't fall for patriotic songs performed by "true believers" who are in fact selling out their Motherland wholesale and retail on the raw-materials markets. We don't believe the most elementary truths, for example that the latest D&G jeans for sale in a boutique on Nevsky are any different from the same style of jeans by Collins, bought in a cheap outlet on Sadovaya at a triple discount. For us nothing is sacred.

I'll wipe the floor with any elf who gets in my way, and will crush the delicate, finely calibrated inner works of his expensive watch on the ground under my dirty old shoe without the slightest reverence. I'm dangerous, it's true. My energy needs to be neutralized—I need to be convinced that I'm a nobody, a loser, that I Do Not Have Anything Against Outlet Stores. That's Plan A. And if that doesn't work, remember, there's always Plan B.

Sometimes Plan A works and I'm overcome with a sense of my own insignificance. And at other times, Plan B works.

The elves' magic is very effective: Ordinary policemen who earn a pathetic salary fervently defend the interests of the wealthy and blatantly ignore us losers. It's just some kind of instinct.

It's not that difficult to toss a stone through the windshield of a Mercedes parked in your building's lot; no one will know who did it. You can even murder the tycoon just outside your apartment building and the investigation will lead nowhere, because it will concentrate on his business competitors and his lover, not some schmuck in the street. But you won't do that. Because he's an elf, and you feel only the most reverent awe in his presence.

You're far more likely to take out your aggression on your drinking buddy by slashing his throat with a broken bottle. He's as much of a loser as you are, and sure enough, they'll track you down with no trouble at all, just by asking around, and before you know it, you're in prison.

The law-enforcement system doesn't defend the weak against the strong; it defends the strong against the weak, and no one bothers to question whether the strong are really as strong as they would have you believe. In spite of their magic, they are weak. And they are afraid. TERROR.

In Terry Pratchett's book, the people defended themselves successfully against the attack and the elves slunk home with their tails between their legs. But the people themselves are no angels. They lie and cheat, are cruel to one another, and they love money; they all really love money. But take a look inside— all they want is earthly happiness, to the extent that this is possible. They want to make their loved ones happy, to let them enjoy a little beauty and comfort in this short, all-too-short life. For them, piety and nirvana are infinitely remote. But they do their duty, they simply do what they're supposed to. And so they are closer, if only by a couple of inches, to Heaven than to Hell.

This world is ours. And in this world, the elves are powerless.

Brother, maybe you're having a good laugh reading these lines. For you cast off all of your doubts long ago and are convinced that your sharp-tipped ears and elfin status are a just reward for those iron balls of yours.

*Or maybe you're still slaving away at your measly ad-
ministrative-assistant job for a few dollars a day. But you're
still young, and everything will change; there's still time.
You'll get another job, you'll be given some responsibility,
and one day someone will bring an envelope to you with
your first kickback, a tidy sum with more than a few lovely
zeroes at the end.*

*You'll take the money. Of course you will, you'll have to.
What then? What will you do next? Invite your buddies to a
bar to celebrate? Send a couple hundred bucks to your cousin?*

Or . . . right, of course. Why bother? . . . They're losers.

Well, go up to the mirror and take a good long look.

Especially at your ears.

Maximus had already reached the end of this lyrical manifesto
when the Cold Plus security officer materialized behind his office
chair.

"Semipyatnitsky! You are in violation of Cold Plus company
policy, which prohibits use of the Internet for non-work-related
purposes."

Maximus didn't have time to close the blog window. And he
wouldn't have tried to anyway. It would've been demeaning, and
it wouldn't have made any difference.

"Your violations have been systematic in nature."

The security officer had brought a printout with him—a report from IT—and he laid it on Maximus's desk. It listed all of
his transgressions against Office Policy: the addresses of websites,
along with the times he'd visited them, and even the exact volume
of his traffic, in megabytes.

"We have no other option but to fine you, in accordance with
the Sanctions Policy, one hundred dollars for every instance of
wrongful personal Internet use, plus ten dollars for every downloaded megabyte."

Maximus thought, that's just stupid. If the Internet didn't exist, these corporate fascists would have needed to invent it. The Internet is the ideal place for employees to pour out all their irritation, anger, and negativity, to let off steam.

If he were in the elves' place, he would even have funded a couple of special websites himself—for extremists and anti-establishment types. Let all these workplace philosophers type away at their blogs, where they can insult anyone they want to—the authorities, corporations, and one another—to their hearts' content. That way they can feel as though they're part of an Opposition, without posing any real threat to the existing order. And when the time comes for an actual revolution, the only people who'll show up will be half-dead retirees who don't have Internet access, and maybe a dozen or so anarchists—completely insane, of course. Some revolution: nothing a few billy clubs in the hands of helmeted OMON "cosmonaut" riot police couldn't deal with.

Maybe the riot police themselves might sponsor such sites. Maybe they already do.

So mused Maximus. But he said nothing. The security chief turned and left. Maximus took out a clean piece of white paper and wrote:

Declaration

On account of my own unimaginably strong fucking desire, I request to be relieved of my job, effective immediately. Any outstanding salary owed me may be used to cover these fines, and the remainder you can shove up your ass. Don't neglect that part; I'm going to come and make sure you do.
Date.
Signature.
Signature deciphered as follows:

Maximus P. Semipyatnitsky, the Great Khagan.
PS I know all about the pills.

When he finished writing, Maximus placed the Declaration on his desk, on top of the IT report. He raked all the coins out of his desk drawer and tossed them into his briefcase. Picked up his car keys. Walked out.

On the other side of the security point he ripped his smart card in two and tossed the pieces into the nearest trash can.

Outside at last, Maximus gazed, enchanted, at the world around him and breathed in deep lungfuls of the intoxicating air of freedom and the unknown.

PILLS AGAIN

Wait!

That's not all.

I admit I was tempted to end not just Part III, but the whole book, with that elegant if slightly clichéd turn of phrase about "freedom and the unknown."

What happened next? You might well ask. Maximus quit his job; the part of his life during which he functioned as a contributing member of society was over. He made his choice. He left, and brought his story to an aesthetically satisfying conclusion. The story is over, the protagonist's fate has been decided, the curtain has come down . . . The house lights come on in the dark theater. The audience rises to their feet; the folding seats snap back into place. Empty plastic soda bottles lie conveniently "forgotten" on the floor, together with cardboard boxes half full of cold, soggy popcorn.

But no!

There's still some unfinished business.

Maximus realized this the moment he stepped outside.

How could he have forgotten?

Given all the fuss, all of his discoveries and worries, such inattention is understandable, but still: How could he have forgotten about the pills?

Peter had taken the pills to the hotel with him. When Maximus met him there, Peter didn't have the pills, only his small carry-on bag. After their visit to the Tribunal, Peter hadn't gone back to the hotel. Maximus had taken him to the train station himself.

So where were the pills?

Maximus got in his car, started the engine, and—following instinct—turned onto Nevsky. Semipyatnitsky muscled his way through the traffic to the Nevsky Palace, then pulled up halfway onto the sidewalk. Ignoring the prominent No Parking sign with its eloquent silhouette of a tow truck at work, he turned off the engine and climbed out.

Maximus walked up to the hotel entrance and stood there for a couple of minutes. Then, still in the grip of the same subconscious impulse, he headed for the Fontanka Embankment. He turned onto the embankment and descended the granite ramp to the canal. At the water's edge he thought, "What am I doing here?" and glanced around.

The answer to his question was immediately obvious. A scrap of paper was stuck on the granite wall on the Fontanka side— part of a label from a carton. The letters were still legible: a big PTH followed by some other letters and numbers.

Interesting. How much time had passed since the Dutch partners' visit? A few weeks at least. But the label, which the waves had pasted onto the granite wall, was still there; it hadn't washed away, hadn't dissolved in the acidic-alkaline solution of the Fontanka canal wastewater. As though it had been placed there for some special purpose, for Maximus himself to come and find it. To find it, to see it, to learn the truth.

And, indeed, as if to confirm Semipyatnitsky's conjecture, the scrap of paper suddenly peeled off the granite, dropped into the water, and disappeared into the cold black depths of the canal.

So Peter had simply dumped the pills in the nearest canal! Tossed them in, box and all! A disaster!

Maximus had a rough idea of how the water circulation system works in a big city: The water goes through a complete cycle. It flows into the sewer pipes, and from there to the wastewater plants where it's purified and sent back into the water supply. Today's urine is tomorrow's tea, and the day after tomorrow it's urine again.

The sanitation process captures the majority of pollutants and toxins and destroys microbes with chlorine, but it was highly unlikely there were any filters effective against PTH. Someone needed to notify the Ministry of Emergency Situations! Warn people of the imminent danger!

Semipyatnitsky's impulse to sound the alarm subsided within a couple of minutes. He climbed back up the steps onto the embankment and took a fresh look at the city around him.

Neon advertisements gleamed on the walls of the surrounding buildings, and the shop windows emitted blinding light; weirdly shaped metal conveyances sped along on the streets with pompous-looking passengers inside, while people strutted by on the sidewalks flaunting their designer clothing. Everyone looked happy. Or almost. At least they knew what had to be done to achieve the happiness they desired. And were highly motivated to take the next step on that path.

Maximus felt sad and relieved at the same time. There was nothing he could do. The pills had already permeated the city's air and the people's blood long before Peter's visit. A couple dozen kilograms more or less wouldn't make any difference. People would stay the same. They wouldn't be willing to return to a life without the narcotic. It made no sense to try and fight it.

There was only one thing left to do: go home and go to bed. Dream dreams. If no more dreams of Khazaria came, then there would be others; Maximus could be sure of that.

So this really is the end.

Our story is over.

But the reader will note that the book doesn't end here; there are a few more pages. What else is there to tell?

Sometimes an author and his readers find it hard to part with characters they've come to know and love. And I've gotten quite attached to Maximus. What about you?

I'd be curious to know what happened after Semipyatnitsky left the office. Besides which, it looks like my contract stipulates a higher word count. Seriously now, only the exterior, visible part of the story has ended. The most important thing still lies ahead. So let us turn the page . . .

PART IV

Poppies

INSOMNIA

Tick-tick-tick-tick-tick-tick-tick-tick-tick-tick-tick . . .
The little metal alarm clock ticked in the silence of the dark room.

Just tick-tick-tick-tick-tick-tick-tick-tick-tick . . . Normally when authors describe clocks ticking, they write "ticktock." But my clock said tick-tick-tick-tick-tick-tick . . . on and on without end, with no "tock" to be heard.

I lay on my bed on top of the covers, and stared blankly into the nowhere of the ceiling. My insomnia was back.

Tick-tick-tick-tick-tick-tick-tick-tick-tick-tick-tick-tick . . .
I hate the sound of clocks ticking in the middle of the night. It keeps me up. My ears snag on the rhythm, noting each tick, anticipating the next.

Every tick is in the right place, each pause measured out precisely, not a single one rushing ahead, not a single one falling behind. But my ear keeps on mistrustfully monitoring the intervals, sound and silence, and the mechanism keeps on ticking.

I needed to get up and silence the damn clock. I could smother it in a pile of laundry or move it out into the kitchen, or I could simply remove the battery and let it fall silent forever. That's what I usually do. Or used to.

One night I was alone in my apartment, which was, I guess, my home, or would have been if I'd been myself at the time, tick-tock-tick-tock-tick-tock, but the noise was deafening. I collected all the clocks in the apartment (there were three) and disabled them. And fell asleep.

Tick-tick-tick-tick-tick-tick-tick-tick-tick-tick . . .
I used to have a home, there used to be people around. But now I'm alone. Alone. Home alone, alone, no home.

The clock might very well have made a different noise if it had been bigger—say, the size of my cupboard. Ticktock, tick-tick-tick. Alone at home, at home alone . . . better alone.

I remembered one of my old jobs, the one before the last, when I—or it might have been someone else—used to be sent on various trips around the country. Pack, unpack, pack, unpack, planes, buses, trains. From plane to bus to train and back again, unpack, pack, unpack, pack.

Life. No, life isn't some kind of show. It's not a game. And not a dream, either. Life is a business trip. Only your company ID has gone missing, and you can't remember what you're there for. You're in some strange place, trying to get something done, but you're not sure what exactly they sent you to do. And so you're waiting for the management to contact you. While also being afraid they will. And even more afraid they won't.

Even without all the baggage, it's not exactly a vacation. And you're dragging around all your things, bags and suitcases full. It's easier to travel light, but before you know it, you've accumulated even more stuff—wife, kids, relatives, friends.

So you kill time, looking for things to do in the evening. You get used to the place, you can find your way around now, and soon you've even forgotten who you are and who sent you and where you're actually from.

And only then do they contact you and tell you it's time to go home.

So it's better to be alone.

Tick-tick-tick-tick-tick-tick-tick-tick . . .

The resolve to try to change something in your life dwindles with every passing year. I used to be able to stop the flow of time. Now I was simply lying around without getting up; I took no action against the clock—it wouldn't make any difference; I wasn't going to fall asleep anyway.

I'd been given the clock at the annual reception that the St. Petersburg branch of one of the maritime shipping companies organized every year for its partners. OOCL. The acronym—the company's logo—was engraved on the top. The clock was shaped like one of those navigation instruments, maybe some kind of chronometer, I don't know; I've never been on one of those big ships. All I know is that the toilet is called the head, the kitchen the galley. That much I know for sure. Though I have no idea where I learned it. Or, more to the point, why.

OOCL is a Chinese company. People had come from their headquarters to serve as hosts for the reception: short Asians wearing European suits and very conservative, embossed neckties. The senior executive gave a brief presentation enumerating the company's achievements over the past year, notably a forty percent increase in container shipments to Russia. Yes, their business was thriving. How could it not, with the yearly increase in imports from Southeast Asia? Russia imports everything: food, clothing, technology; the only growth here is in new shopping centers. Nothing is being assembled here these days except for criminal cases; nothing being invented except new ways to fleece the population.

But what difference did that make to me, naked little creature that I was, lying there in a dark apartment unable to sleep, listening: tick-tick-tick-tick-tick-tick-tick-tick-tick-tick-tick-tick-tick-tick . . .

At the reception I was introduced to a little man with a pock-marked face that resembled the surface of the moon; must be smallpox, or maybe some other pox, since European medicine eradicated that long ago. I seem to recall the man's name was Nick, and he worked in one of the Chinese company's European offices. I exchanged a few words with him in English, and his Russian colleagues hurriedly, with obvious relief, abandoned him to my care for the rest of the evening.

Nick told me about his office in England, which was located, of course, not in London—it's too crowded and noisy there—

but in some little town out in the country. Nick told me about his wife and two little kids, about his dog Lassie and his Toyota. Nick invited me to go to a bar with him after the reception, some place that had music, German beer, and beautiful Russian girls. His eyes gleamed in the darkness like two swamp lights, but I politely declined.

At the reception I ate a whole kilo of salmon and drank four bottles of light white Italian wine. In the process of entertaining Nick, I managed to make a few additional useful acquaintances, told them how thrilled I was with the hotel, complimented the hosts, shook hands with the directors, made eyes at the female managers, and smiled gallantly at the older women who ran companies that did business with or competed with Cold Plus.

I was the very image of *comme il faut*, or so I thought. I floated in the waters of this tastefully dressed and fragrant society like a fish, like that same salmon I'd been consuming, and by the end of the evening I felt as though I'd been washed up onto the shore, onto its scorching sand, into sizzling oil in a red-hot frying pan.

I'm not really a people person.

I staggered out of the hotel and made it somehow to the metro. I descended into its womb and found myself in a car in the company of an entirely different sort of person, hungry-looking, pasty-faced, bad-tempered, reeking exhaustion and beer from plastic bottles. And I realized that I was no better with these people than with the elect.

I've always felt like someone from another planet, from some parallel universe. With some effort I've learned how to smile and hold up my end of a conversation. I read up on soccer and sports cars, visit a couple of vacation spots, and make a point of following the daily weather reports. So I'll always have something to talk about, and I won't appear too antisocial.

I've learned how to keep up appearances.

There are only a few people in the whole world, or I only know of a few, anyway, who are on the same wavelength as I. In their company I can blurt out any heresy that comes into my head, the kind of thing that would send any "normal" crowd into a stupor.

We are a secret society. We recognize one another by smell. We have all lost something, and we are seekers.

Blessed are the poor in spirit.

But this isn't about us. We are on a quest, we are on the verge of discovering some great spiritual treasure; in our pockets we carry spiritual gold cards with no credit limits, as yet unused. The time shall come when we will activate them.

Tick-tick-tick-tick-tick-tick-tick-tick-tick-tick-tick-tick-tick-tick-tick . . .

I wonder what kind of man that Hakan is. I'd guess he's on the wrong side of thirty—anything over thirty is the wrong side—a little overweight, chronically unshaven, and with an unpretentious haircut. Or maybe he's thin and wears plastic-rimmed glasses like a retiree.

Back when I only read his reports on current events, I sensed—by his smell—that he was someone I could get along with. Then I rummaged around on the Internet and found some more of his work, and it turned out to be completely deranged. And this only confirmed my feelings of kinship.

I found his e-mail address in one of his entries and sent him a short note with my essay about Khazaria attached. I got an answer a week later. Hakan wrote:

> *Nice work, bro! Dug your credo. First thing I thought was, that's a helluva lot of words, no way Ill get thru it. But the end was right on—sweet, bro. Score. Flames of Hell! Write back!*
> *Keep m shakin,*
> *Hakan*
> *PS You ask why I call myself Hakan? Who the fuck knows?*

Some Armenian guy in tradeschool gave me the name (among other things. Have no idea what, even now). Cause my beard is red and comes in uneven. Like some Khagan. I told him to go fuck himself, banged him up good. Later I was dicking around on the net and realized that there's nothing wrong with the word. It's even a compliment. Some big shot Tatar or Viking somebody was named that. Anyway, I don't dye my beard and I don't shave, and I go by Hakan. That's the fucking long and short of it.

P.P.S. I was surfing the web just now and saw something about Khazar chemists on some shitty site. I can't make sense of the damn thing, but maybe you'll be interested. Here's the link:

THE SECRET OF FISH PASTE

In thirteenth-century Venice there lived a Khazar by the name of Abongaldyr, who was known as Fish Eye. This nickname was due to a physical deformity; one of his eyes was completely covered by a cloudy film. The name was also due to his profession: This Khazar used to buy fish guts; he'd poke around in them and boil them. Maybe he ate them, maybe they served some other purpose.

This Khazar was believed to be a Jew, most likely because he didn't wear a cross or attend church. He didn't associate with Jews, or with good Christians either for that matter, and he didn't observe Hebraic law. It was whispered that Fish Eye was in fact a sorcerer who practiced black magic.

His eye problem had begun during a time of plague; the black queen of the pox had come to Venice, brought by sailors arriving from distant lands. The sailors infected the harlots working the ports; from them the entire city soon came to know the wrath of God. The people infected with this plague all died because no one knew how to cure the pox. But Fish Eye was different. Though he fell ill, he survived, most likely through some miracle or sorcery. But he retained the mark of Satan, that dead eye, which gave his entire face a ghoulish appearance.

The Jews in Venice were primarily merchants and moneylenders, like the Khazars who fled here from their native land. But Fish Eye didn't lend money and didn't engage in trade; he didn't even own a shop.

But he was wealthy nonetheless. Fish Eye lived in a big house with a garden where he grew brilliant scarlet flowers, which reminded him of his lost homeland. When he went to the market he would buy, in addition to his fish guts, special spices that cost several times their weight in gold, and from the travelers who were always coming and going he bought special stones, which he crushed for some purpose.

Fish Eye wore on his left hand a heavy silver and black enamel ring with a dragon pictured on it, biting his own tail—the sure sign of an alchemist and wizard. It was believed that alchemists could turn any metal into gold. But Fish Eye didn't make gold from lead; his gold came from merchants.

The merchants came to him secretly at night, bringing bags of gold coins, and when they left they took vessels filled with a slimy gelatinous substance that was known as fish paste.

Fish paste used to be produced only in Khazaria. Fugitive Khazars brought the secrets of their craft along with them to Europe, and of them all Fish Eye was the most notorious and successful.

The merchants who bought the fish paste made huge profits, and their business thrived.

Fish Eye sold his paste to anyone who could afford it, but he kept the formula to himself. One Jew was desperate to get the formula at any price, and he offered a huge sum of money. But Fish Eye refused.

Then the Jew bribed some Christians he knew, and they denounced Fish Eye to the Holy Inquisition. The Khazar was accused of trafficking with the devil, and someone even claimed to have found a contract with the Enemy of Humanity in his house, with all its terms spelled out in great detail and sealed with an imprint of the Khazar's ring, inked with his blood.

The Khazar was led out to the great cleansing fire. When bound to the stake he raised his arms to the heavens and cursed: "Woe upon ye, inhabitants of Venice and of all cities! Ye will yet come to know the power of the stolen delights, the seductions of the Prince of this world! And ye will lose your eternal souls!"

Before he perished in the flames, Fish Eye had experienced the rack and a multitude of other contrivances utilized by the

Holy Church for the purposes of taming the flesh and saving the souls of sinners who had strayed from the path. But whether the Khazar gave up the secret recipe and whether the Jew who had betrayed him got the secret from the church officials—on that subject nothing is known.

LIFE AFTER DEATH

Do you believe in life after life?

A Western pop singer wails on MTV. I can't remember her
name; if I get curious I can watch the whole clip; eventually a
credit will show up at the bottom of the screen giving her name
and the titles of the song and of the album it's from. But I'm not
that curious. I'm not much of a connoisseur, frankly. I just listen.
I just keep it on out of boredom.

The credit is sure to be there at the end of the clip. Like a label,
like a toe tag at the morgue.

"Earthly glory is like a toe tag on a corpse."

Some Buddhist lama said that, I think. I don't remember *his*
name either. But I do remember the quote, more or less. I like it.
I didn't even bother to write it down in my special notebook (you
have one of those too, don't you?); it just stuck in my mind. And
it's true. A man dies, and all that's left is a slab with his name and
the high points of his biography: He was born, studied somewhere, got married, won eight Oscars, and then died.

This hag should have kicked the bucket long ago. Or left show
business and spent her final days sitting on a bench in front of her
house, or puttering around in her garden. Anything but gyrating
up there on stage in front of everyone. She's an old lady, same age
as Marilyn Monroe would be now, probably, but Marilyn died at
the right time. This one, though, just keeps on singing. Won't shut
up. Dances too.

I can't wrap my head around that. You've already shown what
you've got, said everything you can say, and earned huge piles of
money; why keep on writhing around on stage like a clown? Go
over your bank statements, count your money, and enjoy the rest
of your life.

I always liked Britney Spears. Now there's someone who did

it right! I recall her debut. A nymphet, a pedophile's dream, in a school uniform and flimsy little white skirts. She danced on a dock by the sea. Sang words of love, first love, pure, timid, and innocent love. And the planet quivered, pierced through by an ultrasound wave of unprecedented force—the sound of men's balls buzzing, the whole world over.

She made it big, became a superstar, sold millions of albums, earned millions of dollars, got up on stage with the whole world watching and sucked face with Madonna. And then sent everything to the devil.

Started having babies, eating sandwiches, getting fat, and vandalizing cars in parking lots, pounding on their hoods like a madwoman.

Of course, malevolent critics will remind you, before this she bombed in the movie *Crossroads*, ruined her personal life, started in on alcohol and drugs. But, hey, up theirs. They're just jealous.

Do you believe in life after life?

No, Britney isn't like that old bag, who will cling to the stage till the day she dies. Look at her, a veritable cyborg! After all the plastic surgery, liposuctions, and implants, there's nothing left of her original body. Like the robot cop from that movie. *Robocop*, that's it. Robo-singer.

The Russian stage has its share of this particular brand of mutant. When they come out on stage for the Police Day concert, it's downright terrifying. These aren't real people, they're some sort of pale zombie who've risen up from their dank graves, called forth by some voodoo sorcerer who fed them a poisonous powder. Or pills, maybe.

To hell with that kind of career! Everyone has to die someday. Sure, you have to be in the right place at the right time to strike it rich. But you also have to know when to make your exit.

Every year new stars appear on the stage. What happens to the old ones? Nothing—they're still up there too. If things keep going on like this, there won't be any room left for the living; all the space will be taken up by walking corpses. The devil should definitely reconsider the terms of his standard contract.

There's no place for the living among the dead, just as there's no place for the dead among the living. I learned that from my wise old grandmother.

Do you believe in life after life?

What the hell is this song about, anyway? I can't get it out of my head. The zombie is howling mournfully. What is she really trying to say? Probably something like.

Do you believe in life after love?

Like, say, her love is over, but she has to go on living. *I will survive.* So many songs by women can be boiled down to that one idea. But what *I* hear is:

Do you believe in love after life?

Yes, that's more like it. And I do believe:

At night I dream of the sky and my star,
People living on water and air,
Free as the wind in the steppe, antelopes,
And that love that comes after the grave.

Love that lasts till death, to the grave, is a fairy tale, an illusion, a lie. Love *after* the grave, though—that's real, it gives me hope. Lines from my own song, something I wrote when I was sixteen:

I grew up near an abandoned slaughterhouse.
We played with the bones of murdered animals.
And it must have been there that I realized
That if we are to live, they must die.

I think that I sang that song once, drunk, to a one-eyed old man, shitface drunk himself, on Zayachy Island near the Peter and Paul Fortress. And he shoved a piece of paper into my hand with his phone number on it, told me to call, promised that he would find me a band, would set up an audition, would make me a star.

Of course I didn't call. People say all kinds of things when they're drunk.

Or, no, maybe what she means is exactly what she's saying:

Do you believe in life after life?

If so, it's clearly autobiographical; the song must be about her experiences after the zombie master hauled her out of the grave.

Though I died too, in a certain sense. I died for the world of advanced capitalism and industrial-trade corporations, the day I walked out of Cold Plus.

The heroes of my favorite books always had "something in reserve" waiting for them before they told everyone to go to hell and set out to pursue their own destinies. Something to "tide them over" for a while.

But when I wrote my resignation and walked out on the company that had fed me, for better or worse, for so many years, I had no savings. Just debts. I stepped into emptiness, *pustota*.

Jumped without a parachute, as one of my friends put it. He'd been complaining to me about his life for as long as I could remember. He didn't love his wife, his job was monotonous and boring, and he was stuck out in some provincial town. I suggested he quit, give everything up at once and move away.

He answered, "I'm already too old to jump without a parachute." Too old. And he wasn't even thirty!

But I jumped. It wasn't a big deal, just a completely meaningless little act of protest. The least a man can do if he wants to live his own life. But that didn't mean I wasn't scared.

When I quit my job without even picking up my last paycheck, I didn't have the slightest idea how or on what I would live. All I had in my wallet was small change enough to cover my immediate needs.

But God, or fate, or the devil—one of them anyway, or maybe all of them together—come to a man's aid when it's time to make a big decision. The next day I went to the bank, which I hadn't visited for along time, and learned that some money had been transferred to my account—a commission for this deal I'd made with some Chinese guys for a friend of mine, using my Cold Plus connections. I took some of it out in cash and went to the supermarket, which was practically empty (it was early and all the usual shoppers were at work). The only people there were stay-at-home wives, retirees, and a couple of young people doing their shopping. I went up and down the aisles and gathered food and drink, four plastic bags full, using up almost all my money.

I left the car outside my building, went up to my apartment, and put all the groceries away neatly on the kitchen shelves and in the refrigerator. Grains on one shelf, save for pasta, which got its own place; processed foods in the freezer; milk products in the fridge door; cheese and butter in the upper rack closest to the freezer; jars of jam and other preserves on the next shelf down; and then finally, on the bottom, fresh vegetables and salad greens. That would last me a week.

Once I'd put everything away, I went into my bedroom and surveyed the familiar disorder. The sight brought a strange sense of relief. Here was something to keep me busy.

First I made the bed. Then I picked up the various objects that were strewn around the room and sorted them out: clean clothes on the cupboard shelves, shirts on hangers. I stuffed my dirty laundry into paper bags: underwear in one, the rest sorted by color.

Then I put on some music and started in on my books. I cleared them all off the shelves, dumped them onto the floor, and started dusting each one individually, then putting them back on the shelves in alphabetical order by author.

The purpose of man's existence is to create order out of chaos. I'm convinced of it. I'm no longer plagued by the need to find the meaning of life; I know the one and only, universal, correct answer to the question of "why." Man lives in order to create order out of chaos.

A Sisyphean task, that's for sure. Across the universe, chaos is growing, expanding every second. This is a principle of physics that follows from the second rule of thermodynamics. The level of entropy increases in any closed system. The time shall come when the entire world will grind to a halt. The stars will go out and the galaxies will disintegrate, leaving no trace. Just dust and stones, flailing in disorder throughout the dead expanse of the cosmos.

But man, himself a chaotic fluctuation of elements, creates his own little world around himself—itself a transitory fluctuation with its own set of rules—and the cheese goes on the upper rack of the refrigerator, and ironed shirts go on hangers in the closet.

Chaos creeps into human existence, into the crannies of a man's apartment, into the dark alleyways of his life. Chaos has its own rules. But man grabs a broom, picks up an iron, a washrag, a marker and notebook, and he sweeps out chaos, dumps it in black garbage bags, gives everything a name, numbers everything, puts everything in its special place.

And so it will be until the very last day, when this man falls on the field of this cosmic battle, dead but not defeated.

Then others will come, will wash and dress him, will tuck him in his coffin in strict accordance with their rituals, will sing the appropriate hymns, make solemn speeches, and will consign his body to earth, or fire, or water, or air—whatever their traditions require. Man is broken down into his component elements, which are no longer orderly but chaotic—and these elements now return to the cosmos, which is itself just another name for pandemonium.

The only thing that will remain of him will be memory. The Upanishads say: "When my body turns to ash, and the breath of my life flows together with the air of the Universe, O my God, remember everything I did for Thee."

Because that memory is with God.

And it is called soul.

The soul is nothing more than God's memory of a man who lived on this earth. And there is no other soul.

> *Before I know it, my eyes will melt*
> *into darkness.*
> *Will there be something*
> *For My God*
> *To remember?*

LIFE AFTER DEATH,
CONTINUED

I went to bed content, thinking about the work I still had to do: polish the floors, do the laundry, clean all my shoes and arrange them in the entryway. I slept soundly. And that night marked the end of my Khazaria dreams.

But then the insomnia set in.

I could never sleep during the day. As long as the sun was up, I had to stay busy. I washed, cleaned, sorted, and arranged things in my little apartment. Or I'd go out and wander the streets or go to Esenin Park and walk along the path by the grandly named Okkervil "River."

Then I started going into the city. I'd put gas in the car and go to exhibits, art shows, and symphony concerts, spend time in cafés. I developed a taste for reading in crowded places. Hoping to stretch my limited resources, I economized wherever I could. Before long I realized that the privilege of being allowed to sit all day at the twenty-four hour buffet in the book megastore on Vosstanie Square, reading without buying anything, only extended so far. You take one title off the shelf and settle down with it in the buffet area; it's especially convenient at night when there aren't many customers and there are lots of open spaces at the tables; it doesn't cost anything just to sit. But occasionally a waitress will turn up at your table and ask, "Will you be ordering anything ELSE?" making it clear by her emphasis of the word "else" and her entire demeanor that if you're sitting in her buffet reading a book that you don't intend to buy, then you'd better order some food. Otherwise, perhaps it's time to think about heading home, sir.

So you order another cup of coffee, a piece of cheesecake, and then some more coffee, and then something else, and ultimately by morning you've dropped more money into the buffet than it would have cost you to buy the book.

It's simpler and cheaper just to take a book along and read it in an ordinary coffee shop, ideally, if there's a place by the window. There are coffee shops in Petersburg where you can sit for two or even three hours without ordering anything. No one will bother you and no one will notice when you get up and leave.

But it's better to go up to the counter and get a cup of hot chocolate—when I was little they used to call it cocoa—or a cappuccino. Take a seat, settle in with your book, and read as long as you want. No need to touch the cup; just let it cool down. That's what I used to do.

If I went during the day, it was hard to find a place to sit. But I could look up from whatever I was reading to admire the flocks of young girls, fresh and dewy-eyed, who'd come from places like Barnaul to get an education in the capital. They sat in the coffee shops, smoking cigarettes and babbling endlessly. They never noticed me. Why should they? Who would be interested in a carelessly dressed, slightly overweight man with a sparse graying reddish-brown moustache and beard? No, I know, you run into all kinds of deviants. But I didn't need anything from them, and so, by the laws of sympathetic magic, I never had any problems with the girls—didn't make them nervous, didn't attract them either. It was as though I simply didn't exist in their dimension, which was filled with the aroma of Rive Gauche perfume (bought on discount with a girlfriend's gold card), with nice-looking boys from their school and dreams of a new life—so close at hand, within their grasp: graduation, a job in a big company with potential for advancement, a nice car (some shade of green, and bought on credit, of course), and vacations in Turkey, or, alternatively, Maldives, if she's lucky enough to catch the eye of a man of means.

Their girlish naïveté didn't bother me, though I didn't envy them either. And I never bothered to drink my hot chocolate. Who knows what they put in it.

When I went late at night there would be older people at the tables, sometimes couples, talking, poring over brochures and spreadsheets, or simply sitting in silence, emitting smoke.

Occasionally I would spend the whole night in a twenty-four hour coffee shop. After the nightclubs closed, the clubbers would come in, exhausted, half-awake, but not ready to give up yet. They would drink cups of hot coffee and stare at their surroundings in silence, eyes glassy.

And I would read. And not feel at all abandoned or alone.

Finally, when (or if) I went home for the night, I would undress slowly, fold my clothes carefully, turn off the light, and go to bed—as though performing some sort of a ritual, particular and prescribed. Order in all things. Nighttime is for sleeping. If a man can't get to sleep, then he needs to just lie there in bed naked, staring blankly at the ceiling. Not violate the order of things.

What came now instead of dreams were thoughts. And memories. Sometimes from a very very long time ago.

THE DARK TEREK

I remember everything vividly to this day. We would take a trip. To the farm! To Zarechnoye! To Grandma's! It was always special. The excitement would start the night before, when my dad would make an announcement: Tomorrow we're going on a trip.

Hurray!

My sister would spend half the night packing all the things a girl needs: all eight dolls; a bag crammed full of paints and books; a separate bag with markers and colored pencils; three dresses, a bathing suit (she has only one, how annoying!), sandals, and belts; a makeup bag with a mirror; some little buckets and trowels, and a rubber duck. And in the morning my mom would get mad and make her leave most of it behind.

I would stand outside next to the car, aloof. Girls! Always dragging all kinds of useless stuff around wherever they go. You need to travel light. Like me: just the clothes I'm wearing and a slingshot in my back pocket.

And my favorite stuffed bear, a head taller than me.

My father called me to help, and—being men together—we loaded the usual gift for Grandma into the trunk: a bag of mixed fodder for her pigs.

Then we piled into the car—a red Moskvich 412—and headed out. My father was a cautious driver. He never even went out on the highway at night. Forty years of driving and not a single accident.

I used to get carsick. But I had to put up with it when we went to Zarechnoye. We drove all the way through Chechnya and Dagestan, to the Cossack settlements. Along the road we would see rows of gypsy encampments out on the steppe. We would drive down alleys full of ancient trees, lime trees, and every time he saw them my father would tell us that those lime trees

had been planted during the reign of Catherine the Great.
For some reason he thought this was a big deal.

But then we would emerge from the dark forest, and a marvelous vision would open out before us: on both sides of the road
the fields were covered with scarlet flowers in full bloom, opium
poppies, *mak*, like my name; they were like a fire blazing, filling
the whole steppe, flames as far as you could see!

And of course we would stop and gather big armfuls. And my
mom wouldn't scold us when we brought the poppies into the car
and when they shed their petals, messing up the seats. She loved
the flowers, and the color red.

Grandma always knew exactly when we would arrive. She
would be outside standing at the gate, holding up her palm as a
sunshade over her wrinkled forehead, looking into the distance.
How did she know that our dusty, rattling old Moskvich had
already reached Zarechnoye? Did the birds tell her?

She didn't stand out there like that all day long, did she?

Inside the hut the air was hot and steamy from two days of
baking: fish pies, potatoes and meat, salad, fruits. And a bottle of
homemade red wine would stand on the table, waiting. Grandma
had a vineyard—twenty *sotki* big! How did she manage it all?

Everything is so delicious! The grownups are lazy; they'll just
sit around gossiping, eating, and drinking the whole afternoon.
But we have things to do. We grab some pie, drink a glass of wine
each—like the grownups—and take off running.

To the Terek.

I could find the path with my eyes closed. Along Grandma's
fence to the end, then across a ditch and a field, and then a ravine
and some woods, and finally there it was: the Terek! The river is
big, smooth, deep. It wasn't like the stream in our village, which
only comes up to your waist, and only up to the grownups' knees.
No, the Terek has a strong current, and you shouldn't swim out
too far or you'll be caught in a whirlpool and that'll be the end of

you. The *vodyanoi* demon will drag you all the way down to the bottom. My sister kept a close eye on me. If I tried anything, she yelled at me. She's the older one. We'd splash around for a while, then make our way back to the hut.

It was dark at night on the farm. Keep your eyes peeled. Though why would you want to peel your eyes? I never got that.

Jackals howled on the other side of the garden, down by the Terek. If a traveler came across them at night, he was done for; they'd surround him and tickle him to death. And when they howled, it sounded like little kids crying, or else laughing really hard. Try and make sense of it. Maybe they had someone in their clutches out there.

I got to sleep in Grandma's room, on a trunk. They'd already made my bed. I loved the trunk! Grandma told me that it was her hope chest; she brought her trousseau in it when she married Grandpa. Her family was rich—the trunk was huge! It used to belong to her mother, and before that, to her mother's mother. Made of oak, with metal bands around it, and decorated with silver trim.

We went to bed. Grandma prayed to her icons first, and then got into her bed with its ornate cast-iron frame. I lay down on my trunk. But I didn't want to go to sleep! I wanted Grandma to tell me stories.

"Tell me a story, Grandma!"

"What do you want to hear?"

"About the old days!"

"What is there to tell? I don't remember anything!"

Grandma dissembled, delayed. That was part of the ritual; she did it every time. She would eventually tell a story, though, however much she protested, and when she did, she would talk and talk until after midnight.

First, for a warm-up, she'd tell about how the Reds came to the settlement. They stabbed Great-Grandpa to death with their sabers, right there in the bed where he lay wounded from battle. Before that, when Great-Grandpa was healthy and able to ride his horse, there was no way the Reds could have gotten into the settlement. Great-Grandpa was the ataman!

But then the Reds came, a shabby, rough sort of bunch—they said there's no tsar anymore, and no God either!

They went around to all the huts and the church, gathered up the icons, and took them to the public square, where they piled them up and set fire to them. They put pots over the fires with the icons and tried to make watermelon honey. But the bottoms of the pots melted through and all the honey leaked out. They tried using different pots, but the same thing happened. And every time they tried a new pot, it would leak when they put it over the fire made of holy icons! So they couldn't make their watermelon honey.

Because there is a God. The time will come when those godless men who sold Christ and their own eternal souls will weep bitter tears.

I'd heard the story countless times before, but I do not interrupt. It got more interesting from there.

"*Ba*! Tell about how it was after the war!"

"Oh, *vnuchek*! It was a terrible time! So many soldiers lay dead on the fields— there was no one to give them a funeral and a proper burial. And the wolves came and multiplied! Fed on the carrion. Only there was something strange about those wolves. The people were strange, too. Everything went to support the war, and famine spread over the villages and cities—people ate one another to survive. It got so you couldn't tell the difference between wolves and men."

"Grandma, you're scaring me! But those were just rumors, right?"

"What do you mean, rumors? I saw it myself."

"Saw what, Grandma?"

"Well I'll tell you. I was on a carriage going out of town. We used to work on the collective farm during the week, just to get our work credits. But to earn money to buy bread for the children, your mother and her sister, and their brother, I used to sell melons at the market. So I'm coming back from the market one night. And two Cossacks are walking along the road, strangers. They say, 'Give us a lift, sister Cossack, take us to the station!' but I really don't like the look of them. They were dragging their feet, and their shoulders looked cramped, somehow, like they were wearing someone else's shirt. Or like they were wearing someone else's body. And their voices had a hollow sound to them. I didn't say anything, just flicked the mare with the switch, giddyup, let's get a move on. She was a good horse, and she took off at a gallop. But the devil made me turn and look back, and I saw two wolves skulking along behind the carriage, green eyes gleaming. No Cossacks in sight. I nearly died of fright. Barely survived. I kept praying and crossing myself the entire way home. That's what saved me!"

"So Grandma, if they were werewolves, then why couldn't they just jump into the carriage and grab you?"

"They weren't really alive, that's why! Remember this, my dear: Spirit creatures can't enter our world completely. They have to trick people into letting them in. All it takes is for you to say just once, 'yes, all right.' And that's it, you're done for. They'll drag you to their lair, they'll swallow your soul! So don't get into conversations with strangers, don't open your door to anyone at night, and don't give rides to people you don't know. Those are the three rules."

"Now tell me about Grandpa!"

"Oh, dearie . . . " Grandma fell silent. She was probably crying. "I loved my husband. He's the only man I ever had. He gave me three children, and I stayed faithful to him my whole life, even after he died. And I was a good-looking girl, the Collective Farm Chairman himself came courting. He was one-eyed and ugly, like the devil. And he said, 'Stepanida, here I am, the last man left in the settlement. Who else is there for you to marry? I'm a good man. I'll take you, kids and all. And if you don't marry me, I'll bring up your White Guard past and ruin you. You'll rot in prison, you and your kids along with you.'"

"What did you say?"

"I was raking hay at the time. So I poked him in his fat belly with my pitchfork and told him, 'It is said: Your first husband is from the Lord, the second from man, and the third from the devil. I had Volodenka, and he was from the Lord, and he died in the war. The Lord giveth, and the Lord taketh away. Now I don't need anything from man, much less the devil. And you're a one-eyed devil at that! Do whatever you want, harass me, try to hurt me, but make no mistake about it, I'm the ataman's daughter, and I fear nothing except the Lord's wrath. I'll scoop your guts out with this pitchfork!'"

"So then what?"

"Nothing. He stopped bothering me after that, the monster."

We lay there quietly and thought to ourselves. A moth beat against the window, attracted by the light inside.

"*Ba*, tell me about how Grandpa died."

"We don't know the details, dear. I got a death notice, that's all. It said he died a hero's death, at such and such a village, on such and such a day, and that was it. After the war I went to the village where they said it happened and tried to find his grave. Couldn't find a thing. Anyway, I already knew that he hadn't been given a proper funeral and burial. And he was a Christian, yet! He'd been baptized! Wasn't some commie."

"How do you know that he wasn't buried?"

"If they'd given him a proper burial, would he have wandered the earth after he died? Would he have come to see me?"

"What do you mean, 'come to see you,' Grandma? Didn't you say he was killed?"

"It happened the usual way. I got the death notice and was sitting in the hallway crying. And my friends came over, all of them already widows, and they told me how to handle it. 'Stepanida,' they said, 'your sorrow is great, but what can you do, it's war. Cry, grieve, but don't bring on God's wrath. Your Vladimir died—that was God's will. And it's not proper for the dead to walk the earth before the Judgment Day. We have our world, they have theirs. The dead don't belong among the living, and the living don't belong among the dead.' That's what they told me. And now I'm telling you the same, *vnuchek*, and don't you forget it!"

"What do you mean?"

"At first I didn't understand either. But they explained: 'Some soldiers who weren't given a proper Christian funeral rise from the fields and walk back home. Their soul is far away, mind you, awaiting God's judgment. But their body finds its way home, by habit. Finds its way by the stars and by the smell. And it comes and stands outside your door and asks you to open up and let it into the hut. Only at night, though. If you get one of these visits during the day, it's more likely to be a deserter than a dead man. Deserters can sneak by while the sun's still out. But dead men hide during the day, lurk behind bushes and in ditches, shunning the light. That's how you can tell the difference. He'll come at night, but all the same, don't let him in! Remember, it's not really your Vladimir, it's a dead man, just an empty body! Your beloved Vladimir, his Christian soul, is at peace—one hopes—in Heaven. Be strong, sister, don't open that door. Remember what happened to Nikitishna; she disappeared a month after she got the notice about Ivan. They found her body out in the woods; the wolves had eaten all the flesh off her bones. It's the living dead—they'll call and beckon, they'll lure you away to the riverbank or into the woods, and leave you there for the wild animals to eat. It always happens that way. And now Nikitishna's two little children are orphans—no father, and no mother either.'"

"So Grandma, did Grandpa come to visit?"

"He did. Ten days after I got the news. It was a dark night. I put the children to bed, and I was sitting there doing the mending. And I heard a scratching at the door, a voice saying 'Stesha, open up! It's me, your husband Vladimir!' And it was definitely his voice. My Volodenka! I jumped up, beside myself, was about to rush to the door and fling it open. But I held myself back, sobbing, and said, 'If it's really you, Volodenka, and you've deserted your unit and are still alive, then go hide in the barn for now, and when the sun comes up, come back in daylight and knock again. Then I'll let you in. And I'll help you hide from the authorities: I won't tell a soul!' But he kept saying the same thing: 'Open up, Stesha! Open up right now! I'm tired, I've missed you. I want to hold you in my arms, make love to you while the children are asleep.' And I was trembling all over! I'm a woman, after all, I need loving! But I looked at the children, and I answered, 'No, Volodenka, I can't! If it were just me, then I'd let you take me anywhere you wanted, to the river bank, or to feed me to the wolves, if only so I could touch your hand one more time! But we have three children, and if you kill me, who will take care of them? They'll starve to death. If you're dead, go away, don't torment my sinful soul!' But he wouldn't leave. He kept on scratching at the door till the sun came up. And when morning came, he disappeared."

"Maybe you dreamed it, Grandma?"

"No, *vnuchek*. It wasn't a dream. I was sewing, remember, so I pricked my finger with the needle on purpose, just to see if it was all for real. I didn't wake up, and in the morning my finger was still covered with blood. But, you know, that wasn't the end of it—he came back again and again. He came every night. Our hut was outside the village. And after midnight I'd hear it again, the scratching at the door, or else he'd be peeking in the window, and he'd keep calling out to me, begging. And there I was crying and praying. It was so hard for me—I have feelings, *vnuchek*! I would have gladly rotted out there with him! But the thought of my children kept me back."

"So how did it end, Grandma?"

"On the fortieth day from when they'd said he died, I asked for a service in the church, and we had a funeral. And after that he stopped coming. He was at peace."

I was too amazed to ask any more questions. I had never before, nor have I since, heard a story about a stronger and more terrible love.

But now I really couldn't get to sleep. And though it was long past midnight and time to stop talking, I kept after her, hoping to hear a story, a fairy tale:

"Grandma, tell me about the *rusalki*!"

"What can I say? I've never seen one."

"Who has?"

"My grandpa shot the last *rusalka* in the orchard, with a flintlock rifle."

"What was she doing in the orchard?"

"What do you mean? Stealing apples of course. For her children."

"You mean they had children?"

"Of course! They had everything people do: husbands, wives, children. But they would go around naked and they didn't speak our human language. They were big and strong and had strong hands. But other than that, you couldn't tell the difference between one of them and a normal person."

"What do you mean, Grandma? The fairy tales say that *rusalki* are girls with fish tails instead of legs."

"That's just in the stories. But I'm telling you the way it really was. Fish tails! What will they think of next? The only fishy thing about the *rusalki* was that fish paste of theirs."

"What fish paste, Grandma?"

"Fish paste! They used to follow our fishermen around and gather up fish guts. The men would go out onto the Terek and catch fish, and they'd clean them right there on the riverbank and toss the guts into the bushes. And the *rusalki* would be waiting out there. They would grab the fish guts and drag them away."

"What did they use them for?"

"Hold on, silly! I'm telling you. They collected poppies, too, *mak*. And they would make paste by mixing the *mak* with the fish guts. They would boil it and then lick it. But woe to anyone who tried to eat it—it was highly toxic. Every once in a while one of our Cossacks tried some of the fish paste and immediately started acting crazy. He wouldn't cover his shame, would stop going to church, would give up working in the fields. And he stopped caring about anything but sucking on the paste. Worse than a drunk! He'd become like a *rusalka* himself. Or would leave and go to the city."

"Wow! And where did the *rusalki* come from?"

"From nowhere. They'd always lived here, they were here before we were. We're the ones who came from somewhere else. Some from Russia, others from Ukraine. Our ancestors came and attacked the *rusalki*, they wiped out the whole tribe. They were strong, but they had no religion, and they had no weapons. Naked as junkies."

"Monkeys, Grandma."

"What?"

"You said junkies. What kind of a word is that? You need to say it right: naked as monkeys."

"Aren't you ashamed of yourself! Correcting your Grandma! As though your Russian's so perfect. Don't forget your father was named Raul!"

"So what if I'm Raulevich? I got an *A* in Russian! And in literature, too!"

"Well, if you're so smart, I won't tell you any more stories, since you know everything already."

Grandma would act offended, but it was just for fun. She loved my father, actually. And my father adored her. Not at all like in those mother-in-law jokes.

"Look, Grandma! I was just saying. It's just a funny thing to say, that's all, junkie. It's not a mistake, just an idiom, I guess."

"You're getting too big for your britches. 'Idiom'—I bet you made that up."

Grandma sounded like she was complaining, but obviously she was proud of my erudition. She would give it some thought, then conclude:

"The old folks used to say that at one time those *rusalki* had their own villages and farmlands, and cities with big bazaars. It was a powerful land! But the fish paste destroyed them. Whenever a person licked some of the paste, whatever he imagined seemed real to him. It was like witchcraft."

"How did it work, Grandma?"

"Here's how. Let's say someone wants some nice new clothes. He can sit down and sew some. But if he licks some paste, he'll imagine that he's all decked out in brocades and silks. He looks in the mirror and admires himself. And the people around him, those who didn't have any of the paste, see that the man is naked. Or say he wants a horse—he'll eat some paste, and he'll imagine that he has a horse. He'll take a switch and gallop around the fields, swatting at his own heels with it. Even food—all it takes is one whiff of the paste, and he'll imagine that he's full, that he's had a big meal of fish, and meat, and fresh bread, and wine. He'll puff his belly out and stagger around! But you can't fool yourself forever. When you don't eat anything at all, and just rely on the paste, eventually you'll swell up from hunger. The only *rusalki* who survived were the ones who ate apples and wild fruits. But they stopped plowing their fields and building houses. They even forgot how to catch fish! All they did was keep on mixing their paste—that was one art they didn't lose, and they never passed it on."

"How could they have told it to anybody if they couldn't talk?"

"It was only later on they didn't know how to speak, but they used to be able to. How could they have maintained their great state without language? Anyway, the *rusalki* kept the secret of their fish paste to themselves. And that gunk ruined them. They died from malnutrition, from exposure, from wars. One of them would eat some paste and suddenly think he's holding a sword in his hand, and he would wave his hand around in the air, and some Cossack just looks on and laughs, then goes up and stabs him to death."

"Were the Cossacks really that mean?"

"What else would they be? Those *rusalki* were just taking up space, doing nothing. They scared off the livestock, destroyed or-chards, and even started harassing good Christian people in dis-gusting ways."

"How did they . . . harass them?"

"You're too young to know about that."

"Tell me, Grandma. Just skip over the details."

"Well, let's say, for example, that the *rusalka* was a male. He'd go out and stand in the street, right in front of our girls. And he'd start strutting around, making crazy faces. He would think that he was decked out in his finest clothes, with striped trousers, a Circassian coat with an ammunition belt, a fur hat, a saber in a scabbard, and that he was mounted on a fine horse to boot—but he's just a stoned *rusalka*! Had too much fish paste. And what the girls see is a naked man out there in the road, and his shame is poking right out at them, saints alive! The girls take off running, and he chases after them, just like that, without a stitch on! And now the Cossacks come out of their huts, the girls' fathers, brothers, and fiancés, that is, and of course they hack the shameless infidel to death."

"Wow!"

"And if the *rusalka* was a female, then she'd go up to the Cossacks when they were hauling in their nets or were busy with some other gainful employment, and start striking poses! It would be obvious that she'd licked some paste—she'd look into the water and see her reflection: an elegant princess, pure as the driven snow, all in silks and pearls, her face veiled like an innocent bride's. But in fact, she has no more shame than the so-called horseman—she's naked and dirty. The Cossack men, at least the ones who were weak of faith, licked their chops. So the Cossack women kept a close watch on them. They would slap the men in the back of the head, and would flog the she-devil with pokers and drive her out into the Terek, into the middle, where it's deep, and drown her."

"That's so cruel!"

"No it's not, *vnuchek*. That's life. And that's how come there aren't any *rusalki* anymore."

"Grandma, your stories are amazing! There's nothing like them in any books! Especially the ones about the *rusalki*. They're more like the abominable snowman! So why do you call them *rusalki*?"

"What do you mean, why? All they could do was bleat and grunt. *Khy-khy, zy-zy, ry-ry. Khy-zyry . . . Kha-zary . . .* they just babbled. Didn't even know their own name. We had to call them *something*. Every creature needs a name . . ."

CONCLUSION

On one of those nights when I couldn't get to sleep, there was a knock on my door; the doorbell was broken. I opened up immediately, without asking who was there. I knew. Who else would come knocking at this time of night?

"Well, let's get comfortable, shall we, Mack?"

"My name is Maximus. Only one person ever had the right to call me Mack. But she left. Like all the others."

Maximus came in and sat down on the edge of my folded-out sofa bed.

"Want her back? I can do that. Or should I make it so she never left?"

I sat down on the swivel chair in front of my desk, the one with the computer I was using to enter my text.

"No, everything is as it should be. I'm meant to be alone."

"So what do you want?"

"I want you to answer a few questions. They've been piling up. How did you find me?"

He smirked and silently showed me my own business card. There was only one word on it: "Creator."

"I feel that things must be coming to a close. You've posed too many riddles. Burdened me with all of your own doubts. Now you need to give me some answers."

"Go ahead, ask."

"May I smoke?"

"No. You quit. So, what's your second question?"

Not paying any attention, he got out a cigarette, lit it using his silver lighter, and inhaled deeply.

"I'll begin with the easiest thing. White and black Khazars, Slavs and Rus, elves and other fairy-tale bullshit . . . who cares what they're called, in the end: Do the elite truly differ in any

279

essential way from ordinary people? Are they different in terms of race, blood, who the hell knows what else, or are they just the same thugs as you or I, just thugs who've simply managed to grab fortune by the tail?"

"Yes and no. It's an illusory distinction, really. Every elite, in order to preserve its place at the top, is faced with two opposing tasks: first, to prove that they're the same as everybody else, and then to prove that they're different. They need to assure the subjugated population that they are of the same flesh and blood, that they identify with them and are concerned about their welfare. But they also have to justify why they, and not some other poor random bastards, occupy their privileged place in society. This is why you see so many contradictory things about them in print . . . the sources just record what was said at any given time when the elite, reacting to whatever situation was at hand, happened to emphasize one argument over another."

"All right then. Here's a different kind of question: Does God love me?"

"The Lord doesn't feel love or hatred for anybody, though it might seem that way sometimes."

"Somehow I knew that that was exactly what you were going to say."

"What do you mean, you knew?"

"That you wouldn't give an answer."

"It's basically from the Vedanta Sutra. There are a lot of commentaries on the subject."

"I see that you're working on one yourself."

"*Vedanta* means 'the end of knowledge.' The end of all knowledge. All subsequent books are merely commentaries upon the Vedanta Sutra."

"Let's come back down to earth. To our sinful, fallen world. All the material goods that we use these days are cultivated, produced, and assembled in 'third world' countries. But all the ideas and dreams continue to be produced in the 'first world.' The only country remaining in the 'second world' is Russia. And Russia doesn't do anything. Just eats and sleeps. Eats other people's food and dreams other people's dreams. How long can this go on? Until all the oil and gas is used up? And then what? I'm concerned, I guess, about Russia's fate."

"Oh, the fate of Russia's not the most important thing, believe me! What's more important is to make sure that your liver doesn't start acting up and that your teeth don't rot."

"Very funny."

"It's not funny at all. People lose their sense of humor when they have a toothache. Personally, I'd rather deal with a debilitating level of anxiety about the fate of Russia than an average level of anxiety about pulpitis or periodontal disease. Not to mention something like indigestion. That kind of thing can really ruin your life."

"Don't pretend to be a doctor. You're only a creator."

"Touché. But since we've started in on the notion of creation, I've recently come to the conclusion that Russia doesn't exist at all. What, in your opinion, is this Russia you're so worried about? This empty wasteland, *pustyr?*"

"*Pustosh.*"

"This emptiness, *pustosh*, was here long before it was given the name Russia. And when Russia is no more, this *pustosh* will continue to exist, so there's no need to be concerned for its sake. If 'Russia' does come to an end, other people will come and settle the land and give it a different name. Is the name all that important to you? Plus, you're not even a Russian, so why are you so concerned about Russia? What's it ever done for you?"

"Ah, so now you'll start in on my Khazar identity. The same old xenophobia—it's an old joke that's not funny anymore, and hasn't been for a long time now. I'm a citizen of my country."

"Oh, if only you knew, my dear friend, what you're really a

citizen of . . . no, I'm not talking about how your soul is one little particle in the Supreme, in Brahman, which is greater than the whole universe. But, look, if you need to hide behind the illusion of some country or other, help yourself. Nothing to it. *Maya!*"

"Could you repeat that? In Russian, this time?"

"All of Russia is between your two ears. And, by the way, that's where China and Holland are too. Take Nils and Guan, they're just concerned about their respective countries' fates. Everyone worries about the future. But as far as what's used up first—oil, rice, or dreams—that's anyone's guess. That's the plain and simple truth."

"I learned the plain and simple truth from my grandma: Don't pick up hitchhikers, don't talk to strangers, don't open your door to anyone knocking in the night. But if you do, at least try to give your visitor some clear answers."

"I'll try."

"Next: How is all of this connected: the pills, Holland, the Khazars . . . ?"

"You haven't figured it out yet?"

"No."

"Not too bright, are you?"

He stubbed his cigarette out unceremoniously and mashed it under his heel onto my freshly washed floor—he hadn't taken his shoes off at the door—and snapped:

"But you're the creator here, not me. Author, writer. What I am is only image and likeness."

"All right, here it is, *The Maya Pill for Dummies.* The Khazars came up with the drug. They made a goo out of fish guts—like the powder from poisonous fish that voodoo doctors feed their victims to turn them into zombies—and mixed it with a poppy-based opiate in whatever special way. The concoction had a slimy, sticky consistency, hence the name "fish paste." The toxic fish extract paralyzes the will and enhances suggestibility, while the opium causes a pleasurable narcotic effect and brings on hallucinations. Soon the Khazars realized that the fish paste could serve as a substitute for actual goods, or, at least, could change the properties of said goods as perceived by the user."

"Wait! So can this mixture actually replace material goods for the user, or does it only create incorrect conceptions of the value of whatever it is?"

"The answer to that question depends on which position you adhere to in that Hindu dispute about the nature of reality—the first or the second."

"Personally, I prefer the third school, the one with the singing and dancing. But you're apparently a secret follower of those luckless philosophers who were poisoned with fly agaric before the dispute began. I can tell that your answers won't lead to anything of substance. Let's close the subject. Go on about the Khazars."

"So Khazaria became a transit center for trade between east and west, north and south. Anything with fish paste added sold much better everywhere. This made Khazaria wealthy and prosperous, but only for a while. The fish paste eventually destroyed the underlying economy. Nothing was as profitable as making fish paste. Gradually the Khazars stopped doing anything else, and concentrated all their efforts on mixing the drug and using the paste to cement their trade relationships. Soon the wealth of Khazaria started attracting attention from hostile nations, and the Khazars were powerless to resist. They had already forgotten how to plow, and make war, and build. In fact, it was the Byzantines who built their last fortress, Serkel. Instead of their native warriors they used mercenaries, and the mercenaries had no particular desire to give their lives for someone else's country. Khazaria fell under enemy attack: Rus from the west, nomads from the east. After their cities were destroyed, many Khazars fled to Europe, taking with them the recipe for the fish paste. In Europe the concoction was modified and refined for specific needs, either by the Khazars themselves or by people who had managed one way or another to get their hands on the recipe. Since the time of the great Khazar migration to Europe, trade began to develop, towns grew into great cities, the bourgeoisie emerged, and capitalism was born. When the mysticism of the Middle Ages fell into decline, sorcerers and alchemists gave way to other pseudo-scientists specializing in such fields as marketing and management. These sciences are essentially the same as their predecessors: They're merely research into the most effective ways to use fish paste. And how to turn everything into money."

"So what did they come up with? How did they use the paste?"

"Every way you can imagine. The Europeans were far more talented and inventive, and made considerably more progress, than the ancient Khazars, who had never managed to turn their product into anything more than a disgusting and smelly slime. As you know, in the Netherlands, which has always been a strong country in the chemical industry, they figured out how to produce the stuff in the form of neat little pink pills with no taste or smell."

"Yes, the pills. I have some. Want a try?"

"No thank you. I have some of my own."

"Fair enough. What happened then?"

"It just took off. At first the chemists were mostly interested in the actual recipe—that is, the specific ingredients that went into it and their proper proportions. Later on, some brilliant thinkers realized that the really important ingredients were actually the four principles of the gunk's effect: suppression of the will, an increase in suggestibility, arousal of pleasure, and the inducement of a hallucinatory state. Here too, of course, you need to know in what proportions to combine these effects: to what degree ought the will be suppressed, ought suggestibility be enhanced, ought the pleasure centers of the brain be activated, and then which particular hallucinations ought to be induced for whatever specific purpose. Once they saw that the paste's value was in these states of mind, not so much in the goo itself, they discovered that they could reproduce them by other means in just about any form you could think of. Those same principles go into every TV broadcast or election speech. Books too, for example. Books are also pills!"

He had no more questions. He just stood up and went out the open door. Didn't even say good-bye.

It was already light outside. I'd managed to get a couple of hours of sleep. Then I woke up, all by myself, without the alarm clock. It had been a long time since I'd set it; what was the point?

I washed, shaved carefully, brushed my teeth, and took a shower. I looked in the cupboard and chose an outfit that would make a good impression, professional but not too formal. And headed for Nevsky Prospect.

Nevsky was already crowded with people and cars. Amid the dense fabric of the city's usual noise I heard a strange sound, something like little bells ringing. I looked down the street in the direction of the noise, and saw a sparse but exotic-looking little procession approaching. Girls wearing bright Indian saris and men draped in what looked like white and saffron-colored sheets. They were all singing and dancing. One boy was beating a drum that hung on a strap around his neck; some of the others were tapping miniature copper cymbals. It was the cymbals' thin, bell-like sound that I had heard from a distance. I thought, there they are, the philosophers of the third school.

The procession came closer and soon drew even with me. Alongside the singers walked a very pretty girl with a red dot on her forehead. She was holding a tray with some round pinkish sweets arranged on it. I stood on the edge of the sidewalk and watched the philosophers of song and dance go by.

She came up to me and held out the tray:

"Take one!"

"What is it?"

"Imagine that it's a pill that will relieve you of doubt and suffering forever."

"But how?"

"It will end your material existence, which is the source of both doubt and suffering."

Well now. So they have pills too. To help one lead a purely spiritual existence. But she's a nice, normal-looking girl! What got her so involved in . . . philosophy? And she's not shy about preaching, apparently—just comes right out with it. Must be new at this.

"No, I'm sorry. I've already heard about you. And I like you, really. I far prefer your methods to those of other schools. But . . . I'm not ready yet."

The walk light turned green and I started across the street. The procession continued on its own way. Within a few minutes, all I could hear was that thin, bell-like sound, mixed in with the noise of the cars and people. And then it faded away, dissolved into the din of the great city.

I walked down the canal embankment that ran perpendicular to Nevsky Prospect, and stopped in one of my favorite cafés, one that was relatively quiet for this part of the city. I waited briefly in line and ordered an espresso.

I didn't really want any coffee.

I needed to gather my thoughts.

Though I had already made my decision.

I needed to find the business card.

And that wasn't difficult.

I knew that it wouldn't be.

Not the kind of business card that you stick in your pocket at some point, and then you decide you need it for some reason and so turn everything inside out looking for it, upending your brief-case, shaking everything out onto the floor, rummaging through your whole apartment, even checking inside books to see if you might have stuck it between the pages. And you still can't find it.

The kind I mean is always with you. And when you finally make your decision, it's right there where you need it.

I took my wallet out of my inside jacket pocket and opened it. There was the business card, in the transparent plastic pocket. Where my debit card used to be. But I didn't feel at all concerned, just then: I figured I must have put the bank card in some other pocket.

There was only one word on this business card too.

And some numbers. A phone number, I presumed.

I didn't have my cell phone with me. I'd stopped using it long ago. Hadn't even thought to bring it along.

There's a telephone on the wall near the counter in the café for customers to use. You can call anywhere in the city for free and talk as long as you want, so long as there isn't some antsy girl waiting in line behind you looking at her watch. And so long as it's a direct number. This number was the most direct imaginable. All seven numbers were the same. I procrastinated a moment wondering if there were even any numbers in our area code with that prefix. But it could have been a new system with its own fiber-optic cables, or something, operating independently from the regional phone system.

I dialed the number. A girl's voice answered. I gave my name, and she said simply: "I'll connect you."

Then a man's voice came on the line. I gave my name again. He said:

"Delighted. Come right over to the office, and we'll go through the contract."

Which caught me off guard.

287

"But I haven't told you what I want yet ..."

His answer didn't quite match: "We knew you would call."

He transferred me back to the girl, who told me how to get to the office. It wasn't that far from Nevsky Prospect; in fact, it was quite close to the café where I was making the call. Soon I was at the address, standing by the door. There wasn't anything special about it, no gothic monograms or anything like that. Just a doorbell. I pushed it.

I heard footsteps on the other side, and a girl opened the door and invited me inside.

"Come with me. I'll take you ..."

Judging from the sound of her voice, it was the same girl who'd answered the phone.

We passed through a large foyer and went down a long corridor to a spacious office, where a man was sitting behind a massive desk. Apparently the girl and this man, her boss, were the only people working here. Such extravagance, thought I, and right in the center of the city, with its insanely high rents for commercial space! They must own the building.

The man stood up when I entered the room.

He didn't look at all like Al Pacino. Young, blond, with soft features. There was absolutely nothing infernal about his appearance. He shook my hand; his grip wasn't too firm, wasn't too limp: just right. He didn't hold my hand for too long, didn't pull back his hand too early, and his palm was dry and warm. Everything was ideal—creepily so.

"Hello! Glad to see you! Have a seat."

He indicated a comfortable chair in front of a small coffee table at the wall, and instead of going back to his desk, he took a seat in a chair on the other side of the table, just like mine, exactly the same height. Perfect manners.

"To tell you the truth, we're a little pressed for time. I have to close the deal today and submit a report."

"I'm ready. I've just been a little busy, finishing up my book."

"Good for you! Was it difficult?"

There was nothing forced or artificial about his tone. Just sincere interest and concern. The question could just as well have been about my decision or my literary labors . . . I preferred to believe the latter.

"How to begin . . . actually, this is harder. When you finish a book, you think that you've already said and done everything you could, and you don't know why you should bother to go on living . . . Time to die, pal, you tell yourself. But the days go by, weeks, months, and you accumulate new experiences, new ideas come to you. Or maybe they're just new words and images for the same old thoughts. And the conclusion you reach is always the same, essentially: Just keep on doing what you're doing. Keep on pushing that boulder up the hill, dance while the music is playing, fight on without worrying about victory or defeat. Everyone finds his own image, the only possible thought for him or her, and tries to communicate it to the world. We have no choice! But a feeling of emptiness at a certain stage is unavoidable."

"I understand. I hope that the fruit of your labor was worth all the effort."

"Sometimes it seems to me that any normal person who'd read my book would have only two questions: First, what was the author smoking? And second: Is there any more?"

He laughed the beautiful laugh of a healthy, genial, self-assured man.

"Well, that's hardly the worst reaction! Your literary experiments are undoubtedly extremely interesting. But let's get down to business. Please take a look at the terms of the contract."

There was a stack of papers lying on the table. He slid it over to my side.

I skimmed the dozen or so pages, which were covered with fine print, and said, "All right. I agree."

"Then let's sign."

I have to admit that I was still a little nervous. I'd made a point of bringing a pen from home. I got it out and pricked my finger with the sharp end.

A single drop of scarlet blood spilled onto the white page next to my signature.

He gave a satisfied smile and, gathering up the signed contract, noted: "That was not at all necessary."

The feisty concoction you've just (perhaps) finished reading is the product of the restless, fertile mind of Russian-Chechen author German Sadulaev. Sadulaev has proven to be one of the most original and prolific writers of the post-Soviet generation; his works have drawn a broad readership and critical acclaim. *The Maya Pill*, his first novel (and second book) to appear in English, was short-listed for both the Russian Booker and National Bestseller prizes, and his subsequent Chechnya-themed novel *The Raid at Shali* was also short-listed for the Russian Booker. *I am a Chechen*, a genre-bending collection of legends, stories, and reminiscences situated amid the wars in Chechnya, appeared in English in 2010, and has been translated into several other languages as well.

The "loose, baggy monsters" of the classic Russian literary tradition offered a broad, realistic picture of the social, cultural, and political life of their times even as they probed inward into the human psyche and outward into the universe. True to those roots, Sadulaev's novel abounds in themes both trivial and profound. His protagonist commutes to work, swipes in with his smart card, scrolls lazily through his inbox, and performs his duties as a cog in the wheel of the new Russian capitalism. On this level, *The Maya Pill* offers as complete a picture of twenty-first century Russian office culture as can be found in modern fiction. But that is just the surface—and Russian thinkers have always mistrusted appearances. Maximus, it turns out, is a dreamer, a writer, an armchair philosopher. In his dreams he is Saat, humble Khazar horse-herder and future great Khagan, spokesman for the common people, ruler of the boundless steppe. Saat's Khazaria, with its wars of aggression, its political intrigues, its neglect of the earth and its injustices to the little man, is Post-Soviet Russia, thinly veiled. Saat is also the child Maximus, who on his trips home to his grandmother, gathers armloads of poppies. And the frozen French fries that his company sells—do they even exist? Or are they, like the material world itself, a product of the imagination, of Maya—pure, distilled illusion? Or perhaps the culprits are Dutch hallucinogenic pills—derived from those very poppies, mixed into a heady fish paste and introduced into Western Europe long ago by itinerant Khazar merchants? Behind it all, the devil is at work, offering fame and fortune in exchange for human souls. Maximus treads a complex path indeed. His duties as a mid-level import-export manager lead him into contact with business partners in Holland and in China. Their paths, it turns out, run parallel to his. All three of them face the challenge of finding love in an alienating, virtual world. Are the women they meet just Maya, illusion, like the imaginary French fries that the Dutch are selling to the Russians? Sadulaev is nothing if not ambitious, and the attentive reader will reap rich rewards as all these plotlines come together at the end, when the devil comes in to close the deal, and when you learn that the novel you have just read has told the story of its own creation.

The Maya Pill took its translator on an exciting ride from Russia's present-day urban reality to its hazy mythical roots and back again. Fresh words abound. Sadulaev's language presents unique challenges that begin with the novel's very title, *Tabletka*. By choosing this title—the word means "pill"—the author foregrounds the little pink hallucinogenic pills of his central plot, which were by some oversight included in a shipment from Holland to the Russian frozen food company's warehouse. A literal translation ("The Pill") would send the English-language reader down a garden path of irrelevancies; in spite of the novel's abundance of themes, birth control is not one of them. "The Tablet," too, would suggest wildly unrelated matters, from trivial items like notepads and computers to such profundities as Moses's

Ten Commandments. The Dutch pills lead Maximus to confront the nature of reality and perception—the classic Russian theme of beauty, which may or may not save the world—in the form of the Goddess of Sex, Spring, and Fertility who appears to him in the office elevator. She is the Hindu goddess of illusion, that force that veils true reality, and her name is Maya. Hence the English title. The titles of the novel's four parts are also worthy of note: Itil, Samandar, and Serkel are names of lost cities of Khazaria, and Part IV, "Mack" (*mak*), is both the Russian word for poppy and the protagonist's tabooed nickname.

Sadulaev's rich and varied language reflects the novel's themes. When referring to pop culture, the Internet, the streets and eateries of St. Petersburg, and the modern workplace, the style is jazzy, modern, and witty. A completely different diction takes the reader into Saat's life in ancient Khazaria. Saat is illiterate, his perceptions visceral, his moral compass true. He is the classic wise fool who serves and suffers in an unjust economy and an unjust war. Saat bears witness to "misfortune, woe," in short sentences that are the more powerful for their clumsiness. Saat's naïve and awestruck perception of life in the Khazar capital bears the novel's political allegory. Blue flashing lights attached at their horses' tails clear the roadways for the oppressors as they sweep through town, just like the lights on Kremlin officials' vehicles speeding through Moscow. The military requisitions officer confiscates Saat's horses, including a tender foal that is of no use for the war effort, but will make a perfect pet for his children. Through it all, Saat observes and tries to understand. Sadulaev's satire is light and humorous, but carries a bite. As always, wordplay and humor present a challenge to the translator. The best example is the description of the elections in ancient Khazaria, to which the voters proceed in a zombielike state, with their brains divided into segments supporting different political parties. Sadulaev found these "party-portions" out in a field somewhere, in a dialect word for manmade beehive boxes—*bortii*—which, yes, do sound sort of like "parties"—*partii* in Russian, a word as alien to Saat as *bortii* is to the compilers of the Oxford Russian-English dictionary, not to mention to a host of otherwise convenient Internet tools. The solution to this problem comes from author himself, who dubs them, in English, "peehives." Various words conveying empti-ness—*pustota, pustosh, pustynia*—which serve the novel's theme of perception and reality, present another challenge. What seems to a Russia in economic thrall to nimbler neighbors west and east to be an empty, barren landscape—*pustosh*—fills, in dreams, with economic, cultural, and philosophical potential.

Even when English is a good servant to Sadulaev's Russian, some elements transit over uneasily. Not everyone, notably the female half of our readership, will savor the sex scenes with equal relish. All three male protagonists illustrate distinctive cultural attitudes toward sex, and in all cases, the reality of the experience is mediated through a particular form of storytelling: literary, oral, and virtual. Readers of all tastes are urged, however, to ap-preciate the easternmost lovers' use of (genuine) ancient Chinese poetry as foreplay. Sadulaev situates his China scenes within the perspective of the country's millennia-long history, which colors his characters' attitudes toward business as well as to sex and fam-ily life. The big picture above all; and above all, patience. It may also help to keep in mind that Maximus's lover Maya functions more as muse than mistress, and the Dostoyevskian story she tells of sordid child abuse is not meant to be taken literally. Maximus, after all, is a writer, and the book in your hands is a story about its own creation—and the devil's role in that creative process. More treacherous still for contemporary Western readers is the Dutch partner's foray into the Internet sex chat room staffed by a Russian girl, with all its attendant nuances. More often than not, the sex scenes are better interpreted as reflecting cultural dif-ferences and attitudes toward illusion and reality than as serving some prurient purpose or social message. As for Sadulaev's political themes, they participate in a gritty Russian literary tradition that wallows in the mud as it strives to solve the great problems of ontology, and for all that, exerts an unmistakable fascination upon its often bewildered readers—as it always has.

As they conduct their international business transactions, Sadulaev's characters resort to the universal language of trade—English. Maximus's dreams occasionally leave traces of the ancient Khazar language in his consciousness as well; the reader—like the translator—is unlikely to be able to decipher them, though readers proficient in Arabic may fare better. Russian novels have always been hospitable to heterogeneous intrusions, and *The Maya Pill* is no exception. Here can be found various interpolated histories: of the post-Soviet economy, of Khazaria, of the mythical origins of Rus. A dip into the chaos of the Internet yields a series of posts by a barely literate blogger that, for all their misspellings and crude vocabulary, do manage to lead Maximus to the secret of the fish paste, and from there, to the true nature of the pink pills.

The Maya Pill, like its hallowed literary predecessors, offers a panoramic picture of the contemporary social and economic world even as it probes deep into our assumptions about the nature of reality. True to the novel's ambitions, the eternal "accursed" questions of Russian literature lurk quietly on every page. Here, though, they come with an understated irony that should endear itself to a modern readership that has heard and read it all before, or thinks it has.

Carol Apollonio
Durham, NC, 2013

GERMAN SADULAEV was born in 1973, in the town of Shali, in the Chechen-Ingush ASSR, to a Chechen father and Terek Cossack mother. In 1989, aged sixteen, he left Chechnya to study law at Leningrad State University. Today he lives and works as a lawyer in St. Petersburg.

CAROL APOLLONIO is Professor of the Practice of Russian at Duke University. She is the author of *Dostoevsky's Secrets: Reading Against the Grain*, and is a translator of Russian and Japanese literature.

SELECTED DALKEY ARCHIVE TITLES

MICHAL AJVAZ, *The Golden Age.*
The Other City.
PIERRE ALBERT-BIROT, *Grabinoulor.*
YUZ ALESHKOVSKY, *Kangaroo.*
FELIPE ALFAU, *Chromos.*
Locos.
IVAN ÂNGELO, *The Celebration.*
The Tower of Glass.
ANTÓNIO LOBO ANTUNES, *Knowledge of Hell.*
The Splendor of Portugal.
ALAIN ARIAS-MISSON, *Theatre of Incest.*
JOHN ASHBERY AND JAMES SCHUYLER,
A Nest of Ninnies.
ROBERT ASHLEY, *Perfect Lives.*
GABRIELA AVIGUR-ROTEM, *Heatwave and Crazy Birds.*
DJUNA BARNES, *Ladies Almanack.*
Ryder.
JOHN BARTH, *LETTERS.*
Sabbatical.
DONALD BARTHELME, *The King.*
Paradise.
SVETISLAV BASARA, *Chinese Letter.*
MIQUEL BAUÇÀ, *The Siege in the Room.*
RENÉ BELLETTO, *Dying.*
MAREK BIEŃCZYK, *Transparency.*
ANDREI BITOV, *Pushkin House.*
ANDREJ BLATNIK, *You Do Understand.*
LOUIS PAUL BOON, *Chapel Road.*
My Little War.
Summer in Termuren.
ROGER BOYLAN, *Killoyle.*
IGNÁCIO DE LOYOLA BRANDÃO,
Anonymous Celebrity.
Zero.
BONNIE BREMSER, *Troia: Mexican Memoirs.*
CHRISTINE BROOKE-ROSE, *Amalgamemnon.*
BRIGID BROPHY, *In Transit.*
GERALD L. BRUNS, *Modern Poetry and the Idea of Language.*
GABRIELLE BURTON, *Heartbreak Hotel.*
MICHEL BUTOR, *Degrees.*
Mobile.
G. CABRERA INFANTE, *Infante's Inferno.*
Three Trapped Tigers.
JULIETA CAMPOS,
The Fear of Losing Eurydice.
ANNE CARSON, *Eros the Bittersweet.*
ORLY CASTEL-BLOOM, *Dolly City.*
LOUIS-FERDINAND CÉLINE, *Castle to Castle.*
Conversations with Professor Y.
London Bridge.
Normance.
North.
Rigadoon.
MARIE CHAIX, *The Laurels of Lake Constance.*
HUGO CHARTERIS, *The Tide Is Right.*
ERIC CHEVILLARD, *Demolishing Nisard.*

MARC CHOLODENKO, *Mordechai Schamz.*
JOSHUA COHEN, *Witz.*
EMILY HOLMES COLEMAN, *The Shutter of Snow.*
ROBERT COOVER, *A Night at the Movies.*
STANLEY CRAWFORD, *Log of the S.S. The Mrs Unguentine.*
Some Instructions to My Wife.
RENÉ CREVEL, *Putting My Foot in It.*
RALPH CUSACK, *Cadenza.*
NICHOLAS DELBANCO, *The Count of Concord.*
Sherbrookes.
NIGEL DENNIS, *Cards of Identity.*
PETER DIMOCK, *A Short Rhetoric for Leaving the Family.*
ARIEL DORFMAN, *Konfidenz.*
COLEMAN DOWELL,
Island People.
Too Much Flesh and Jabez.
ARKADII DRAGOMOSHCHENKO, *Dust.*
RIKKI DUCORNET, *The Complete Butcher's Tales.*
The Fountains of Neptune.
The Jade Cabinet.
Phosphor in Dreamland.
WILLIAM EASTLAKE, *The Bamboo Bed.*
Castle Keep.
Lyric of the Circle Heart.
JEAN ECHENOZ, *Chopin's Move.*
STANLEY ELKIN, *A Bad Man.*
Criers and Kibitzers, Kibitzers and Criers.
The Dick Gibson Show.
The Franchiser.
The Living End.
Mrs. Ted Bliss.
FRANÇOIS EMMANUEL, *Invitation to a Voyage.*
SALVADOR ESPRIU, *Ariadne in the Grotesque Labyrinth.*
LESLIE A. FIEDLER, *Love and Death in the American Novel.*
JUAN FILLOY, *Op Oloop.*
ANDY FITCH, *Pop Poetics.*
GUSTAVE FLAUBERT, *Bouvard and Pécuchet.*
KASS FLEISHER, *Talking out of School.*
FORD MADOX FORD,
The March of Literature.
JON FOSSE, *Aliss at the Fire.*
Melancholy.
MAX FRISCH, *I'm Not Stiller.*
Man in the Holocene.
CARLOS FUENTES, *Christopher Unborn.*
Distant Relations.
Terra Nostra.
Where the Air Is Clear.
TAKEHIKO FUKUNAGA, *Flowers of Grass.*
WILLIAM GADDIS, *J R.*
The Recognitions.

SELECTED DALKEY ARCHIVE TITLES

JANICE GALLOWAY, *Foreign Parts.*
 The Trick Is to Keep Breathing.
WILLIAM H. GASS, *Cartesian Sonata*
 and Other Novellas.
 Finding a Form.
 A Temple of Texts.
 The Tunnel.
 Willie Masters' Lonesome Wife.
GÉRARD GAVARRY, *Hoppla! 1 2 3.*
ETIENNE GILSON,
 The Arts of the Beautiful.
 Forms and Substances in the Arts.
C. S. GISCOMBE, *Giscome Road.*
 Here.
DOUGLAS GLOVER, *Bad News of the Heart.*
WITOLD GOMBROWICZ,
 A Kind of Testament.
PAULO EMÍLIO SALES GOMES, *P's Three*
 Women.
GEORGI GOSPODINOV, *Natural Novel.*
JUAN GOYTISOLO, *Count Julian.*
 Juan the Landless.
 Makbara.
 Marks of Identity.
HENRY GREEN, *Back.*
 Blindness.
 Concluding.
 Doting.
 Nothing.
JACK GREEN, *Fire the Bastards!*
JIŘÍ GRUŠA, *The Questionnaire.*
MELA HARTWIG, *Am I a Redundant*
 Human Being?
JOHN HAWKES, *The Passion Artist.*
 Whistlejacket.
ELIZABETH HEIGHWAY, ED., *Contemporary*
 Georgian Fiction.
ALEKSANDAR HEMON, ED.,
 Best European Fiction.
AIDAN HIGGINS, *Balcony of Europe.*
 Blind Man's Bluff
 Bornholm Night-Ferry.
 Flotsam and Jetsam.
 Langrishe, Go Down.
 Scenes from a Receding Past.
KEIZO HINO, *Isle of Dreams.*
KAZUSHI HOSAKA, *Plainsong.*
ALDOUS HUXLEY, *Antic Hay.*
 Crome Yellow.
 Point Counter Point.
 Those Barren Leaves.
 Time Must Have a Stop.
NAOYUKI II, *The Shadow of a Blue Cat.*
GERT JONKE, *The Distant Sound.*
 Geometric Regional Novel.
 Homage to Czerny.
 The System of Vienna.
JACQUES JOUET, *Mountain R.*
 Savage.
 Upstaged.

MIEKO KANAI, *The Word Book.*
YORAM KANIUK, *Life on Sandpaper.*
HUGH KENNER, *Flaubert.*
 Joyce and Beckett: The Stoic Comedians.
 Joyce's Voices.
DANILO KIŠ, *The Attic.*
 Garden, Ashes.
 The Lute and the Scars
 Psalm 44.
 A Tomb for Boris Davidovich.
ANITA KONKKA, *A Fool's Paradise.*
GEORGE KONRÁD, *The City Builder.*
TADEUSZ KONWICKI, *A Minor Apocalypse.*
 The Polish Complex.
MENIS KOUMANDAREAS, *Koula.*
ELAINE KRAF, *The Princess of 72nd Street.*
JIM KRUSOE, *Iceland.*
AYŞE KULIN, *Farewell: A Mansion in*
 Occupied Istanbul.
EMILIO LASCANO TEGUI, *On Elegance*
 While Sleeping.
ERIC LAURRENT, *Do Not Touch.*
VIOLETTE LEDUC, *La Bâtarde.*
EDOUARD LEVÉ, *Autoportrait.*
 Suicide.
MARIO LEVI, *Istanbul Was a Fairy Tale.*
DEBORAH LEVY, *Billy and Girl.*
JOSÉ LEZAMA LIMA, *Paradiso.*
ROSA LIKSOM, *Dark Paradise.*
OSMAN LINS, *Avalovara.*
 The Queen of the Prisons of Greece.
ALF MAC LOCHLAINN,
 The Corpus in the Library.
 Out of Focus.
RON LOEWINSOHN, *Magnetic Field(s).*
MINA LOY, *Stories and Essays of Mina Loy.*
D. KEITH MANO, *Take Five.*
MICHELINE AHARONIAN MARCOM,
 The Mirror in the Well.
BEN MARCUS,
 The Age of Wire and String.
WALLACE MARKFIELD,
 Teitlebaum's Window.
 To an Early Grave.
DAVID MARKSON, *Reader's Block.*
 Wittgenstein's Mistress.
CAROLE MASO, *AVA.*
LADISLAV MATEJKA AND KRYSTYNA
 POMORSKA, EDS.,
 Readings in Russian Poetics:
 Formalist and Structuralist Views.
HARRY MATHEWS, *Cigarettes.*
 The Conversions.
 The Human Country: New and
 Collected Stories.
 The Journalist.
 My Life in CIA.
 Singular Pleasures.
 The Sinking of the Odradek
 Stadium.
 Tlooth.

JOSEPH MCELROY,
  Night Soul and Other Stories.
ABDELWAHAB MEDDEB, *Talismano.*
GERHARD MEIER, *Isle of the Dead.*
HERMAN MELVILLE, *The Confidence-Man.*
AMANDA MICHALOPOULOU, *I'd Like.*
STEVEN MILLHAUSER, *The Barnum Museum.*
  In the Penny Arcade.
RALPH J. MILLS, JR., *Essays on Poetry.*
MOMUS, *The Book of Jokes.*
CHRISTINE MONTALBETTI, *The Origin of Man.*
  Western.
OLIVE MOORE, *Spleen.*
NICHOLAS MOSLEY, *Accident.*
  Assassins.
  Catastrophe Practice.
  Experience and Religion.
  A Garden of Trees.
  Hopeful Monsters.
  Imago Bird.
  Impossible Object.
  Inventing God.
  Judith.
  Look at the Dark.
  Natalie Natalia.
  Serpent.
  Time at War.
WARREN MOTTE,
  *Fables of the Novel: French Fiction
  since 1990.*
  *Fiction Now: The French Novel in
  the 21st Century.*
  *Oulipo: A Primer of Potential
  Literature.*
GERALD MURNANE, *Barley Patch.*
  Inland.
YVES NAVARRE, *Our Share of Time.*
  Sweet Tooth.
DOROTHY NELSON, *In Night's City.*
  Tar and Feathers.
ESHKOL NEVO, *Homesick.*
WILFRIDO D. NOLLEDO, *But for the Lovers.*
FLANN O'BRIEN, *At Swim-Two-Birds.*
  The Best of Myles.
  The Dalkey Archive.
  The Hard Life.
  The Poor Mouth.
  The Third Policeman.
CLAUDE OLLIER, *The Mise-en-Scène.*
  Wert and the Life Without End.
GIOVANNI ORELLI, *Walaschek's Dream.*
PATRIK OUŘEDNÍK, *Europeana.*
  The Opportune Moment, 1855.
BORIS PAHOR, *Necropolis.*
FERNANDO DEL PASO, *News from the
  Empire.*
  Palinuro of Mexico.
ROBERT PINGET, *The Inquisitory.*
  Mahu or The Material.
  Trio.
MANUEL PUIG, *Betrayed by Rita Hayworth.*

The Buenos Aires Affair.
Heartbreak Tango.
RAYMOND QUENEAU, *The Last Days.*
  Odile.
  Pierrot Mon Ami.
  Saint Glinglin.
ANN QUIN, *Berg.*
  Passages.
  Three.
  Tripticks.
ISHMAEL REED, *The Free-Lance Pallbearers.*
  The Last Days of Louisiana Red.
  Ishmael Reed: The Plays.
  Juice!
  Reckless Eyeballing.
  The Terrible Threes.
  The Terrible Twos.
  Yellow Back Radio Broke-Down.
JASIA REICHARDT, *15 Journeys Warsaw
  to London.*
NOËLLE REVAZ, *With the Animals.*
JOÃO UBALDO RIBEIRO, *House of the
  Fortunate Buddhas.*
JEAN RICARDOU, *Place Names.*
RAINER MARIA RILKE, *The Notebooks of
  Malte Laurids Brigge.*
JULIÁN RÍOS, *The House of Ulysses.*
  Larva: A Midsummer Night's Babel.
  Poundemonium.
  Procession of Shadows.
AUGUSTO ROA BASTOS, *I the Supreme.*
DANIËL ROBBERECHTS, *Arriving in Avignon.*
JEAN ROLIN, *The Explosion of the
  Radiator Hose.*
OLIVIER ROLIN, *Hotel Crystal.*
ALIX CLEO ROUBAUD, *Alix's Journal.*
JACQUES ROUBAUD, *The Form of a
  City Changes Faster, Alas, Than
  the Human Heart.*
  The Great Fire of London.
  Hortense in Exile.
  Hortense Is Abducted.
  The Loop.
  Mathematics:
  The Plurality of Worlds of Lewis.
  The Princess Hoppy.
  Some Thing Black.
RAYMOND ROUSSEL, *Impressions of Africa.*
VEDRANA RUDAN, *Night.*
STIG SÆTERBAKKEN, *Siamese.*
  Self Control.
LYDIE SALVAYRE, *The Company of Ghosts.*
  The Lecture.
  The Power of Flies.
LUIS RAFAEL SÁNCHEZ,
  Macho Camacho's Beat.
SEVERO SARDUY, *Cobra & Maitreya.*
NATHALIE SARRAUTE,
  Do You Hear Them?
  Martereau.
  The Planetarium.

SELECTED DALKEY ARCHIVE TITLES

ARNO SCHMIDT, *Collected Novellas.*
Collected Stories.
Nobodaddy's Children.
Two Novels.
ASAF SCHURR, *Motti.*
GAIL SCOTT, *My Paris.*
DAMION SEARLS, *What We Were Doing and Where We Were Going.*
JUNE AKERS SEESE,
Is This What Other Women Feel Too?
What Waiting Really Means.
BERNARD SHARE, *Inish.*
Transit.
VIKTOR SHKLOVSKY, *Bowstring.*
Knight's Move.
A Sentimental Journey: Memoirs 1917–1922.
Energy of Delusion: A Book on Plot.
Literature and Cinematography.
Theory of Prose.
Third Factory.
Zoo, or Letters Not about Love.
PIERRE SINIAC, *The Collaborators.*
KJERSTI A. SKOMSVOLD, *The Faster I Walk, the Smaller I Am.*
JOSEF ŠKVORECKÝ, *The Engineer of Human Souls.*
GILBERT SORRENTINO,
Aberration of Starlight.
Blue Pastoral.
Crystal Vision.
Imaginative Qualities of Actual Things.
Mulligan Stew.
Pack of Lies.
Red the Fiend.
The Sky Changes.
Something Said.
Splendide-Hôtel.
Steelwork.
Under the Shadow.
W. M. SPACKMAN, *The Complete Fiction.*
ANDRZEJ STASIUK, *Dukla.*
Fado.
GERTRUDE STEIN, *The Making of Americans.*
A Novel of Thank You.
LARS SVENDSEN, *A Philosophy of Evil.*
PIOTR SZEWC, *Annihilation.*
GONÇALO M. TAVARES, *Jerusalem.*
Joseph Walser's Machine.
Learning to Pray in the Age of Technique.
LUCIAN DAN TEODOROVICI,
Our Circus Presents . . .
NIKANOR TERATOLOGEN, *Assisted Living.*
STEFAN THEMERSON, *Hobson's Island.*
The Mystery of the Sardine.
Tom Harris.
TAEKO TOMIOKA, *Building Waves.*

JOHN TOOMEY, *Sleepwalker.*
JEAN-PHILIPPE TOUSSAINT, *The Bathroom.*
Camera.
Monsieur.
Reticence.
Running Away.
Self-Portrait Abroad.
Television.
The Truth about Marie.
DUMITRU TSEPENEAG, *Hotel Europa.*
The Necessary Marriage.
Pigeon Post.
Vain Art of the Fugue.
ESTHER TUSQUETS, *Stranded.*
DUBRAVKA UGRESIC, *Lend Me Your Character.*
Thank You for Not Reading.
TOR ULVEN, *Replacement.*
MATI UNT, *Brecht at Night.*
Diary of a Blood Donor.
Things in the Night.
ÁLVARO URIBE AND OLIVIA SEARS, EDS.,
Best of Contemporary Mexican Fiction.
ELOY URROZ, *Friction.*
The Obstacles.
LUISA VALENZUELA, *Dark Desires and the Others.*
He Who Searches.
PAUL VERHAEGHEN, *Omega Minor.*
AGLAJA VETERANYI, *Why the Child Is Cooking in the Polenta.*
BORIS VIAN, *Heartsnatcher.*
LLORENÇ VILLALONGA, *The Dolls' Room.*
TOOMAS VINT, *An Unending Landscape.*
ORNELA VORPSI, *The Country Where No One Ever Dies.*
AUSTRYN WAINHOUSE, *Hedyphagetica.*
CURTIS WHITE, *America's Magic Mountain.*
The Idea of Home.
Memories of My Father Watching TV.
Requiem.
DIANE WILLIAMS, *Excitability: Selected Stories.*
Romancer Erector.
DOUGLAS WOOLF, *Wall to Wall.*
Ya! & John-Juan.
JAY WRIGHT, *Polynomials and Pollen.*
The Presentable Art of Reading Absence.
PHILIP WYLIE, *Generation of Vipers.*
MARGUERITE YOUNG, *Angel in the Forest.*
Miss MacIntosh, My Darling.
REYOUNG, *Unbabbling.*
VLADO ŽABOT, *The Succubus.*
ZORAN ŽIVKOVIĆ, *Hidden Camera.*
LOUIS ZUKOFSKY, *Collected Fiction.*
VITOMIL ZUPAN, *Minuet for Guitar.*
SCOTT ZWIREN, *God Head.*